THE

SEAGULL

CALLED

ME HOME

THE SEAGULL CALLED ME HOME

Jenny Hewett Smith

DEDICATION

This book is dedicated to my daughter Jade, who gave up her summer to weigh the words of this novel. Her commitment and expertise has shorn off the rough edges, allowing it to shine. Thank you Jade, for using the many red pens I bought you, to polish this work and make it the best it could be. You are amazing.

ACKNOWLEDGMENTS

I want to thank those who have helped me in my writing career:

To my husband, Derick, who always helps me with the tedious work and never complains. Thank you for believing in me and for your endless encouragement.

To my children, Shana and Jade, thank you for inspiring me with real life scenarios, which in turn creates new stories. To my precious son-in-law Justin, thank you for setting up my website. I am blessed.

To my Father, Jerry Hewett, you always ask me what I am writing. Thank you for your ceaseless interest, which pushes me forward. To my Mother, Loretta Hewett, thank you for the many cups of tea between breaks. I look forward to them and the warmth your love brings me.

I offer special thanks to Bill Hart who always believes in me, and without whom, I may not have written. You are always the first to read my work and support me. I'm grateful to Nancy O'Brien for her eyes, and to my daughter Jade for being my catcher. Your work has been invaluable.

A note to Jeff Sheldon. This novel would not have been completed without your generous and timely gift. Thank you.

Most of all, I want to thank the Lord for using me as a vessel for His glory. I pray that all who read this work will feel his companionship in a more tangible way. He is always near.

1

Tessa sat on the white balcony of their castle-like house and looked down upon the crystal sea. Clad only in her bikini, she studied the water below and waited to spot the dolphins that often played around the huge boulders that protruded out of the majestic ocean. She always marveled at how the Pacific and Indian oceans met here and battled with each other until huge waves clashed and roared, making the ground quiver beneath her.

This piece of South Africa was idyllic and Tessa felt like a beautiful princess who lived in a magical haven. She often imagined that her handsome prince would find her on this white stone ledge, and she waited for him there every afternoon. Yes, life was perfect she thought, as she squinted her green eyes in an effort to catch a glimpse of the playful dolphins.

Her mother's sharp voice shattered the serenity and she couldn't help thinking that perhaps life was actually not quite *that* perfect. She hurried into the kitchen to find her mother impatiently tapping her fingers on the counter.

"Why have you not started dinner yet?" she snapped. "You're always daydreaming and wasting time at the water's edge!"

What her mother didn't understand was that down on the beach, time stood still and everything was alive and magical. *I can be anything I want to be down there*, Tessa thought, but didn't dare utter the words out loud.

Her mother was an old woman who had birthed her late in life and apparently resented her arrival into the world. Tessa always felt a keen sense of disapproval from her mother and tried to hurry as she poured the rice into the cast iron pot. Either her mother was finding fault with her, or she was completely ignoring her. She spent many nights laying in her bed wishing above all else that her mother would just talk to her, but all she heard day after day was a deafening silence or a harsh reproof.

"Hurry up and make me a cup of tea," her mother shouted as she hobbled out of the kitchen, her cane tap-tapping against the cold stone floor.

After washing the supper dishes, Tessa quietly slipped out the back door and ran down the cobblestone path that led to the beach. The wind had picked up and her white skirt tangled around her legs, almost tripping her as she hurried down the steps. She knew there were exactly ninety-three steps that wound their way through the heavy brush and onto the sparkling white sand.

"Where is he?" She whispered into the wind. Her brother knew the rules! If he missed dinner he would go to bed hungry again for mother never bent the rules. Although Jeremiah was five years older than her mere eighteen years, she always found herself mothering him. But who could blame her? He was her best friend, after all, and seemed to be the only one who truly loved and

10

protected her. She adored him. Their father had abandoned them many years ago and she was sure this attributed to the coldness that exuded from her bitter mother.

It was dusk now as she ran along the beach and onto the narrow wooden bridge that led to the big boulders beyond. Under the bridge, the dark water churned angrily and spewed up white foam that soaked the hem of her skirt. *Surely he can't still be fishing from our hiding spot,* she worried. There were many nooks and crannies that had provided fine hiding places for them over the years. The enormous rocks created little caves that shielded them from the baking summer sun, and from the harsh winter winds that could slice to the very bone at times. She shivered at the thought and was careful not to lose her footing on the wet, slippery path. Creeping through the small opening of the cave, she was disappointed to find it empty.

She quickly retraced her steps back onto the pathway but stumbled over the old seaweed that had washed up earlier in the day. The smell of rotting seaweed assaulted her as she looked up at the moon, which now was her only source of light. A half-moon shone down on her and she wondered why, just once, her brother couldn't have gone missing during a full moon! She was getting angrier as the minutes passed. *I should just teach him a lesson and feed his dinner to the fish!* But she held the little bag of food closer as she rushed along the moonlit path.

A rustling in the trees nearby made her instantly wary. She was used to the mischievous monkeys that swung in the branches above, and often stole the fruit off their trees, but she didn't want to come face to face with the huge baboon that came down the mountain every so often and scared everyone to death. He was not as polite as the monkeys and demanded more than fruit. The last time he had made an appearance was when he had walked into the Black Marlin Restaurant on the corner nearby and stood up on two feet, baring his fangs as he snatched food from the plates of the terrified customers.

The rustling grew closer and she couldn't decide if she should run for her life or stand dead still. She tried to remember what the rule was when facing a baboon. Was it the same as when facing a dog? Or was she to run like hell? The hair on her neck stood up in fear as she peered into the nearby bushes. She screamed as she saw something big lurch out and felt herself being dragged to the ground. But instead of looking into the white fangs of a gorilla, she was looking at a row of perfect white teeth as her brother laughed hysterically.

"You should see your face," he howled.

She shoved him away roughly. "That's not funny you big baboon. Where have you been anyway?"

"I was snorkeling out at the inlet and lost track of time. The giant octopus was out again and-"

"That octopus is going to eat you for dinner one day! And speaking of dinner..." she pulled out the little sack of food and saw that the green peas lay strewn between them.

Now they were both laughing. "Never mind, I ate so many mussels I am stuffed anyway."

He always made her laugh, and she felt safe as they walked up the steps together. The many hours of fishing and snorkeling had made him grow into a muscular boy and he towered over her at six foot four. The summer sun had bronzed his body and she had noticed the girls in town smiling up at him as he walked by. She didn't want to accept that he was now a man and not a young boy who would stay with her forever.

What would I do without him, she wondered, as they climbed the ninety three steps up to their 'castle'.

2

Tessa opened her eyes and rolled out of bed. After throwing on her swimsuit and splashing water on her face, she hastily put on the pot of coffee her impatient mother would be expecting before breakfast.

"Hurry, hurry," she urged the bubbling black liquid and poured herself a cup as soon as it was done. She took the steps down to the beach two at a time and again wondered why there couldn't have been only twenty-three steps instead of ninety-three!

Tessa wiggled her toes as she stepped into the cool sand. She closed her eyes and breathed deeply, inhaling the fragrance of the salty sea air. A seagull cried above her, begging for a scrap of some sort. "I have no stale bread today," she called back to the seagull that circled around her head.

She turned her head and looked past the steep hill to their home, which stood proudly on its perch protruding out from the side of the mountain. It was really just a simple home that appeared to be a castle because of the oversized white stone balcony and the huge wide windows that opened up above the ocean. Her eyes lingered on the impressive structure and she started praying as she did every day.

"God, thank you for my home and for the ocean. Thank you for walking with me on this beach every morning. Thank you for everything, but please help my mother find something to love about me today."

Tessa always felt God's presence here at the water's edge, like he was right here with her. She imagined him waiting patiently on the beach for her every morning, and that was why she hurried down to the sand regardless of what the weather was doing. But today she didn't have to worry about bad weather and she slipped into the turquoise water for a quick swim. The salty water licked her skin as she swam out to the first boulder.

She remembered the day she and Jeremiah had been spear fishing and he had come eye to eye with a shark at that very same boulder. The shark had stared at him with those dead grey eyes and Jeremiah could do nothing but stare back. Time stood still as they eyed each other. Who would be the prey? Apparently a stand-off was called between man and beast because they turned away from each other and swam off in different directions. She liked to think it had something to do with those early morning prayers that she uttered every day.

*****

The alarm kept beeping and Tessa groaned as she watched the clock flash 5:00 a.m. It was Tuesday and Tessa hated Tuesdays. As a matter of fact, she hated Thursdays as well. These were the days she had to go into Fish Hoek and work at the hair salon. She knew that jobs in South Africa were scarce and so she had taken whatever was available, but really…this job was tedious and boring. Sweeping up hair all day long and making tea for grouchy old ladies was not her idea of fun. And to top it off, she had to listen to all kinds of strange gossip.

Tessa waited impatiently for the train to arrive in Simonstown. She didn't mind the ten minute train rides because she loved watching the waves splash over the tracks ahead, except of course for the days when leap tide came in and threatened to wash the train and all its passengers into the angry waves below. Now she rubbed her cold hands together as she peered down the barren train tracks and strained to hear the sharp sound of the whistle. The weather was starting to change and the constant Cape winds would soon be turning into gale- force monsters. She wished that summer would never end and dreaded the long cooped-up winter, when all she could do was stare out of the oversized bay windows of their castle, and watch the swells reach massive heights before thrashing themselves against the rocks below.

Entering the ancient musty salon, Tessa pinched her nose closed. The fumes from the *perm* bottles swirled around her and almost knocked her breath away. The room was filled with little old ladies who had perm rollers in their short gray hair and long cigarettes hanging off their painted red lips. Their brown leathery skin witnessed that they had spent many years on the beach worshipping the golden sun. "Note to self: use more sunscreen," she mumbled to herself.

"It's about time," Betsie hollered from across the room. "I'm ready for a cuppa so put the tea kettle on."

Am I sentenced to a life of serving tea to unappreciative people? Tessa thought. Immediately the scripture she had read earlier that day came back to her.

Whatever you do, work at it with all your heart, as working for the Lord, not for men.

"I'm sorry, Lord," she breathed. She had made it a habit to whisper these little prayers to God throughout the day and it gave her comfort to know that he was never far. Sometimes it felt like he was standing right next to her.

Tessa stood in the little kitchen and lined up the mismatched tea cups. While she waited for the kettle to whistle she twirled her shoulder-length dark brown hair into a loose bun and pinned it on top of her head. She looked into the oval mirror that hung on the wall and examined her face.

What do people see when they look at me? Tessa wondered. Blake, her brother's friend, had told her she was beautiful a few months ago, and it had made her *feel* beautiful. She turned her head to the left and then to the right. The sun shining through the window brought out the deep mahogany color in her dark hair, and she noticed that she *did* have beautiful green eyes, although mournful at times. Her heart-shaped face was silky smooth and her lips were a cherry red. She could have felt more beautiful, had it not been for the scar on her left cheekbone. It wasn't necessarily an ugly scar, but the dent marred her otherwise flawless skin. Still, Blake had called her beautiful!

Tessa couldn't help thinking about his dark brown eyes and olive skin. He always spoke to her about God and encouraged her whenever he was around. He found things funny, and she loved to watch him throw back his head and laugh uninhibited. Oh, he was so handsome! But the sad truth was, she liked Blake, she liked him a lot, and if she was truly honest... she actually loved Blake.

For many years she had secretly wished that he would be the Prince she sat waiting for on that white ledge of the balcony. Tessa sighed as she poured the boiling water onto the teabags. Did he really even see her? Except for calling her beautiful a few weeks before, he had never shown her anything more than friendship. Or...were the long looks she sometimes caught him giving her a sign of something more? It was all so confusing!

She carried the tea tray out and watched Betsie pick up the petite, flowered teacup with her fat ugly hand. Her nails were bitten down into the quick and had been stained a bright purple from all the years of coloring hair. She brought the cup to her orange lips, which matched her short orange hair, and drained the cup in one single swallow. Without a word of thanks she turned back to the wavy gray hair she was working on and continued on in the senseless chatter.

By noon Tessa was starving. Her belly growled with hunger as she swept piles of fallen hair into the filthy dustpan. Eventually, Betsie reached into the register and pulled out some money.

"Go and get us some meatball sandwiches," she said.

It was the same meatball sandwiches every day, but Tessa hurried across the road to the café and watched them toast the tiny bread buns and add one single meatball to each. That and another cup of tea would suffice for lunch and carry her through to dinnertime. She wondered how Betsie could stay so fat on these meager rations.

All afternoon she listened to the familiar gossip, only this time it didn't seem like empty gossip but true ugly fact.

The unrest in South Africa had led to escalating violence. A state of emergency had been declared in many areas as the civil unrest increased and produced angry, riotous mobs.

Tessa wished she could shut her ears to the horror stories that were being told. She watched the clock tick 5:05 p.m....5:30...5:45...5:55, and now finally it was 6:01 p.m. She locked the door of the worn-out salon, sat in the closest chair and rubbed her tired feet. A knock on the door made her jump, but she smiled with delight when she saw Jeremiah leaning against the doorframe.

"I made mother an early dinner so we can go out tonight," he smiled.

Tessa looked down at the old drab work clothes she had on.

"I know, you look *horrible*," Jeremiah said as he held up a beautiful new dress. "Now put this on so we can get out of here, I'm starving!"

3

Jeremiah always bought Tessa little gifts to make up for the lack of comfort their mother extended to them. By calling pretty things 'pure vanity' their mother had withheld many vital necessities, and Jeremiah realized that his sister had suffered more than he had. He was glad that he had made some extra money down at Kalk Bay Harbor and now desperately hoped that the dress would fit.

Slipping on the silky dress, Tessa was amazed at the transformation she saw take place in the mirror. The white dress clung to her narrow waist and curved around her shapely hips, causing her long legs to be accentuated. She smiled as she looked down at the tiny blue embroidered flowers. She was no longer a 'girl', but a stylish young woman.

"What's taking so long?" Jeremiah called.

Tessa quickly applied another layer of red lipstick and was glad that she had when she entered the Black Marlin restaurant and saw Blake already seated at a table against the wall. His dark eyes held hers before he gave her a warm hug.

"Enough, enough of the hugging. I'm famished," Jeremiah said as he hastily waved over the waitress.

Tessa and Blake dined on olive oil basted lamb chops, seasoned in fresh garlic and rosemary, while Jeremiah ordered glazed ostrich in a sweet and sour apricot sauce. The fresh bread was almost too hot to touch, and the mashed potato and sweet carrots were scrumptious. After dinner they drank strong coffee and ate apple tart heaped high with fresh whipped cream. *If only I could stop watching Blake's every move*, Tessa thought as she *continued* to watch Blake's every move. *His every mannerism is so captivating ...*

"I am leaving tomorrow for three weeks," Blake said unexpectedly between mouthfuls of apple pie, "My uncle has work for me on his wine farm in Stellenbosch."

"Well, be sure your work consists of working with the vines and not drinking the wines," Jeremiah laughed at his own joke. "But I hear the girls in Stellenbosch are gorgeous," he winked at Blake.

Tessa put her spoon down, her appetite suddenly evaporated. *Three weeks. Three long weeks with gorgeous girls!*

As they got up to leave, Jeremiah saw some friends from the harbor sitting at a nearby table and walked over to them as Tessa and Blake continued out the door. It was late already and a heavy fog circled around them as they waited on the pebbled pathway for Jeremiah. The fog encapsulated them, and for a single moment in time, nothing else existed but this moment with Blake. Tessa heard the waves swishing nearby and was aware of the full moon that tried to pry through the misty air. She heard the foghorn's cry in the distance as it warned the sailing ships away from the hidden jagged coastline. But none of this mattered as Blake turned to her and looked deeply into her eyes. Tessa held her breathe. *Could this really be happening? My dream is coming true.* She had been waiting so long...

The fog twirled around them as a soft breeze blew up from the water below. "Tessa," he paused as he took her hand between his large calloused ones. Never had Tessa felt more alive than in this moment, and she shivered at his touch. He spoke quietly, "There is something I've wanted to say to you for a while now. I've been thinking that-"

"Sorry for keeping you guys waiting out here in this creepy fog!" Jeremiah yelled as he walked up and playfully slapped Blake on the back. The magical spell was broken and Tessa sighed inwardly. Jeremiah continued to chatter and was oblivious to the look that passed between his sister and his best friend.

"I'll see you in three weeks," Blake said as he hugged them goodbye. "Maybe we can finish our conversation then" he added, as he looked back at Tessa one last time before turning away. She watched his broad back disappear into the dark night and felt sadness settle over her. *Stop being so melancholy,* she chided herself, *it's only three weeks.*

*****

June arrived with a wintery blast. In the three weeks that Blake had been gone, the northwesterly winds had ushered in the famous freezing rains and stormy seas. The Cape of Storms held true to its name, and Tessa was reminded why the Cape was called 'the graveyard for shipwrecks' as she walked down the winding steps and prayed on the beach every morning. The winds were angry and fierce as they stole her words right out of her mouth while they were being uttered, and she hoped that God heard her frantic prayers. It was essential that He heard her, because she prayed for Blake every day. More specifically, she prayed that he would not meet any gorgeous girls in the vineyards and that, if he did, they would not make him forget her!

The evil wind picked up the sand and stung her flesh so that she sought refuge in the secret cave where she prayed for Jeremiah's safety, since the angry weather did not stop him from snorkeling in the rough seas.

When Tessa could stand the cold no longer she hurried back up to the 'castle' where she found her mother in an even worse temper than before, because the cold winter weather made her stiff leg ache continuously. The sound of the tapping cane against the stone floor was like the constant dripping of the rain outside the kitchen door, and it grated on Tessa's nerves during these endless winter days.

Drip drip drip…   Tap tap tap...   Drip drip drip… Tap tap tap.

The next morning, Tessa sat behind a boulder on the beach as long as she dared and continued to pray for patience towards her mother. She turned her thoughts back to Blake and smiled. He would be returning home today. She had asked Jeremiah to call his house and leave a message for him to come and join them for dinner tonight. The weather predicted a bad storm but Blake could sleep over as he had many times before.

The weak afternoon sun shone through the window as Tessa poured rich gravy over the pineapple chicken that baked in the oven. The golden pineapple rings glistened as she basted the plump chicken. Tessa welcomed the warmth from the oven that filled the kitchen and hummed softly as she set the table.

"You may as well take my placemat off," her mother snapped from the doorway. "I have decided to drive into Simonstown to pick up my medicine and eat dinner at Mabel's."

Tessa was surprised that her mother wanted to drive herself, because for the last year she had relied on Jeremiah to give her rides into town. She understood that her mother was lonely and wanted to see the only friend she had. Mabel had been a loyal friend since their high school days, but the steep winding mountain roads could be intimidating, especially at night.

Tessa chose her words carefully, "Perhaps you should wait for Jeremiah to come in from checking the nets and have him drive you."

Her mother glared at her, "I'm not a complete invalid!" she angrily retorted.

"I know...but there is a really bad storm blowing in tonight and-"

"Don't tell me what I should and shouldn't do, I am your mother!" her mother bellowed as she hit her cane on the ground.

Then act like one, Tessa wanted to scream, but instead she turned back to the table and removed her mother's place setting. She blinked and hoped her tears would not splash over onto the table to cause her further shame. *You're a mean old woman*, she thought, *and you're so stubborn, you deserve what you get! I don't care what happens to you anyway.*

Then Tessa heard that still small voice,

Love is patient, love is kind. It is not rude, it is not self-seeking, it is not easily angered, and it keeps no record of wrongs. Love always protects, always trusts, always hopes, and always perseveres. Love never fails.

The quiet words ministered to Tessa and she knew what she had to do. "God, help me please. I can't do this on my own..." she breathed as she swallowed the lump of raw pain that was sitting in her throat.

Tessa walked over and put her arms around her mother. "I love you, Mother," she said. For a brief second Tessa thought she felt her mother relax in her arms, but just as quickly she stiffened and pulled away. Without another word she hobbled out of the house.

Tessa looked at the clock on the kitchen wall and forgot all about her mother. She ran to her bedroom and put on her newest pair of jeans. She shivered as she tried to pick out a long sleeve top. *I want to be warm... but I have to look pretty, too.* She settled on a red sweater and put on some red earrings and lipstick to match. She smiled at herself in the mirror and noticed the playfulness in her green eyes. *Tonight is the night that Blake is going to ask me to be his girl; I just feel it.*

Jeremiah, Tessa, and Blake sat at the table and dined together, just as they had done three weeks earlier. To Tessa, however, it had felt more like three months of endless waiting. She hoped that Jeremiah would get distracted at some point and give her and Blake some time alone. It didn't look hopeful as Jeremiah and Blake kept talking about how to catch fish and how to prune vineyards...how to fix cars.... and how to play cricket. Tessa felt like rolling her eyes but instead tried to appear interested and nodded from time to time.

"Mmm, this chicken is delicious!" was the only direct comment she got from Blake during the whole dinner. Then the phone rang…

From that day forward, Tessa always marveled at how one phone call could change one's life. The weather had turned ugly, as predicted, and her mother had lost control of the car on the mountain pass.

"How is she?" Jeremiah had asked the nurse on the phone.

"You need to come up to the hospital as soon as you can," was the vague reply.

Now they sat in these sterile hospital chairs and waited for the doctor to come out.

"She didn't make it, I'm sorry." And with those six little words, Tessa's mother disappeared from the earth.

"Are you OK?" the doctor asked Tessa, who said nothing but continued to sit quietly in the white hospital chair

4

It had been a month since their mother had been buried in the frozen ground. Tessa replayed the scene over and over in her mind. The day had been much like this day, with the grey clouds hovering overhead. The seagulls had been restless and constantly squawked in the frigid sky. She could still smell the upturned damp earth as it lay in a neat pile at her feet, waiting patiently to cover the silver coffin. Her only solace in the bleak day had been Blake. He had stood close to her and she had sensed, rather than felt, his light touch on her back. She wished he would draw her to him and hold her close, but even the light touch soothed her troubled soul.

Now Tessa rubbed her red chapped fingers and brought them up to her lips. She cupped her hands and blew on them in an attempt to warm them before reaching into the laundry basket and hanging another icy item on the washing line. The wind whipped the white sheet up towards the grey heavens, and she added another clothes peg to keep it from hurling down the steep hill and into the ferocious sea below. The weight of her guilt, rather than the force of the arctic winds, kept Tessa bent over as she hurried back to the house. *Why had she not stopped her mother from leaving?* She had known the weather would be bad...*Had she shown her mother enough love? Could she have tried to sit and talk to her mother during afternoon teatimes, instead of always rushing off to explore at the surf below?* But then the more tormenting questions would arise... *Why had her mother not loved her? Was she truly unlovable?* These were questions that constantly rattled around in Tessa's mind and never seemed to land on an answer.

It is time to get back into some kind of routine, Tessa chided herself, and even though the tap-tap-tapping cane was not there to urge her on, she decided to cook Jeremiah his favorite meal. He would be home soon, and he deserved a hearty meal after working at the harbor since the crack of dawn. As Tessa peeled potatoes her mind wandered back to Blake. He had been her constant companion in the weeks that followed her mother's death. Not wanting to be insensitive, Blake had not broached the subject of their relationship but had instead spent time encouraging her to turn to God for the answers she was seeking. He had prayed with her often and during those times she had truly sensed a deep peace settle upon her. She felt safe with Blake and missed him terribly between visits.

With her mind still on him, Tessa pulled the piping hot chicken and mushroom pie out of the oven as she heard the front door slam.

"Jeremiah, you're just in time...hurry up and--"she stopped mid sentence as she saw Jeremiah's pale and drawn face. He looked haggard as he leaned against the wooden door frame. Tessa did not speak as she watched him struggle with the words that would not form. She nervously twisted the dish towel she held in her hands as she waited for him to speak.

He walked over to a chair and sat down heavily, his shoulders slumped.

"I've been called into the military. So has Blake. After our three month basic training, we will be sent to patrol the northern border."

"No, not now! Not *both* of you!" Tessa cried out, "Besides, there is a war at the border against the terrorists!"

"I'm sorry Tessa; we knew it would happen someday…"

Angry now, Tessa demanded, "But why? Why now?"

"I don't know…I'm sorry," he said again.

Tessa sank into the chair across from Jeremiah, "When?"

"Soon," was his one word response.

No more words followed and Tessa understood that there was nothing left to say.

They ate in silence.

*****

It was the middle of the night and Tessa tossed and turned on her bed. She knew that the two-year military training was mandatory and Jeremiah had to go, but she searched every corner of her mind in an effort to find a way to keep him home. After hours of fruitless agitation, she peered out of bleary red eyes and saw the first pale hues of dawn sneaking in her open window. She had forgotten to close it last night and now a cold breeze blew in and swayed her pink curtains back and forth. Tessa snuggled deeper under her pink and white comforter and watched the graceful curtains dance. The serene morning seemed peaceful, and the day was starting like any other, but Tessa felt...different.

There's no point in trying to sleep any longer. She pulled on some warm pants and grabbed a jacket on the way out the back door. It was still dark under the heavy foliage, but Tessa knew the path so well she could have found her way easily, even if she were completely blind. *Well, I feel blind,* she thought cynically. *I don't understand why this is happening; I will be lost without them.*

As her feet hit the white sand she started praying as she did every morning. "God, thank you for this day..." but no words followed.

What was there to be thankful for? She had lost her mother, and now she would lose the two people she loved most in the entire world. Tessa felt guilt wrap itself around her at these traitorous thoughts. *There has to be something good I can say to God today.*

She respectfully tried again, "Thank you God for this day...," a long silence followed, "But...I'm just wondering why you allowed all this to happen to me?" Tessa's voice grew louder, "Why couldn't you have stopped this? Do you even care *at all* that I am being left all alone?" Silence followed as Tessa gazed around the beach. "Haven't I served you faithfully? What have I done to deserve this?" The only sound she heard was the waves that crashed at her feet. Even the seagulls seemed shocked at these disloyal questions and sat unusually still on the boulders nearby. They watched her with accusingly beady eyes. Tessa allowed the anger that had been bubbling inside to rise up, and it spewed out as she screamed "God, are you even out there?"

The startled seagulls squawked loudly.

"Oh shut up!" she flung back at them as she stalked away.

The next morning Tessa decided to sleep in, and skipped going down to the beach. The day after that she decided to catch an earlier train to work.

There just won't be enough time to go down to the beach this morning, she reasoned. On the third morning she realized that it had been a while since she had taken the hiking trail that led to her Zulu friend's hut. Instead of wasting time on the beach trying to talk to a God who was silent, she would take the thirty-minute walk along the winding trail to Nolwazi's hut. The flattened path had originally been cut by the bare feet of the old Zulu woman, as she traipsed back and forth daily between Tessa's house and her own little hut.

Nolwazi had been their maid and Tessa's nanny for many years until her mother decided that Tessa was old enough to take on the responsibilities of cooking and cleaning. Tessa remembered the day that Nolwazi had arrived at the back door, only to be rudely dismissed by her mother. Nolwazi had turned and waved to Tessa before closing the rusty iron gate at the far end of the yard. Tessa had cried for days but to no avail…her mother would not allow Nolwazi back into the house. Soon after that, Tessa had snuck out early one morning and followed the broken weed path that led to the door of the little thatched roof hut. Since then Tessa had often found herself on the path that led to Nolwazi's fat, comforting arms.

Tessa smelled the woodsy fire before she saw the little hut. The Zulus constantly burned wood in big metal drums, and the smell was familiarly soothing. The mixture of salty sea air and smoke from the fire made Tessa long for the summer days when she smelled the same fragrance waft down the mountainside and surround her as she sunbathed on the rocks below. She breathed in deeply, filling her senses with the pungent scent.

Rounding the corner, Tessa came upon Nolwazi who was standing outside of her hut stirring a pot of mielie meal that hung over the fire. The white maize porridge bubbled wildly as Nolwazi swayed her big body from side to side. She was humming a tune and stirring the porridge in time to the rhythmic tribal melody. Tessa stood still and watched; she was mesmerized by the delightful sight. It dawned on her that Nolwazi had so little compared to most people, yet she radiated an inner peace that made her charmingly beautiful.

Tessa knew that Nolwazi spoke to God all day long and whatever secret things passed between them seemed to permeate every area of her life with a deep serenity. Her kindness towards Tessa had been tangible, and it had helped her learn how to love others. Nolwazi's quiet trust made Tessa long for the peace she now couldn't seem to find. It was gone, and she didn't know how to get it back. She frowned at these thoughts and sighed, *when did things get so complicated?*

5

Nolwazi set the pot of porridge on a stone to cool. She sensed someone watching her and turned to see Tessa standing on the edge of the path. Nolwazi's bright orange and red tribal skirt restricted her movement as she ran up to Tessa.

"Sawubona, sawubona!," Throwing her fat brown arms around Tessa she twirled her around and around, causing her matching orange and red head cloth to droop to the side.

Tessa laughed, "Good morning to you too!"

Nolwazi drew back and looked into Tessa's brilliant emerald eyes but immediately noticed the lack of sparkle that usually shone out of them.

Sompthinks wrongg, she thought.

Nolwazi looked Tessa up and down as though she was purchasing a piece of meat from the nearby butcher and pronounced, "U-kakhulu ondile."

Tessa defended herself with, "I'm not too thin!"

"OK, weze eat now," was Nolwazi's response as she dragged Tessa towards the pot of porridge. Holding the pot in one hand and dragging Tessa into the hut with the other, they entered the one-room dwelling that consisted of a bed and kitchen, separated by hanging strands of colorful beads.

Tessa sat down on the rickety chair at the little table. The tablecloth was made out of old newspaper that had been cut along the edges to create a pretty scalloped border. The only other thing in the kitchen was a wooden shelf that contained a dented silver pot, a few tin mugs, some assorted bowls, and a handful of mismatched utensils. As Tessa waited for her bowl of porridge, she noticed how spotless the little dwelling was. The dirt floor had been swept recently, and beyond the beaded separation, the bed was neatly covered with a colorful, albeit tattered, blanket.

Nolwazi sat across from Tessa and spooned in big mouthfuls of white porridge. She didn't speak but looked at Tessa with old wise eyes. When her bowl was finally licked clean, she spoke in her broken English "Tessa, God good book say ...we has trouble in these lifes," she paused searching for the words, "so wees have sometime *many* trouble."

She looked at Tessa intently and nodded as if it was all suddenly taken care of. Then she added, "It OK. Trouble OK." As if that was the end of the conversation, she got up and started picking up the empty bowls.

Tessa interrupted her by saying, "I don't understand, how is it OK?"

"Cos He wist us, child....in here," she added while holding her heart with both hands. "He no ever go away, he stay in here wist you. He no go anywhere!"

A toothless grin followed as she patted Tessa's hand.

"But I don't feel him anymore," Tessa whispered.

Nolwazi simply smiled and replied, "It OK."

As Tessa took the winding path home she pondered on the strange conversation. Nolwazi's name meant 'The One with Knowledge'- *but really,* Tessa thought, *sometimes she just doesn't make any sense!*

Tessa knew the 'good book' too, and thought, *What happened to the scripture that says,* "I have a good plan for you, says the Lord, plans for welfare and peace and not for evil."

"So, what about that?" She flung up to the empty sky above her; but the heavens remained brass and her words echoed back to her, mocking her.

*****

The next morning, Tessa woke up to another wailing winter storm. The ocean below heaved and sighed, threatening to rise up and swallow everything in its path. The wind howled around the corner of the house with a woeful moan. Just when Tessa thought the storm might abate, it picked up and the low moaning turned into a high pitched wail, setting her already taut nerves on edge. She was standing in the kitchen stirring a pot of chicken soup when the back door flung open and loudly banged against the wall. The wind had snatched it right out of Jeremiah's hand and he stood panting at the door. Water dripped from the end of his nose and he was drenched.

"You look like a wet dog." Tessa said and threw him a towel.

"Are you going to leave me standing out here all night?" came a voice from behind Jeremiah. Tessa did not have to see him to know that it was Blake. She had branded his voice into her memory and now subconsciously smoothed her hair with fluttering hands. Blake shoved Jeremiah into the kitchen and closed the door. "Mmm, I smell bread baking," he said and bent down to peek into the oven.

"Not before you two clean up," she playfully scolded as she saw the muddy puddles forming around their feet.

Tessa couldn't stop the rapid beating of her heart as she looked across the table at Blake. He'd had his head shaved in preparation for his departure into the military. When she had commented on it, he had mumbled something about not trusting the military barbers with their sheep shears. Looking at him now, Tessa thought him more handsome than ever. His dark eyes were intense and his olive skin glowed in the candlelight. Tessa was so thankful that she had pulled the bread out of the oven only moments before the storm had stolen their electricity. Now she watched Blake spread his hot bread with butter, which melted immediately, causing him to apply another dollop of rich butter to the bread before taking a big bite.

For a moment, everything seemed perfect again and she could forget her troubles. The three of them even found things to laugh about, and the previously eerie wind now seemed to laugh with them as it danced around the corners of the 'castle'. But this respite was short lived as Jeremiah spoke, "Tess, you know that Blake and I are leaving soon. I've been thinking…you cannot live here on your own. It would not be safe…one never knows when the riots will get out of control. Besides, I haven't wanted to tell you this, but we can't afford this big old house. I have to put it up for sale."

Tessa stared at Jeremiah as if he were speaking a foreign language.

"…But this is our home… I don't want to… leave…" she stammered. It was the only constant thing she would have in her life after they left. She looked at Blake for support, surely he would agree with her, but he remained silent and his dark brooding eyes were unreadable.

"I'm sorry Tess, but it's all arranged."

Jeremiah slid the envelope across the table. "Here is a bus ticket to Auntie Rina's farm in the Orange Free State." He glanced away quickly when he looked into Tessa's accusing eyes. "Auntie Rina is excited about you coming to help on the farm. There is much to take care of since her boys have been enlisted too. It will all work out for the best."

"I wish everyone would stop telling me that everything is going to work out for the best! I don't want to go to the Orange Free State. I hate the Orange Free State! It's like a desert and I--"

Jeremiah interrupted, "I'll come and visit you on the first weekend I get off."

Tessa saw the stubborn set of his jaw and knew that any more arguing would be fruitless.

6

Two weeks later Tessa stood at the busy bus depot at Cape Town Station and tried to still the unease that wrestled within her chest. She had only been away from home for a couple of hours and already she felt misplaced. The strangers that swarmed around her with their noisy clamor made her head pound. She watched as Jeremiah spoke to the conductor of the big greyhound bus and arranged a seat for her right up front, behind the driver's seat. He assured her that she would be taken care of during the journey which consisted of an overnight trip over the mountain pass.

Blake had called the house as she was leaving to say that his car had a flat tire. He had promised to hurry and would do his best to make it. Tessa now sat in the overfull bus and anxiously scanned the crowd for a glimpse of him. She could not believe that she may not see him after all. Jeremiah was standing outside the window, his hands stuffed inside his pockets. The wind lifted his dark hair off his forehead and he looked forlorn. Meeting Tessa's eyes through the glass he exaggerated a brave smile which did not quite reach his big green eyes.

Tessa swallowed hard and smiled back. With her hands she made the sign of "I love you" as the bus slowly pulled out of the station. She kept waving until Jeremiah was only a tiny figure in the distance, and then she allowed her first tear to roll down her cheek. She was glad for the privacy the window seat offered her and allowed her tears to fall as she watched the sun set across the golden fields. As each mile passed Tessa felt like she was being pushed further and further from her beloved Cape, and even the beautiful red Protea flowers that reflected the orange and gold sunset, brought her heart no joy.

The bus wound its way along the narrow mountain road and with each turn it inched higher and higher up the side of the mountain pass. Darkness eventually enveloped the bus and Tessa shivered as she draped her coat around her shoulders. Her body ached with fatigue and sadness and she willed herself to sleep. She woke up with the bus lunging from side to side and peered out the window. The lights from the bus only gave a few feet of illumination, but it was enough for Tessa to see the sharp drop that fell away from the narrow shoulder of the road. She peered at the bus driver and thought, *"He looks tired...what if he falls asleep?"* From then on she kept vigil over the driver as she tried to stop the vivid imaginations of the bus careening over the side of the mountain and being smashed to pieces on the rocks below. *No one will ever find us;* Tessa trembled at the thought.

The long black night seemed never ending and at the first glimpse of dawn, Tessa yawned with relief. She was cold and stiff but felt relieved that she had survived the grueling night. The bearded man across the aisle, who had leered at her from time to time, was now snoring loudly. *What a creep! It's a miracle I survived the night!*

Tessa stumbled off the bus at the little gas station and watched the orange sunrise push back the eerie darkness. Her stomach growled loudly and she felt nauseated as she shuffled along with her weary companions until she was seated at a sticky wooden table. She rubbed her tired eyes and ordered coffee along with a bacon and egg breakfast. In two hours they would be at their destination and Tessa's heart sank. The air here was crisp and dry and everything felt dead. She could already feel her skin shriveling up like a prune. She licked her dry lips and looked out onto the barren land. Not a single tree broke the barren horizon. The only foliage she spotted was the dry grassland that stood dead still in the frigid morning air. *It's probably frozen stiff...like me.*

Back on the bus Tessa closed her eyes and imagined her morning walks on the beach. She was amazed at how much she missed the seagulls' cries and regretted not going back down to the beach one last time to say goodbye to them. Surely they were perched on the salty boulders, waiting for her...or at least waiting for their bread crumbs. Her stubbornness had kept her from walking down those winding steps, but now, a new thought assaulted her. *What if God was still on the beach, waiting for her...*

She knew that this was a silly thought because she knew that God was everywhere, and He had promised never to leave her, but it really did seem that his presence was most strongly felt down on that sandy beach. Tessa felt a lump form at the back of her throat, but quickly pushed it away with other thoughts. *Surely there has to be something fun about living on a farm?*

Exiting the bus at 1395 meters above sea level, Tessa struggled to breathe in the arid desert air. *The Orange Free State... in all its majesty*, Tessa thought sarcastically.

"There you are!" Auntie Rina hurried over to her and threw her arms around Tessa, who suddenly felt self-conscious and shy around this Aunt who seemed more like a stranger. On the ride back to the farm, Tessa glanced nervously at her Aunt who was driving too fast down the gravel roads. She studied the older woman's pleasant face and noticed the deep dimples in her cheeks when she smiled. She was a jovial woman with bright, wise eyes; but Tessa got the distinct impression that she was no fool and probably ran the household with an iron fist.

Tessa realized that her mind had wondered and tuned back in to hear her Aunt saying, "...So both my boys, your cousins, have gone to the border to fight. I need help at the farm with the chores, and you and Charmaine will get along just fine! Our neighbor's son, Wayne, also comes over to work a few days a week. He is a sweet boy!"

Tessa heard herself repeat the empty words she had heard so often over the last few weeks, "I'm sure everything will work out fine." Her voice trailed off as she wondered what exactly 'farm chores' meant. She was by no means a typical 'city girl' but would definitely not consider herself a farm girl...

The first thing Tessa encountered as she stepped out of the car was the angry pack of dogs that circled the car. "Don't worry about them," Auntie Rina said as she smacked the first dog in the head. "They are our protection and therefore your new friends! With all the violence and crime around here, we cannot be too careful, now can we?" The wolves circled Tessa and she wondered if *they* knew that she was a new friend.

7

Tessa was relieved to actually find a new friend on the farm. Her cousin, Charmaine, sat on her bed and talked to Tessa as if they were long lost friends. In fact, Tessa had only been on the farm once before, and that had been when she was a little girl. She could scarcely remember her cousin who now dominated the conversation.

"So since we are sharing a room, let me tell you the rules. You can have that bed over there," she said as she pointed to the narrow bed against the opposite wall, "...and you can use the two bottom shelves of the dresser." She smiled widely and completed the instructions by adding, "We're going to be great friends!"

Tessa felt completely exhausted, but looked at her cousin and smiled. Charmaine was a pretty girl with inquisitive hazel-colored eyes. She was petite and looked cute in her white and pink flannel pajamas. The candlelight formed a golden halo around her long blonde hair. This brought Tessa's attention back to the candle that sat on the dresser between them. She could not believe that this old farmhouse had no electricity! There seemed to be some kind of generator for the kitchen and living area, *thank goodness*, but the rooms and bathroom stayed dark unless she walked around with a candle.

The shadows on the walls gave Tessa the creeps and she hurried to unpack her suitcase so that she could jump into bed and escape the ghostly figures she imagined walking the halls of this old farmhouse. She looked over at Charmaine who was brushing her hair and smiling at herself in the handheld mirror. *Apparently she is oblivious to the monsters in this house,* Tessa thought, *or maybe she is just used to them...*

Once her head hit the pillow Tessa was plunged into absolute blackness. It was so dark that when she held her hand up to her face she could not see it.

Charmaine had blown out the candle with a cheery, "Goodnight, see you at 5:00 a.m.!"

Now Tessa lay in the dark and listened to the silence that was deafening. There was not a single sound, and she now realized how loud the roaring of the ocean had been. How she missed that hissing sound...*Shhhh swish shhhh...*

She shivered and tried to warm her toes by rubbing her freezing feet on the cold white sheets. *I need to get up and find some socks. I'll never fall asleep with these frozen feet.*

Reaching over she felt around the nightstand for the candle, but accidentally bumped the matches off the table. There was no way she was getting out of bed to creep around on the cold wooden floors. *No telling what I may find in this spooky farmhouse under this bed.* So instead Tessa pulled the blanket up over her head and just lay in the darkness, allowing her mind to wander. Before, on nights like tonight, she would have spent her time praying and found comfort in that, but tonight the silence between herself and God was tangible. *So this is your good plan for me?*

Tessa thought about her brother and Blake. She tried to picture them lying in their army bunks and wondered if they too lay awake thinking about her. She had hoped that she and Blake would finally have been able to say something meaningful to each other before they were separated. She could have told him that she was willing to wait for him, but she had not even gotten to say goodbye, and now the unfinished conversation tormented her. Not knowing for sure what Blake felt in his heart was almost unbearable. Yes, she could guess and she could hope, but she needed to know! Tessa tried to console herself with the thought of letters that were bound to arrive any day.

If I could find the damn matches, I could write a letter instead of lying here rehearsing these unspoken words that are floating around in my head...

At three o'clock the rooster crowed outside the bedroom window and Tessa almost fell out of the bed from the shock of it. It took her a second to figure out where she was and what the loud noise was. At five o'clock Charmaine stumbled out of bed and stubbed her toe on the corner of the iron bed.

"Ouchhh", she shouted as she hopped around on one foot. "Where are the matches?" she angrily demanded.

Tessa held her pounding head and retorted, "Be quiet! I'm trying to sleep; it's the middle of the night!" The rooster crowed again and she heard the dogs barking ferociously. The windmill creaked in the field nearby and Tessa groaned as she pulled her pillow over her head. *Please just let this be a bad dream...*

Charmaine unceremoniously grabbed the pillow off her head and flung it across the room. "Breakfast is in fifteen minutes; if you miss it, you will only eat at noon. I suggest you get yourself to the table if you don't want to starve out in the cold barn."

Tessa pushed herself up on her elbow and yawned. Her lack of sleep had made her feel irritable, "And what am I going to be doing in the cold barn, pray tell?"

"Well, milking the cows of course!" with that Charmaine tossed her golden hair over her shoulder and stomped out of the room. Tessa sighed and got out of bed thinking she really shouldn't have been so grumpy with her cousin on her first day at the farm. She hurriedly threw her gown on, and stuffed her icy feet into slippers as she rushed down the drafty hall towards the kitchen. The wooden floors creaked as if they too were not ready to be awakened at this ungodly hour.

The sight she came upon as she entered the kitchen was welcoming however. There was a pot of strong black coffee that was percolating on the stove. The aroma filled the kitchen and Tessa's stomach growled. Next to the coffee percolator was a bubbling pot of mielie miel porridge that reminded Tessa of the last time she had seen Nolwazi at her hut.

A few pieces of sausage sizzled in a cast iron pan, making Tessa's mouth water. The ancient farmhouse kitchen held a warm glow. Tessa greeted her aunt who stood in front of the stove warming her hands over the pot of porridge.

A maid was setting the table and didn't look up until Auntie Rina said, "Tessa, this is Sinethemba."

The brown girl was short and plump, much like Nolwazi, but many years younger and she had a tiny infant strapped to her back by a colorful blanket. She wore no socks and her bare feet were stuffed into men's shoes that were far too big for her. The shoes had no laces so they slopped along the floor as she walked. She looked at Tessa with guarded eyes and said, "Ngiyakwemukela." *Welcome*.

Tessa surprised her by answering in Zulu, "Ngiyabonga." *Thank you*. "How old is the baby?"

Auntie Rina answered, "The baby is two weeks old. Sinethemba's husband, Bogani, usually works the fields and does many of the chores, but he got his hand caught in the tractor's engine and now has infection in the wound. He has been running a fever for weeks now, and the doctor is doing all he can. With the boys away in the military, we will have to keep up the chores outside. Sinethemba does the housecleaning and cooking."

Tessa wanted to clap her hands with delight. *No cooking? No laundry?* This was going to be better than she imagined. She looked around the old farmhouse kitchen. It was a large room with many rough cabinets. The stove and fridge were ancient and the long wooden table looked homemade. On one side of the table stood some heavy wooden chairs, and on the other side was a long bench. The table could easily seat sixteen people.

"My husband made this table himself and finished it just before he died in that horrible car accident," Auntie Rina said as she noticed Tessa observing the table.

Tessa looked at Charmaine who was seated at the enormous table for a sign of how to react to this random confession; but Charmaine only shrugged and continued sipping her hot coffee.

"So," Auntie Rina continued the previous conversation as if her dead husband had not been mentioned, "Tessa, you will have to learn how to milk the cows and feed the horses. Have you ever fed chickens?" Without waiting for an answer she waved her hand and added, "Never mind, I will feed the chickens today. In the spring we plant a vegetable garden but the ground is frozen for now, so never mind about that either…" She continued giving instructions as she plopped huge portions of bubbling porridge into the bowls. Tessa followed the others' example and poured a heavy whipping cream into the porridge. After that she added a dollop of butter and a heaping tablespoon of golden syrup.

"This is the best porridge I've ever eaten," she said as she swallowed the hot creamy porridge. *It's probably because I didn't have to cook it myself!*

An hour later Tessa sat on a three legged stool and tried to milk a cow. Her stomach ached and she regretted eating all that rich cream on her porridge, especially as the warm milk accidently squirted her in the eye. She wiped her eye with the back of her sleeve and looked at Charmaine, who didn't seem to have a care in the world. *Obviously, her stomach is not hurting!*

In fact, Charmaine looked very fashionable for milking cows. She wore a tight pair of jeans and a black sweater. Tessa looked down at her own clothes. Her feet were stuffed into an old pair of galoshes that she had borrowed from her aunt. It appeared that those wicked dogs had gotten to them first because they were torn and tattered, but at least they protected her from the mountains of manure that littered the pasture. As it was, Tessa had to hold her nose closed for the longest time to adjust her senses to the 'cow odor'.

After a relatively unsuccessful attempt at milking the cows, and two spilt buckets of milk, Charmaine finally said, "OK that's good enough, you can try again tomorrow."

She smiled at Tessa who was relieved that the morning frustrations had been forgiven. But then, things didn't go much better with the horses. Tessa was afraid of them and kept backing away with their buckets of feed, which only made the horses more forceful. Backing away from them, she tripped and fell, causing the buckets of feed to spill out onto the grass.

Charmaine tried to remain patient and said, "You've got to show them who's the boss. Make them respect your space. Slap them like this...," she said as she walked over to the gelding and smacked him hard on the neck. He yanked up his head and took a few steps backwards. "See..." Charmaine said pointedly.

"Yes, I see," Tessa replied. *Apparently my new job in life is to slap dogs and horses! What's next? Good thing I am not feeding the chickens or I suppose I would have to slap them too...*

"Now we have to straighten the barn and feed the pigs. My brothers used to do all this but they belong to the government for the next two years," Charmaine continued the instructions.

Pigs? Pigs? No one had mentioned pigs!

By lunch time Tessa was totally exhausted from feeding the obnoxious animals. Her hair was tangled and her clothes were slimed with cow saliva. She had a streak of dirt across her cheek and she was starving. *I don't belong here.*

She plodded up the porch stairs and into the kitchen, bone weary and close to tears. It took her by surprise when she bumped into the young man that stood leaning against the counter. He was tall and devilishly handsome as he grinned at her with a crooked smile. His teeth were a pearly white and shone from behind perfectly formed lips. Most striking, however, were his sapphire blue eyes that observed her as if she was the only person in the kitchen. Tessa felt her cheeks grow warm under his scrutiny and pushed back the hair that had escaped the crooked pony tail. "I'm sorry," she mumbled.

"Tessa," Auntie Rina said, "this is Wayne, our neighbor I told you about. He will be helping us around here until the boys get back."

She looked back at Wayne who was casually leaning against the counter and had his long legs crossed in front of him. She expected a polite 'hello' but instead she heard him say, "Apparently you need help around here. She looks like she has been in a wrestling match with those pigs."

At those words Tessa's head snapped back in disbelief and anger at Wayne's rude remark. Seeing her reaction, Wayne threw back his head and laughed loudly. Auntie Rina laughed too, "He's just teasing, Tessa."

Coming through the back door, Charmaine pushed past Tessa and threw her thin arms around Wayne's neck in an exaggerated hug. Tessa used this moment to escape down the hall and into the bathroom, where she saw her green luminous eyes staring back at her in the mirror. She looked cold and pale and was basically…a mess. She washed her face and applied a thin layer of pearl pink lipstick to her lips. She brushed her long dark hair and then slammed the brush down on the counter.

Who does he think he is? She wiped the pink lipstick off of her mouth and wrestled her hands through her manicured hair until it looked a mess.

"There, that's perfect," she said.

Back in the kitchen, Tessa listened to the conversation that was taking place around the long table. Auntie Rina was saying, "In the spring we need to plant some more lucerne for the horses to eat. We also need to keep an eye on the weather and plant our spring garden as soon as possible." Tessa thought that perhaps the conversation was turned to spring, to give the occupants at the table hope that the almost unbearable winter months would not last forever.

Wayne ate his food and conversed with Auntie Rina and Charmaine, but totally ignored Tessa throughout the meal. He didn't so much as look at her. *He is so rude*, Tessa thought. From time to time Tessa would sneak a peek at him and she again noticed how ruggedly handsome he was with his dark hair and fair skin. But it was those brilliant blue eyes that captivated Tessa the most.

Aunt Rina looked at Tessa and said, "After lunch I want you to go with Wayne and have him teach you how to pump water from the bore hole. We don't have city water on the farm, so it has to be pumped. You need to learn how to do it."

Later in the afternoon Tessa found herself leaning over the water pump. Wayne finally spoke to Tessa, "You don't want to be here, right?"

"You mean here at the pump with you, or here on this farm?" she sarcastically retorted.

"Both" he replied. Tessa didn't see the need to respond and remained silent.

Wayne surprised her by adding, "I know how hard it is to be away from home." He looked at her with solemn eyes.

"Why do you say that?" Tessa asked.

"I was sent away to stay with my Uncle in Durban for a couple of years when my mother got sick. I was just a young boy and enjoyed the ocean, but I missed my family terribly. After a few months my mother recovered and I came home. It was the best day of my life."

Tessa relaxed a little and said, "I miss my brother and Blake terribly."

"Who is Blake?" Wayne asked.

"Well, it's hard to explain…but we are going to be together soon." Tessa paused but felt Wayne's questioning eyes watching her, and she hurriedly added, "We have an understanding."

"How do you know you are going to be together? Did he *say* that?" Wayne interjected.

"Well no, not in that many words, but we have an understanding," Tessa repeated herself.

"Oh OK," Wayne's mocking voice belied his words and Tessa felt herself blush. Now that she had said it out loud, it sounded foolish even to her own ears, and she silently berated herself for saying anything to this stranger. It did not help to see a smirk cross Wayne's handsome face.

"Well are you going to show me how this stupid pump works, or am I supposed to stand out here and freeze to death for no reason?" she snapped.

8

That night Tessa lay in bed and felt a little more prepared for the overnight drop in desert temperatures than she had the night before. An extra box of matches was safely tucked under her feather pillow and her feet were warmed by not one, but two pairs of fluffy socks. The only similarity from the night before was that she could not sleep. Wayne's words came back to haunt her in the blackness of the night. "Did he say that? Did he say that you would be together? Do you really have an understanding?"

Tessa had to admit to herself that Blake had not actually *said* it.

"Then could it be possible that you just imagined it?" her mind whispered cynically. It felt like months ago since they had stood in the foggy air and held hands outside of the Black Marlin restaurant. Tonight Tessa felt more alone than she ever had. Her brother was many miles away, her mother was dead, and the man she loved perhaps didn't care about her at all. Indeed, it seemed like God himself had left her and she was completely abandoned.

After many hours she dozed off and her sleep was filled with vivid dreams. She was walking with Blake down a country lane and she was happy. Then she noticed that the cows were talking to her and saying, "Did he say that? Did he say that?" She looked at Blake and he smiled at her, but there was something wrong...his eyes were not their usual dark brown but had turned a sapphire blue and were boring holes into her with the fire that came out of them. Tessa screamed and woke up. She was shaking and her heart was beating wildly. She felt for the hidden stash of matches under her pillow and quickly lit the candle. Charmaine had her head covered with a pillow, and Tessa was glad that she had not woken her.

Tessa quietly tiptoed over to the drawer that held her few belongings and pulled out her writing paper. The room was dark and cold and Tessa sat in her bed and pulled the blanket around her shivering shoulders. The single candle gave out just enough light for her to see the faint scribbling on the paper as she began,

Dear Blake,
I am fine. How are you?

She crumpled the paper up and threw it across the room. That would not do! It sounded like she was writing to a stranger, rather than to her future husband. She tried again,

Hello Blake,
I have been thinking about you all the time and was wondering if you think about me at all?

Another ball of paper hit the far wall at the end of the room. *Too needy*, Tessa thought. She put the pen down and sat for a long time thinking before she wrote,

Hi Blake,

I hope this letter finds you well. I was disappointed that we did not get to say goodbye to each other, but perhaps it was for the best. Goodbyes are too sad and I am sure we will see each other very shortly. But I really wish above all else that we had been able to finish the important conversation we had started outside of the restaurant that night. Jeremiah said that the two of you would come and visit me on your first weekend off. Perhaps we can finish our chat then? I am looking forward to seeing you both!

How is military life treating you? I know that change is hard and I'm sure you miss home...as I do, but we have much to be grateful for and it helps keeping one's mind on the positive things. I am learning how to feed horses, chickens and pigs. Can you imagine that? But at least I do not have to pluck the chickens for our dinner. So you see things can always be worse.

I am also blessed to have a break from the cooking and laundry, as Auntie Rina's maid does all that. Her husband, the gardener, hurt his hand in a farming accident recently and cannot help with

the chores right now. We have a neighbor who comes over and helps with chores, although I must say that he works on my nerves with his arrogant opinions...

My cousin Charmaine is friendly enough but seems to be more wrapped up in herself than anyone else. It's hard to have a serious conversation with her because she is always fixing her hair and applying makeup. Anyway, it's just as well since I don't feel like talking that much these days.

Tessa reread the letter and pondered on what to say next. She didn't want to sound lonely and unhappy and yet she didn't want to lie and pretend she was happy here. The truth was that she felt lonely and wanted nothing more than to return home to her 'castle' at the beach. She longed for the seagulls cry and craved to see the roaring waves. But would Blake even care about that? She was sure that he was probably having a worse time being cooped up in boot camp in the middle of winter. She decided to keep the first letter short and wait for his response so she ended the letter with:

I really miss you and Jeremiah. Can't wait to see you again,

Then she wondered how she should sign off. Should she say,

From your love,
Tessa.

Or would that be presumptuous at this point? Should she end the letter with,

Sincerely,
Tessa... or was that too formal?

"Oh this is all Wayne's fault!" she groaned. "I would never have had a problem with ending this letter if I had not heard those four little words out of his sarcastic mouth... 'Did he *say* that?' "

Tessa eventually scribbled, *love Tessa* at the end of the letter and stuck it in an envelope. She wrote Jeremiah a short letter too and told him she would be watching for his letter every day.

Feeling much better after having written the letters, Tessa blew out the candles and soon fell into a deep sleep. She was certain that she would hear from Blake any day now and that he would proclaim his undying love for her in his romantic letter. She dreamed of him again, but this time they were holding hands and he mouthed the words, "I love you, Tessa" as he gazed at her with his dark chocolate eyes.

"I love you too," she mumbled.

"Oh that's sweet," she heard Charmaine's voice, "but you are going to be late for breakfast again." As usual Charmaine was standing in front of the mirror brushing her golden hair.

It's a wonder her hair doesn't fall out with all that brushing, Tessa thought as she turned over and decided for once to skip breakfast with the hope of falling back into the same beautiful dream she had just came out of.

By midmorning Tessa was starving and irritable. Everything Wayne said irritated her and he seemed to think it was funny, which annoyed her even further. "So maybe you will learn not to skip breakfast!" she heard him saying. "You can't work on a farm in winter on an empty stomach. Any fool knows that," he added. Tessa wondered if she had imagined the change in Wayne's tone. The playfulness seemed to have been replaced by an edge in his voice.

"So now you're calling me a fool?" Tessa questioned, as she stamped her boot on the frozen ground, all the while hating the gesture because it reminded her of her mother when she would stamp her foot angrily on the stone floor in their kitchen. However, the ugly gesture brought a reaction from Wayne, and Tessa was surprised when he threw down his tools and stalked over to her. She found herself taking a small step backwards. She hadn't realized before just how tall he really was and now he towered over her. His eyes flashed angrily and he opened his mouth to say something, but seemed to change his mind at the last moment.

Instead, he gently laid a hand on her shoulder and smiled as he said, "I'm sorry, apparently I'm grouchy too. Let's go over to my house and grab a sandwich; I need to pick up another tool anyway."

Tessa found herself replying, "I'm sorry too, a sandwich sounds good. I'm famished." They started walking down the country lane towards Wayne's house and he chatted as they went, but Tessa felt unsettled. Had she imagined that flash of anger?

She relaxed once they were sitting at the kitchen table eating their sandwiches. When the tea kettle whistled on the old stove, Tessa jumped up out of habit, but Wayne said, "You sit and eat, I will fix you the best cup of tea you've ever had!" He flashed her a brilliant smile as he put the teacups on the counter. "You'll have to come back one day when we have time. I want to show you my bird collection."

"Oh, I didn't know you had birds?" she replied between bites of her sandwich.

"There are a lot of things you don't know about me," he grinned mischievously.

"OK I'll bite…like what?"

"Did you know that I'm an excellent dancer? And did you know that I can speak four languages?" he hesitated and then added, "Most importantly, did you know that I am the best kisser you'll ever meet?" which was followed by an exaggerated wink.

"Oh brother!" Tessa dropped her head into her hands to cover the smile she felt playing on her lips. "No, I didn't know those things, but what I do know is that you are a little conceited. Now give me my tea before I choke on this dry bread!"

As they walked back down the country lane, Wayne put his arm around her and said, "Just in case you slip on the patches of ice on the road."

"I didn't see any patches of ice while we were walking towards your house…"

"Trust me," Wayne grinned and pulled her closer to him and Tessa enjoyed the warmth and did not pull away. He had been so sweet and caring all afternoon and Tessa wondered if she had judged him too harshly. He really was not conceited at all, but merely playful.

*****

"Ahhh, that was delicious," Tessa sighed. They were sitting around the dinner table and Tessa felt truly content for the first time in a long while. Sinethemba had cooked a beef roast with fried potatoes and sweet carrots and was now pulling out a piping hot ginger pudding. The ginger and cinnamon seasoning made the kitchen smell warm and welcoming. Charmaine and Aunt Rina sat across from Tessa and Wayne, and they had found many things to laugh about tonight. But in all honesty, the warmth that Tessa felt came more from the hand that Wayne had laid on her knee under the table.

Tessa ate her tasty dessert and tried to hold onto the sense of contentment she felt. She glanced at Wayne and saw the mischief in his beautiful blue eyes. He squeezed her leg and Tessa tried not to jump. She felt a twinge of guilt rise up in her, but quickly reminded herself that Wayne was just playing and it was all in innocent fun.

Later that night Tessa and Charmaine lay in their beds talking, and Tessa was enjoying having a girl to chat to. She told Charmaine all about Blake and how much she missed him. Then Charmaine whispered into the darkness and told her how her ex-boyfriend had broken her heart a year ago. Tessa felt sorry for her as she heard Charmaine's voice break, and realized that Charmaine was still hurting over the breakup. Then Charmaine added, "Have you noticed how handsome Wayne is?" Tessa suddenly felt hot and was glad the darkness concealed her blushing cheeks. "Um…" she stammered as she thought of something to say. What bothered her more than the question was the sharp jealousy she felt rising up in her.

Thankfully at that moment Charmaine yawned loudly and said, "I'm really tired. Goodnight, Tessa."

The warm contentment that Tessa had felt all evening suddenly evaporated. *What am I doing? I love Blake! I shouldn't let Wayne flirt with me like that! I'll just talk to him tomorrow morning and set him straight.*

The familiar loneliness came rushing back as Tessa fell into a restless sleep. The next morning she woke up and found Charmaine standing in front of the mirror in a beautiful black and silver dress. Her high heel shoes matched the dress perfectly and she looked striking.

"Where are you going?" Tessa croaked.

"You mean where are *we* going?" Charmaine retorted, but continued to stare at herself as she curled her golden hair around the hair roller and then added, "It's Sunday, and we're going to church of course!"

"But I don't want to go to church!"

This response caused Charmaine to turn around and look at Tessa suspiciously; her curler now paused in mid air. "Of course you do! We all go to church every Sunday. Now get up and get dressed or you're going to be late as usual."

Tessa felt too weary to argue and a few minutes later she too peered at herself in the mirror. She stood clothed in the dress that Jeremiah had bought her before their last dinner at the Black Marlin. Now it brought tears to her eyes as she longed for her brother.

"Wow, that is a gorgeous dress!" she heard Charmaine say behind her, and Tessa smiled sadly and answered,

"Yes, it is, isn't it?"

9

Tessa sat on the wooden church pew and shivered. The icy air cut through her thin dress and turned her nails blue from the cold. She finally draped the mismatched coat around her shoulders. She tried to concentrate on what the preacher was saying, "The bible says that in this life we will have trials, but God promises that He will never leave us nor forsake us. God says He hears us when we call! Our enemy is always accusing God to us. He whispers that God doesn't care and that he is an unfaithful God, but I say: draw near to God and He will draw near to you!"

Tessa felt herself taking a deep breath, as if she were trying to breathe in the old familiar presence of God. The colored glass in the window sent shimmering images across her skin as the weak sun filtered through, and Tessa watched the patterns dance across her hands. She turned her palms up in an attempt to catch the sparkles and instead she found herself trying to capture this elusive God. Tessa closed her eyes and whispered, "God, I miss you so much, I have been living in a barren place in my soul. Are you still out there?"

"I've never left you Tessa. Come back to me…" a still small voice beckoned to her and a fresh peace filled her heart and mind.

"God, I just don't understand. Why can't you prevent bad things from happening to us? Why did you allow these things?"

"You have to trust me, Tessa."

Before Tessa could finish her conversation with God, she heard the preacher say, "Amen."

Everyone got up quietly and shuffled out of the musty church. Squinting into the feeble sunlight Tessa observed Wayne and Charmaine standing with a group of young people near the church gate. She wandered over and shyly stood at the edge of the crowd. She hoped that she would get a chance to speak to Wayne about his display of affection from the day before, to set things straight. To remind him that it was all just playing and that her heart belonged to Blake. But today Wayne glanced at her as if he had never seen her before. There seemed to be no recognition in his eyes and Tessa wondered if she had imagined his hand on her knee the previous evening. Since meeting Wayne, she seemed to be questioning herself a lot.

Tessa noticed a young woman who stood rather close to him and laughed loudly at his jokes while constantly touching his arm and smiling up at him with adoring eyes. She was a pretty girl but Tessa thought that her smile was too big for her skinny face. This was probably due to the fact that she was extremely scrawny, which usually made people look like they had too many teeth in their mouth. But her brown hair was cut into a stylish bob and her short red dress matched her red painted nails which gave her an enticing, worldly appeal. Charmaine finally had the good manners of introducing Tessa and said, "This is my old high school friend, Sharon."

"Hey there," Sharon oozed with a wide smile. Tessa was just going to respond when Sharon swung her head away causing her bob to bounce up and down. She was again enraptured with Wayne who now seemed to be flirting with another blonde that had joined the group. Tessa tried not to feel rejected and hurt but wondered what on earth Wayne was thinking, or if he was indeed thinking about her at all!

"So let's all go down to the steakhouse for lunch," she heard Charmaine say, and it was met with a cheer from the hungry group as they all turned to leave.

As it happened, Tessa was seated next to Wayne at the restaurant and Sharon sat opposite them. There was more laughter and jokes as they waited for their lunch. Tessa wanted to feel like she was a part of this group and tried to act jovial, but found it tiring to be so exuberant. Her laughter sounded hollow even to her own ears but it seemed as if Sharon had no problem as she laughed hysterically at Wayne's joke and slapped the table in an attempt to catch her breath.

Wayne completely ignored Tessa until she started a conversation with the boy seated on the other side of her, who introduced himself as Hendrik van Vuuren, an Afrikaans boy who worked on his parent's farm nearby. He was tall and solidly built from years of manual labor. His short blonde hair and light green eyes made him look like a German boy, but he greeted her in Afrikaans and said, "My naam is Hendrik; dit is goed om jou te ontmoet."

Tessa replied, "My name is Tessa, I am glad to meet you too." Before they could continue their conversation Wayne draped his arm around Tessa and drew her close to him, while he looked over at Hendrik with steel blue eyes. On one hand Tessa felt pleased at this sudden public display of affection, but she also felt embarrassed and tried to push away from Wayne who tightened his grip on her.

Hendrik looked away as if he, too, was embarrassed with the intimate embrace and looked down into his coke as if suddenly mesmerized by the bubbles. A few minutes later he mumbled an excuse and picking up his coke, went to join a friend at the end of the table. As soon as Hendrik moved, Wayne dropped his arm from Tessa's shoulder and blew a paper wad out of his straw at Sharon, who burst out laughing when it landed on her thin arm. As she watched them, Tessa's previous hunger pangs were replaced with nausea and a desperate need for fresh air. She too, like Hendrik, whispered a vague excuse to Charmaine and picked up her purse, leaving the group who didn't seem to care about her hasty departure anyway.

Roaming the empty streets of the foreign town Tessa felt forlorn as she watched a single bramble weed slowly roll across the deserted street. There had been no rain and no wind in this dry wilderness since she arrived, and an icy breeze now stirred Tessa's long hair. She trembled as the cold bit into her flesh but relished the feeling of the wispy wind on her skin. She never thought she would have missed those Cape winds that had the power to throw trucks onto their sides, but today she longed for those winds to descend on her and blow the cobwebs out of her head. She smiled at the thought, as she remembered Jeremiah standing on their favorite boulder as the wind howled angrily and the waves crashed around him. He would throw his hands up towards the purple sky and shout at Tessa who hid in the cave nearby, "Come out of there and let the wind blow the cobwebs out of your head!"

Tessa watched the wind whip the dry leaves across the road and thought about how much she missed Jeremiah and Blake. She felt alone and out of place here. She needed to talk to them and turned toward the bus station. She would go home and finish the letters that she'd started, maybe she would feel a little more connected to them as she put pen to paper.

When she got home, Tessa sat quietly at the kitchen table and wrapped her hands around a mug of strong English tea. She continued writing the second letter that she had started to Blake.

"... I missed the ocean so much today. I long to feel the wind on my skin, as my ears strain to hear the crashing waves. But mostly I miss the smell of the salty sea air.

I wonder what you miss most. I haven't heard from you or Jeremiah and can only imagine that you have not had time to write. I hope that this letter crosses yours in the mail and I find a letter in the mailbox soon.

P.S. I made some new friends today...I think.
I miss you,
Tessa.

*****

It was six o' clock in the morning and Tessa stood inside the chicken coop wearing her fluffy slippers, on which the tiny chicks sat. She had two chicks on each slipper and they

65

looked up at her as they waited for the grain to fall into their tiny gaping mouths. The bigger chickens clucked loudly and flapped their wings as they hungrily gobbled up the corn that landed near them.

Tessa had fallen into a rhythmic routine with the caring of the animals and felt herself growing attached to them. The milking of the cows was a much easier task now, and the horses didn't scare her anymore. But the one animal she had grown to love was her Golden Labrador puppy who had adopted her. He was one of the many pups born at the barn and had attached himself to Tessa within weeks. Now he followed Tessa everywhere and was her constant companion.

Tessa had named the dog 'Bullet' because of how fast he took off running after anything that moved in the fields. She smiled now as she watched Bullet sitting outside of the chicken coop impatiently waiting for her to finish. He watched the tiny chickens and barked at them every now and then. "You want to eat these chickens for breakfast, don't you boy?" Tessa spoke to the dog who had quickly become her best friend. Her throat hurt and she rubbed her neck in an attempt to soothe it.

Her mind wandered to the events of the day before. Why did Wayne act so aloof sometimes and then act so affectionate at other times? Worse still was the question …why did it matter anyway? She loved Blake and could not wait to see him again. He was honest and steady. Yes, it was true that she was concerned about the fact that she had not heard from him. And the thought had crossed her mind that he had perhaps changed his mind about her after all, but what if he had not?

On the other hand, Wayne was very handsome, almost in an arrogant sort of way, and Tessa could not always read what he was thinking. She sensed that he had a dark side but, if she was totally honest, it intrigued her. She had seen him for a few minutes at breakfast and he had not said anything about her leaving early from lunch the day before. Had he not noticed? Or did he not care? Tessa emptied the basket of grain and gently moved the now sleeping chicks off her slippers.

By mid afternoon Tessa felt worse than ever. She could hardly swallow and her head pounded unbearably. Her cough sounded like a bark, and Bullet stared up at her with inquisitive eyes every time she coughed. "Let's go lie down for a while," she rasped.

Auntie Rina didn't allow dogs in the house so Tessa snuck Bullet in through the side door and now they lay side by side on the bed. When Tessa heard the creaking of the floorboards in the hallway she quickly threw a blanket over Bullets head and hoped he would be still. Auntie Rina opened the door and entered the room, "Not feeling too good, are you? These winter colds can be fierce out here in this semi-desert area. I'll send you some chicken soup and medicine from the kitchen in a little while. Try and rest."

She turned to leave but stopped at the door and said, "I usually don't make exceptions to my rules Tessa." Tessa thought for the first time that Aunt Rina sounded just like her stern mother when she continued, "but I know how lonely you have been since you got here and I will allow the dog to stay, while you are not well."

She smiled slightly and added, "So you might as well uncover him before he suffocates."

Before Tessa could respond her Aunt had left the room. Now she lay and scratched Bullet between the ears and was comforted by the warmth that her four legged friend brought into her life in more ways than one.

10

Blake lay on his army bunk in the dark and sighed. He did not have many regrets in life, but he regretted not having finished the conversation he had started with Tessa. Why had he not found a way to tell her how he felt about her? Why had he not told her that he had already paid off the jeweler in Fish Hoek for that beautiful engagement ring she had once casually pointed out to him, while they wiled away a sunny afternoon together. She had always been the one…and he had always *assumed* she knew that.

But now he felt troubled and tried to figure out what was wrong. He didn't have much time to think during the day, what with the grueling training and the screaming of the officers that never seemed to end. Why they had to shout so much, he just couldn't figure out. He fell into bed exhausted at night, and had to be up before the cock crowed in the morning. He shook his head as he thought about that saying…"before the cock crows." Up until now it had just been a saying he used, but he was literally awakened every morning by a cock that crowed loudly enough to make a man fall out of bed. The first morning at his new barracks, he woke up thinking, "What the heck was that?" but since then he had gotten accustomed to the strange sound. It always made him think of Tessa, and he wondered how she was doing on the farm. He wondered if she too woke up with a cock crowing. Now he lay and wondered why he felt so restless. Was she OK?

He had received a letter from her a few days ago that sounded distant and vague, not at all like the Tessa he knew. He wondered if she had received his letter. He realized that he was doing a lot of 'wondering' and that was getting him nowhere, so he decided to pray instead. Since he had been moved to this new camp in the middle of nowhere, he had not seen Jeremiah and therefore felt like he had completely lost the link to Tessa. To make matters worse, the mail that came in and out to this secluded camp was snail mail. Blake did not like the feeling he had though; no, he did not like it at all. Something was wrong, and he prayed for hours before falling into a sleep that was filled with strange dreams.

*****

Charmaine willed the bus driver to drive a little faster! They were almost at her stop near the farm and she almost jumped off the bus as it slowly ground to a halt. From here it would only take her fifteen minutes to walk down the gravel road to the farm. She found herself wanting to dance with sheer excitement. She had bumped into her ex-boyfriend, Jack, at the market and he had actually asked if he could visit her sometime. She had been speechless at first, having given up all hope that Jack still cared for her, but she quickly recovered and invited him to dinner. He would be arriving in an hour and she wanted to look her very best. She had a good feeling about tonight, a very good feeling indeed!

It was dusk and freezing by the time she turned onto the lane at the farm. She opened the mailbox and flipped through the letters as she continued down the path. There were three bills for her mother, two letters for Tessa, and a big brown envelope with her name on it that had a return address in New York. She stuffed the other mail into her purse and opened her envelope because she was just too inquisitive to wait and see who could possibly be sending her something from New York, of all places!

Inside was a catalog to an upscale boutique, and a letter telling Charmaine that she had won a gift certificate to the boutique. She would be allowed to choose a dress and a pair of shoes from the catalog and it would be mailed to her door! Charmaine could not believe what a lucky day it was. She had never won anything in her life, and now she would have a fabulous dress for the big spring dance that was coming up. *Won't Jack think that I am absolutely gorgeous then?*

The thought of Jack made Charmaine check her watch and hurry down the lane. She threw down her mother's mail in the kitchen and yelled out, "Jack's coming for dinner, OK?" as she hurried down the hallway to the bedroom. Passing the bathroom she stopped in and started running a bath with hot water. The cold porcelain tub that perched on iron feet looked tired and worn and never kept the water hot. This usually irritated Charmaine who loved to soak in bubbles and read her treasured beauty magazines, but nothing could put her in a bad mood tonight. No, today was a lucky day. As the water ran into the bathtub she went to the bedroom to pick out her clothes. "Oh, you look awful!" she said to Tessa in a cheery voice. Charmaine shrugged her shoulders when she got no reply from Tessa and went to the closet to find the perfect outfit. She hummed a tuneless melody and finally picked out some clothes when she suddenly remembered that the bath water was still running.

She quickly opened her purse to find a matching lipstick for her outfit and saw Tessa's two letters. "Oh yeah" she mumbled to herself and tossed them onto the nightstand as she turned and hurried towards the bathroom. Her mother would be really angry with her if she found the water running unattended again. Charmaine had almost flooded the house once before, by getting distracted, after turning on the bath water and walking away.

Tessa heard Charmaine leave the room and was glad that the annoying humming had ended. This was the third day that she was lying under the covers shivering. Her nose was red and she kept coughing. Bullet lay next to her and only left her side for short periods of time during the day. His little body brought some warmth to Tessa, and she missed him when he left the room. She opened her eyes and was thrilled to see a single letter laying next to her bed on the nightstand. She prayed that it would be a letter from Blake as she sat up in the bed. Her disappointment was great when she recognized Jeremiahs handwriting. Not that she did not love letters from her dear brother but ...if *his* letter could get through the mail to her, then she could no longer use the mail as an excuse for Blake's silence. Blake simple did not want to write to her; it was time she faced the facts. Wayne had been right all along, they did not have an agreement at all. She had assumed something that was not true and as this realization dawned on Tessa, the tiny flame of hope inside of her finally flickered and died.

Tessa heard the floorboards creak in the hallway and turned to the wall, pretending to be asleep. She just could not take another dose of Charmaine's cheerfulness tonight. She heard the door open and felt someone tapping her on the shoulder. She lay dead still hoping she would be left alone.

"Hey…" she heard Wayne's husky voice.

She turned over and looked into his brilliant blue eyes.

"Hey…" Tessa replied and self consciously ran her hands through her hair.

He handed her a bowl of stew, "I brought you something to eat."

Tessa sat up and although she was not hungry she tried to nibble on the food. *He is being so sweet.*

Wayne sat on the end of the bed and watched Tessa eat. *She doesn't know how stunning she is.* Tessa looked up at him and smiled but put her hand over her cheek to cover the slight scar that lay there. It was something she always did when she felt shy and Wayne thought that it made her even more adorable. He doubted that she was even aware of the cute habit. He liked Tessa, he liked her a lot…but then again he liked girls in general. He loved the power he felt when they looked up at him adoringly. God had blessed him with striking good looks and a strong body. He could not help it that girls found him so attractive. Besides, he had a way with words and flirting came easy for him. Why not use what came so naturally to him? It wasn't his fault that there were a few broken hearts left along the way. Sometimes girls just began to read things incorrectly; they became too clingy, and he could not abide a clingy girl. He had to be free and could not imagine being tied down to *one* girl. What would the fun be in that? But Tessa was different. She was beautiful and carried herself with dignity. Her calm ways created a sense of tranquility around her that was almost contagious. Yes, he had to admit that there was something special about her. He had tried to make her jealous at lunch on Sunday, but she hadn't said anything to him about it. He wasn't sure how she felt about him and he wasn't used to not having the upper hand.

I wonder what it would be like to kiss her? To hold her on a cold night? To have her warm my bed?

His mind drifted away with a fantasy, and then he thought about the boy Tessa had mentioned before...*Blake*. He felt a surge of jealousy rise up inside of him. He might not be ready to settle down but that didn't mean he wanted Blake to have Tessa either. *I probably don't have anything to worry about. Judging from Tessa's sad eyes...she almost certainly hasn't heard from him at all.*

"You're deep in thought," he heard Tessa say.

"Sorry, just thinking about my pigeons. I have a couple that are sick right now," he lied. *Nothing wrong with getting a girl to be sympathetic.*

He continued, "But I'm more concerned about getting you well. I miss you and the animals are missing you too. You should see how depressed the chickens are today!"

Tessa found herself laughing and although it sent her into a fit of coughing, she felt much better for having Wayne's company.

"OK, how about a cup of tea?" Wayne asked as he picked up the unfinished bowl of stew.

"*You're* going to make *me* a cup of tea?"

"I am at your complete service, my dear!" Wayne bowed deeply with an exaggerated sweep of his hand. He then clicked his heels together and attempted a fake salute as he swiveled and marched out of the bedroom. Tessa smiled as she got out of bed and went over to the mirror.

She had to steady herself against the wall for a minute as she felt a wave of dizziness sweep over her. She peered into the mirror and saw that her hair was disheveled and her face was pale. She had lost weight and her green eyes looked too big in her thin face. She changed into a fresh set of pajamas and brushed her hair, then applied a thin layer of pink lipstick to her pale lips. *There, that's at least a little better.*

Wayne spent the rest of the evening sitting on the end of Tessa's bed, and they talked easily about their lives. He told her about all kinds of interesting experiences he had had while hunting in the open fields. They laughed about silly things that they had done in their pasts but also talked intently about 'serious' things, like the state of the world they live in. When Tessa grew tired, Wayne got up to leave but walked over to her and softly stroked her face. He bent down and placed a light kiss on the scar she had earlier tried to hide.

Now, as Tessa lay in the dark, she still felt a tingling on her cheek where his lips had touched. His caress had been so gentle that Tessa had almost not felt it... but it had been a sensual touch. It could not be mistaken for a hand of friendship. Tessa felt the familiar twinge of guilt but then reminded herself that she did not have to feel guilty. She was a single young woman who had no other suitors. What was wrong with enjoying Wayne's touch? Blake's face came to Tessa's mind, but she angrily pushed the image away. *It's best that I forget about Blake...since he has forgotten about me.* She took another dose of cold medicine, hoping that it would help her fall into a deep sleep. As she dozed off, Tessa imagined Wayne's muscular arms encircling her slender body and she felt safe and loved by the picture she saw in her mind's eye.

11

By the following week Tessa had recovered completely and was back to her routine of feeding the animals. She saw Wayne often and looked forward to their time together. Bullet stayed close to her during the day, but seemed to stray away when Wayne was around. Tessa put it down to coincidence and thought that the dog was probably just enjoying some free time to explore the many acres of farmland that surrounded them.

Late one afternoon Tessa found herself walking around the farm calling for Bullet. She hadn't seen him since the morning, and he had never strayed for so long. She was beginning to really worry about him. As she thought about how much Bullet meant to her, Tessa felt a knot form in her stomach and she had to hold back the tears that threatened to spill from her eyes. The fields behind the farm were large barren lands and who knew what wandered around out there. Tessa widened her circle of search and finally passed the last piece of farmland she was familiar with. An ostrich walked beside her on the other side of the wire fence and watched her with strange blinking eyes. Its eyelashes were long and dark, as if it had just applied a layer of extra 'long–lash' mascara. The ostrich swaggered with pride as the long neck swayed, causing the narrow head to bop back and forward. "Go away Ozzie," Tessa said impatiently, "I'm not feeding you now!"

Soon Tessa found herself edging down a narrow path she had never seen before. The red mud path under her feet had hardened into a smooth surface from regular use. Tessa held her hands out on both sides and allowed them to graze the tops of the long reedy highveld grass, which the harsh winter had turned into a dead grey color.

"Bullet!" she called as she continued along the winding path.

"God, where is he?" she breathed and then realized that she desperately needed to talk to God.

"Please help me to find him," she continued "and let him be alive," she added, deciding that she needed the prayer to be short and specific. After a few minutes Tessa emerged from the path into a clearing. She stopped short as she saw the three huts that stood in a semicircle. A fire burnt in the middle of the clearing and a few skinny dogs skulked around. There were a couple of poorly clad children that ran around pushing cars made of thick twisted iron wire. The air was thick and smoky, and the smell of burning wood almost overwhelmed Tessa as memories of Nolwazi's hut washed over her.

The little children spotted her and froze from the shock of seeing a white woman standing in their circle. She took a step forward and smiled at them, which caused them to run towards her, their dark faces grinning widely. Holding out their brown hands they all chanted together, "Sweeties, sweeties!"

It was then that Tessa remembered Aunt Rina saying that she brought the children of the farm workers sweets every week.

Tessa felt bad as she showed them her empty pockets and saw the disappointment in their large eyes. She touched their curly heads and said, "I'll bring some sweeties next time." Just then Sinethemba walked out of the hut with a pot in her hand. She kept her eyes on Tessa as she hung the pot over the fire. Tessa smiled but found no response from the big brown eyes that stared back at her. She walked over to Sinethemba and said, "My dog is missing, I was looking for him and the path led here. Have you seen him today?"

The baby cried from inside the hut and Sinethemba silently turned to go, leaving Tessa wondering what to do. She had to know if anyone had seen Bullet so she took a chance and gingerly entered the hut. It was almost dusk now and the shadows outside had grown long. A few tall white candles gave off a murky light inside the stuffy hut. Sinethemba had picked the crying baby up and was rocking backwards and forwards, softly singing an old tribal lullaby in Zulu. Now that Tessa's eyes had grown accustomed to the dim light, she glanced around the hut that appeared to be much like any other Zulu shack.

Old newspaper served as a tablecloth to the little worn table that stood in the corner of the tiny kitchen. The bead curtain that separated the bedroom from the kitchen was tied together with a tattered red ribbon. Tessa's eye caught movement in the room and her eyes locked onto those of a giant Zulu man, who was lying on top of a rusted iron framed bed. The bed had been hoisted two feet off the floor by many bricks that had been stacked under each foot of the bed. His pitch black skin made the whites of his eyes seem unnaturally bright as he stared at Tessa without blinking. Tessa felt unnerved and shivered in the warm hut. As she dragged her eyes from the man she noticed the bloody bandage that was wrapped around his right hand and extended up to his elbow.

"What's wrong with him?" Tessa whispered to Sinethemba who replied, "He fall off tractor....tractor eat arm."

It was then that Tessa remembered Auntie Rina telling her that Sinethemba's husband, Bogani, had had an accident on the farm. "He gone die soon, witchdoctor no help!" Something in Tessa's spirit stirred and she heard that soft inner whisper. "Pray for him."

She knew the Zulu's believed everything their witchdoctors told them and had accepted that he would die.

"Why are those bricks under the bed?" she asked Sinethemba whose eyes went huge with terror and whispered, "For tokoloshe!" and then put her finger to her lips to show Tessa not to continue talking about it.

Tessa had heard that Zulu mythology taught them that the tokoloshe was a dwarf-like spirit, who was mischievous and evil. It had a gremlin appearance and could not see because it had gouged out eyes. The bed had to be high enough, so that the tokoloshe could not reach the toes of the sleeping person, as it was his habit to bite them off! Tessa hated the many superstitions that kept these people bound in fear.

She turned her eyes back to the elevated bed and saw that Bogani had dozed off into a feverish sleep. He moaned and sweat beaded on his forehead as he shivered and pulled the colorful blanket up to his neck, all the while making sure his toes were not exposed for the roaming tokoloshie. Tessa thought it odd that such a giant of a man would be so afraid of an imaginary blind gremlin.

"He gone die soon," Sinethemba repeated as she shrugged her shoulders.

"No, Sinethemba! Let's pray for Jesus to heal him. Jesus can make him better."

For a moment hope flashed across Sinethemba's face and then she frowned and said, "Witchdoctor's bones say he gone die…"

"Jesus is stronger than witchdoctor bones." Tessa replied then walked over to the high bed and softly put her hand on the injured arm. She hoped that the big man would not wake up with her standing at his bed. What would he do if, in his feverish state, he mistook her for the dreaded tokoloshe? He already had not seemed pleased to see her in the hut to begin with. But Tessa again heard that still whisper, "Pray for him."

As Tessa prayed for healing and light to come, a tranquil presence filled the little hut and Bogani fell into a peaceful sleep. The squirming baby too had become quiet and was now contentedly playing with a dented tin cup. Sinethemba looked at Tessa with adoring eyes and said, "You magic power like witchdoctor!"

"No, Simethemba! No magic." Tessa sighed and wondered how she would make Sinethemba understand. She decided to tell her about Jesus and how he loved and died for her. She ended the conversation by saying, "The Bible says that God is a jealous God. He doesn't want to share us with witchdoctors and magic. You have to choose him only and trust him." Tessa's own conscience pricked her as she realized that she had been distancing herself from God. She had been questioning his love for her and whether he was trustworthy…but deep down in her heart she knew that God was completely faithful. She could also see that Sinethemba had felt the presence of God in the hut as they sat huddled together talking, and she was pleased to hear Sinethemba say, "I take Jesus now," as she patted her heart.

It had been a while since Tessa had led someone through the prayer of forgiveness and salvation. Now, she was delighted to see Sinethemba's shining face as she prayed and accepted Jesus as her Savior.

*****

Tessa suddenly noticed that the hut had become even darker than what it had been when she had entered it. It was almost completely dark now and she realized that she had stayed too long. She stood to go and as she stepped out of the hut, Sinethemba grabbed her arm and pulled her close. She looked around and then hurriedly whispered, "A man take Bullet in ol' barn. He have sjambok!" Sinethemba's eyes were large with uncertainty and fear at mentioning the dreaded leather whip.

"I don't understand…why would a man take Bullet to the old barn? Maybe you are mistaken and Bullet just followed him into the barn?" Tessa immediately saw a change in Sinethemba's expression as she nodded in feigned agreement.

Sinethemba then pressed a candle into Tessa's hand, "A light for path," she whispered as she pointed to the worn narrow path, and then hurriedly shut the hut's door, almost distinguishing the fragile flame. After following the path for a few minutes, Tessa was glad that she had the tiny flame to light her way. It didn't give off much light but brought her comfort as she peered into the black bushes along the path. The full moon that she had spotted earlier in the evening was now creeping behind an ominous cloud, and with its disappearance came the terrible chill of the desert night air, which made Tessa's chapped lips burn. Her dry skin itched and she again longed for the ocean, for the damp sea air to spray a moisturizing haze upon her thirsty skin.

The howling sound that came from the grassland nearby caused all thoughts of the ocean to evaporate. She started to run along the path and hoped with each turn to catch a glimpse of the lighted farmhouse.

She missed Bullet terribly and again mumbled, "Where could he be?"

As she rounded another bend on the path she tripped over something and fell, the candle rolled once and then the flame flickered and died. Now Tessa was plunged into utter darkness. She could not see the path and started to panic. She heard the howling again, *does it sound closer?*

Then she heard another sound, much closer. A soft whimper...

"Bullet!" Tessa's eyes started adjusting to the darkness and she wished that the moon would come out from behind the heavy clouds. She made out a shadow lying across the path. She had tripped over Bullet! *Has he been trying to follow me? Why is he just lying there like that?* Tessa crawled on her hands and knees and felt for the warm soft fur. She picked him up and held him to her as she kissed his head. "Where have you been boy? I've missed you..." Bullet let out a soft whine but didn't move.

I have to get Bullet home, she thought and staggered to her feet.

"God, I can't see, please show me the way home."

Tessa felt tears springing up in her eyes. She was cold, tired, and hungry and now she was terrified that Bullet was hurt. His breathing seemed uneven and for the first time she wondered if he was dying in her arms. This thought caused her to muster all her courage and she started shuffling down the path in the general direction of the house. A few minutes later her arms started aching with the weight of the dog and she wondered what she was going to do if she did not see the farmhouse soon. Her hands felt warm and sticky and she hoped that he wasn't bleeding, but soon she became nauseated by the smell of blood.

"Please God, help me and don't let him die!"

That is when she felt the first icy drop of rain. She remembered that Auntie Rina had heard a warning on the radio about a series of unusual winter storms, which had already burst a dam and caused a river to overflow. The floods had caused many farmers to evacuate, but up until now, their town had not seen a single drop of rain. Now the hard rain stung her face as she threw her head back and yelled, "NO! Why now!"

Her arms were shaking from Bullet's weight and Tessa groaned. *I'm going to have to put him down.* As she bent to lay Bullet down she heard the howling again. This time it was much closer and Tessa wondered if a pack of wolves had picked up the scent of the blood trail she was leaving behind. *They'll tear him apart if I leave him here!*

Tessa felt like she would be sick and couldn't think clearly. *Who am I kidding; they will tear me apart too.* Her prayer had turned to a continual whisper, "God, I need you. Help me…show me what to do!"

Suddenly a scripture came into her mind, "Do not turn to the left or the right but set your face like a flint." Immediately Tessa knew what to do. She had been trying to follow the path but now she pushed directly ahead. She left the path as it curved around another bend and started edging her way through the long grassveld. The tiny hard pellets of rain hit her face and blurred her vision, but she kept shuffling forward. She was tempted to verge to the left of the huddle of thick brush she was entering but continued to repeat the scripture, "Do not turn to the left or the right but set your face like a flint."

Just when she thought she could not hold onto Bullet a minute longer she saw the looming shadow of the barn.

"Thank you God!" Tessa's tears now mingled with the rain drops and splashed on Bullet's face.

12

Inside the barn, Tessa lay Bullet down on a pile of hay. She quickly threw off her sodden jacket and felt around for the matches that usually lay on the shelf near the door. Her fingers shook and it took three strikes before the little match lit up. It took another three matches before Tessa located the kerosene lamp and got it burning. Tessa had never been so happy to see a glowing flame and immediately felt reassured. She carried the lamp over to Bullet and gasped in horror as the light illuminated his gaping wounds. What could have done this to him? Had he gotten mangled in some sort of trap? But no, the wounds looked too clean and precise. It looked like he had been....beaten. Some of the wounds had stopped bleeding but others still oozed fresh blood. Tessa tried to move Bullet onto some thicker hay but he yelped in agony, which made her face her worst fear. *Were these just external wounds or were there broken bones?*

Tessa grabbed an old ripped blanket off a shelf nearby and lay down next to Bullet. She covered them both with it and gently rubbed his head. His breathing was shallow but his eyes never left her face as she said, "Hey boy, thank you for being my dearest friend on this farm."

His brown eyes blinked and then held her eyes again and Tessa choked back tears as she continued, "You were a faithful dog. Your work here on earth is done...and you did it well."

Bullet whined and closed his eyes.

Tessa cried then. She cried over all the losses she had recently faced. She cried for her dead mother, for her far away brother, and for the silence of her beloved Blake. She cried for the loss of the ocean. She cried for her dog that was slipping away from her. She continued to rub Bullet's ears and kissed him on the nose. *I can't imagine that this innocent puppy's life is being extinguished. Who could possibly have been so cruel? Haven't I been taught in church that the truth always wins over evil! That if I did what seemed right...I would be happy and life would be relatively trouble free?*

But then Tessa remembered the preacher teaching a series based on the scripture that said, "In this life we will have troubles..." and she admitted to herself that the honest truth was that she had always wanted to believe in fairy tales. She always wanted life to work out just right, like in those fairy tales, and all her prayers had been to that end. *That* is why she had been angry with God lately. She had so much as told him that she only trusted him when she got exactly what she wanted.

While Tessa lay in the cold barn, under a tattered blanket, watching Bullet die, she was jolted by this hard truth. She had not really surrendered her life to God, not completely. True surrender meant trusting even when things didn't make sense, believing that God was in control even in the dark nights...like tonight.

Tessa felt a peace settle around her as she started praying, "God please forgive me for accusing you when things don't work out the way I want them too....when life seems painful. I want to choose to trust you in the good times and the bad." And then she added as an afterthought, "I give Bullet into your hands right now and I trust you with his life."

Tessa, I will never leave you or forsake you.

"Thank you God, you *are* faithful," she whispered as tears slid down her cheeks.

Tessa lay still and listened as the storm picked up and the angry rain pounded on the tin roof. She shivered as the wind blew through the broken window at the far end of the barn, and she lay as close to Bullet as she could without hurting him. His little body gave off a circle of heat and Tessa lay her head in his warm neck and finally dozed off.

Something was wrong, but Tessa couldn't remember what it was. Her head pounded and every time she tried to pry open her puffy eyes, the early morning light assaulted them and made her wince. Every muscle in her body hurt and she was cold and stiff. Then she felt a warm tongue lick her nose and she forced her eyes open and smiled, "Bullet!"

Bullet was alive!

"You're a sight for sore eyes boy," Tessa whispered. The dried blood had made his hair clump together in patches and his wounds were still raw and gaping. *I need to get him to the vet,* Tessa thought as she stood and looked around the barn. Perhaps she could push him in the wheelbarrow that stood against the wall. It had stopped raining but the ground outside the barn was sure to be completely water logged. *Should I try and carry him to the house?*

Just then the barn door flew open and Tessa jumped with fright.

"Where the hell have you been?" Wayne demanded as he stormed in. "Auntie Rina's had us up half the night looking for you!"

Tessa was taken aback by his loud accusing voice and didn't know what to say. Wayne noticed Bullet when he gave out a high pitched cry and said, "What's all this?"

"I'll explain later. Can you help me get him up to the house? I need to get him to the vet."

"He probably won't make it. I can put him out of his misery with one bullet," Wayne replied.

"No, he is going to make it!" Tessa heard herself shout. "Now either help me or get out of the way."

Wayne's blue eyes flashed as he looked at Tessa for a long moment, and then bent down and none too gently, scooped Bullet up into his arms. He strode out of the barn and didn't look back. Tessa hurried to keep up as his long legs strode across the sodden grassveld. "Why are you angry with me," Tessa asked as she trotted behind him.

Wayne stopped abruptly and turned to Tessa, "I am not angry at all. I just think you need to learn farm ways. Dogs are not pets here...they are here for the purpose of protecting or hunting. You have spoiled this dog and he serves no purpose on the farm. You should invest your affection in someone who can give it back, not on a filthy dumb animal."

"But he does give it back! He is a loyal friend."

Wayne's voice was softer when he spoke this time and his eyes held deep emotion, "I won't leave either Tessa. Have you ever thought of that? I just don't want you to get hurt. Sometimes accidents happen on a farm, and these dogs don't always stay around."

He suddenly bent down and placed a gentle kiss on her cheek. "I'm sorry for yelling earlier, but I was worried about you, alright?"

Tessa nodded and smiled slightly at Wayne who stood waiting for a reply. She didn't want to waste time arguing about this. They turned and continued walking in silence towards the farmhouse. Bullet lay still in Wayne's arms but kept his eyes pinned on Tessa. She wanted to reach out and stroke his head but decided against it. It would probably only annoy Wayne whose jaw was set as he strode purposefully through the long wet grass.

As she stepped through the kitchen door, Tessa was pounded with questions from Auntie Rina and Charmaine. She explained quickly what had transpired the night before to which Auntie Rina replied, "You shouldn't go to the Zulu's living quarters. They won't appreciate you invading their privacy. Now what happened to Bullet?"

"I don't know, it looks like he was beaten. Who would do such a horrid thing?"

Tessa noticed Sinethemba, who had been standing at the stove stirring a pot of porridge, look up and settle her eyes on Wayne who was staring into his cup of coffee. When Sinethemba saw Tessa looking at her she quickly turned away and pretended to be busy by adding a dash of salt to the porridge.

Auntie Rina shrugged and said, "Well, we best get him to the vet. I'll take you into town."

Later that afternoon Tessa felt much better. Although the vet had confirmed that the dog had indeed been beaten, he assured Tessa that the wounds would heal with the ointment and medicine he had sent home with them. Now Tessa sat next to Bullet on a blanket and sipped on a cup of hot cocoa. The weak sun had finally broken through the mottled clouds and now filtered through the bedroom window. The sunlight warmed the blanket and bathed Tessa in a sense of wellbeing. *Everything is going to be alright*, she thought, as she gently stroked Bullet's soft fur and watched him sleep peacefully. *Yes, everything is going to be alright.*

*****

Two weeks later Tessa stood in front of the mirror and brushed her long hair until it shone. She felt invigorated! The icy fingers of winter were finally pulling away and allowing a fresh promise of spring to appear. The dead grey grass was at last turning green and the farmland was sprinkled with the first buds of flowers. This had been the longest winter she had ever endured, and a new sense of hope surfaced as she looked at herself in the mirror. Her green eyes sparkled as she anticipated the day ahead. Wayne had been very sweet all week and had taken care of most of her chores while she nursed Bullet back to health. She could hardly conjure up the memory of him being angry the day he had found her and Bullet in the barn.

She wondered if perhaps, because she had been so tired, she had simply blown things out of proportion that morning. After all, he had been nothing but helpful and kind since that day.

Today he was taking her to his house to tour the many bird cages he kept. His favorite birds were his homing pigeons, and she always saw his excitement when he spoke about them. He had also promised her a delicious lamb roast for lunch, which was already simmering in the oven.

Tessa added a little blush to her pale cheeks and pressed her red lips together in an attempt to even out her ruby colored lipstick. Charmaine had given her a white dress with tiny yellow daisies on it, and the dress seemed perfect for a day like this. Tessa smiled at herself in the mirror, but suddenly a picture of Blake popped into her mind. In her mind's eye, Tessa saw him so clearly that he could have been standing next to her. His dark eyes looked sad and her heart skipped a beat. *Blake*, she whispered as a tear gathered at the corner of her eye.

"No!" Tessa angrily wiped the tear from her eye.

"You are not going to spoil this day," she spoke out loud to the vision of Blake as if he were there standing in front of her.

"You forgot about me…and now I will forget about you." Tessa's voice cracked as she met her own gaze in the reflection of the mirror. The earlier sparkle was gone and in its place was an empty stare. She flipped her hair over her shoulder and turned away from the betraying eyes.

*****

Wayne was casually leaning against a post on his porch when Tessa walked up the pathway towards him. His lingering gaze drifted over Tessa's body causing her to feel self conscious. She never really knew what he was thinking and it was rather frustrating.

"Do you know how beautiful you look?" he said as he stepped towards her. Thinking that she wanted to ask him the same question, Tessa giggled. He had always been handsome but today he was beautifully handsome. His blue eyes were almost luminous in the morning light, and he wore a white button down shirt and blue jeans that fit perfectly over newly shined boots. His aftershave was more noticeable in the crisp spring air.

"What's so funny?" Wayne asked as he reached out and confidently took Tessa's hand.

"Nothing...I'm just glad to be spending the day with you," Tessa replied shyly.

"Me too," Wayne whispered in her ear and did not let go of her hand but led her toward the bird cages. Tessa looked with amazement at how many birds sat nesting and pecking at their food. They continued on to another cage that was separated from the others. "This is called a loft. These pigeons are my trained racing pigeons and have won me some good money in the past." Wayne said proudly.

"How do they know how to come home once they have been let out for the race?" Tessa questioned.

"They have been trained and are able to find their way back from almost a thousand miles away. On a calm day they can fly thirty seven miles an hour, and with tail winds they can fly eighty miles per hour. Can you believe that?" Wayne explained passionately.

"That is impressive," Tessa replied as she shielded her eyes from the sun, "but are these birds your pets? Do you worry about them on the flight back? Do you ever lose them to predators?"

Wayne shrugged as if he was getting bored with all the questions and kept silent for so long that Tessa thought he may not acknowledge her questions.

Then he said, "Some of them don't get back...but they are only birds after all and can be replaced."

Tessa remembered Wayne saying the same thing about Bullet but decided to say nothing further on the subject. Not everyone loved animals as much as she did and that was not a crime. Wayne had so many other strengths she could focus on.

She looked over to where Bullet sat patiently waiting for her outside of the fenced area. He had recovered well except for a slight limp, but what worried Tessa was that the beating had taken the 'puppy' out of him and he had become very docile and submissive. The old Bullet would have been yapping at the cooing pigeons, but today he just sat quietly observing them. She hoped that Bullet would reclaim some of his sparky personality as time went by. Wayne drew her attention back by saying, "Are you hungry yet?"

"I'm starving," Tessa replied as her stomach growled at the thought of food.

The lamb roast, curried potatoes, and sweet green peas were wonderful and Tessa felt truly spoiled. Wayne was a charming host and entertained her with funny farm stories as they ate their dessert. The afternoon also turned out to be delightful as they strolled across the wildflower-covered ground that led to a huge pond. The blue water sparkled and Tessa saw a fish jump and then scoot away playfully, as if it too felt the new hope of the changing season. Tessa thought about the ocean and imagined herself going down to her cave as she had always done at this time of year to explore the new plants that were sure to be pushing up through the thawing ground around the rocky path.

Wayne stopped and looked at Tessa, "Why are you sad?"

Tessa was impressed that he was so attentive and perceptive that he could read the slightest change in her mood.

"I miss home, I miss the ocean."

Wayne lifted Tessa's chin and looked deeply into her eyes, "This is home now. You could be happy here. I would miss you if you went away…"

Tessa was conscious of his arms that surrounded her and did not resist when he pulled her close to him and gently brushed his lips across her temple. The affectionate gesture gave her chills. He pulled away and smiled, "I've wanted to do this since the first day I laid eyes on you."

His mouth captured hers and set Tessa on fire as the weak sun waned in the blue sky.

She surrendered to the passionate kiss and didn't resist. It felt good to be wanted. It felt good to be held. It felt good to belong. She felt Wayne's warm breathe as he whispered into her ear, "I think I love you, Tessa." His voice was husky and his strong hands were urgent as he drew her closer.

Somewhere in the background she heard Bullet barking and the sound pulled her back to consciousness. She took a shaky step backwards and said, "Let's take a walk."

"No, don't go," the mesmerizing voice rasped as he kept up his caress by slowly tracing Tessa's jaw line with his thumb. "I need you here with me," his luminous blue eyes looking into Tessa's soul. Somewhere deep inside, Tessa heard another voice say 'no', but Wayne's firm hand was already pulling her down onto the soft blanket…

Tessa hesitated for only a moment but Wayne's mouth had already arrested hers. His kiss was hungry and electricity shuddered between them. It seemed a magnificent experience and Tessa finally abandoned herself and let passion have its way.

Now Tessa lay wrapped in the blanket and watched Wayne who lay with his head propped up in his hand. His eyes roamed across the water that lazily swirled in the pond as he chewed on a long piece of grass. She couldn't help but wonder what he was thinking, yet she had the distinct impression that he was far away and that he was no longer aware of her lying next to him. *I'm probably just being oversensitive and insecure.* Tessa chided herself for spoiling the moment with troubling thoughts, but the intimacy that they had shared should surely have felt fulfilling, and yet Tessa felt more alone than ever before. As Wayne's silence and indifference continued, the hollow feeling in Tessa increased.

Why had she allowed herself to be seduced by someone as complex and unreadable as Wayne? Yet maybe she was overreacting? She had read in a magazine one time that men didn't really like to talk after intimacy. *Yes, that is it....he is just content, that's all.* As if on cue, Wayne turned and looked at her and smiled. Relief swept over Tessa. *It was all just my imagination. He does love me.*

Wayne started to say something when they heard the wheels of a car crunching the gravel on the road that led up to the farmhouse. Tessa sat up quickly and ran her fingers through her messy hair. Wayne was already on his feet and walking back to the house. Tessa folded the blanket and called for Bullet who had continued to keep his distance and was lying under a tree on the other side of the pond. When she got near the house she saw Charmaine waving frantically.

"Tessa, I have a big surprise for you," Charmaine grinned from ear to ear. "Jump in...hurry!"

13

Tessa froze in her tracks as she entered Auntie Rina's warm kitchen. There standing in front of her was her long lost brother Jeremiah! Her shock turned to unbridled joy as she ran into his arms and held him tightly. Her brother seemed taller and leaner and the muscles of his arms bulged as he hugged her.

"See I told you!" Charmaine threw her hands up and almost shouted, "Isn't it a grand surprise?" This brought laughter from the whole group and when everyone had greeted him she introduced Wayne to Jeremiah. As they shook hands she thought she saw Jeremiah's face harden.

Auntie Rina quickly hurried them into the living room and said, "You young people catch up while Sinethemba and I whip up some dinner." Wayne put his hand on the small of Tessa's back to guide her to the sofa and Tessa felt uncomfortable as she again saw Jeremiah's jaw tense. She knew him well enough to know that something was wrong and Tessa found herself feeling guilty. Why had Jeremiah shown up today of all days? She hadn't even had the time to figure out how she felt about what had just happened, and she already felt vulnerable. Then Tessa found herself feeling angry as she thought about the silent treatment she had received from Blake. *I have nothing to feel guilty about... I am not committed to anyone and I can like whoever I want to.*

Soon the smell of frying fish wafted into the living room and Jeremiah rubbed his growling stomach, "I'm starving! I haven't eaten since I started hitchhiking before dawn this morning."

"How long can you stay?" Tessa asked.

"I have to be back on base by Tuesday, so I have tomorrow and part of Monday with you."

"That's too short! I haven't seen you in months!" Tessa heard herself complaining even though she knew that Jeremiah had no control over his time off, so she quickly added, "But I am so glad for the time we have together!"

After a delicious supper of fried red snapper and hot chips covered with salt and vinegar, they all sat around the table with steaming mugs of hot chocolate. Everyone had a turn to ask Jeremiah questions about the military and how he was surviving. They congratulated him on becoming a corporal and then listened to his interesting stories of military life and the challenges he faced. He shared with them how much he missed the Cape and how he dreamt about the raging seas at night. "Sometimes, just before I wake up completely, I smell the salty sea air and think I am back home. Those are the worst mornings for me."

Tessa felt moisture in her eyes as she identified with Jeremiah's experience. How many times had she not woken to the same thing and then had to face the great disappointment of the reality of living in a frozen desert. How the ocean crept into one's soul, Tessa didn't know...but it did, it surely did.

96

By midnight everyone was yawning and one by one they got up and drifted towards their beds. Wayne was the last to push away from the table. He took Tessa by surprise and lowered his lips onto hers with a lingering kiss. Then he turned to Jeremiah with a crooked smile that seemed more like a smirk, and gave a fake salute before he shuffled out the back door into the cool evening.

Jeremiah tensed as he watched Wayne's retreating back disappear in the darkness. He turned his attention back to Tessa and said, "I don't like him! I don't like him at all! What are you doing with him?"

Tessa saw Jeremiah's anger in his flashing green eyes and matched it with her own, "What do you mean you do not like him? You don't even know him! You don't know what it has been like to be stuck here. I've been desperately lonely and Wayne has made it bearable. He has been a good…friend to me. Actually, he loves me."

"Loves you?" Jeremiah shouted and hit his fist on the wooden table causing the mugs to rattle. "I'm telling you Tessa, I don't trust him. There is something about him…and what about Blake?"

Tessa shifted on her seat and then tossed her long hair over her shoulder before folding her hands and answering, "Blake has forgotten about me. I have not received one letter from him in all these months. I need to go on with my life."

Jeremiah took a deep breath and fought against his frustration. He knew that Tessa would not hear him while he spoke angrily, it would only cause her to dig her heels in and defend that scoffing idiot Wayne.

He reached across the table and took Tessa's hands, "I'm sorry for getting mad. But it is impossible that Blake has forgotten about you. Before we were separated he told me about his deep love for you and that you were the one for him. Since we don't have a father he asked for my blessing in taking your hand in marriage. *Blake* loves you."

Tessa pulled her hands away and rubbed them together so Jeremiah would not see them shaking. She felt sick to her stomach. Blake wanted to marry her! He really did love her! Tessa thought about what she had done this very afternoon, and she felt her cheeks grow warm at the memory. Suddenly it didn't seem romantic at all and she couldn't remember the reasons for giving in to Wayne. But the truth was that none of that mattered now anyway. It was simply too late.

Tessa felt Jeremiahs eyes questioning her and she quickly said, "Blake has a fine way of showing it! I haven't heard from him in all this time. If he loved me he would have written or come to see me by now."

Tessa stood up abruptly from the table causing a half full mug of hot chocolate to topple off the table. The mug broke and hot chocolate spewed all over the kitchen floor. She grabbed a kitchen towel and knelt down to start cleaning up the mess, glad that it was giving her something to do with her hands and a moment to think. She was sure that Jeremiah could see her shame and she was relieved that she no longer had to look into his probing eyes. He knelt down next to her and started picking up pieces of the broken red-clay mug. Without looking at him Tessa said, "I'm tired and I don't want us to spend our time arguing. I'm beginning to be happy here and Wayne is good to me. Please Jeremiah…give him a chance."

Jeremiah saw how tired and sad Tessa looked and regretted not having waited until the morning to talk to her. Things always seemed worse at night. After they finished cleaning up the floor Tessa lit herself and Jeremiah each a candle and led him to the little spare room that was tucked away under the staircase that led to the attic.

Auntie Rina always made sure that the room was spotless and dusted in the event that they got an unexpected guest. The single bed was neatly made and the blanket, although a ghastly green color, looked warm and fuzzy. Jeremiah turned around in the tiny room and had to stoop from hitting his head on the low wooden beams. "I'm sorry, it's really small," Tessa giggled.

"Are you kidding?" Jeremiah replied and grinned. "It's dry and cozy and the best part is, I'm not sharing a room with twelve other guys! I just appreciate my own room!"

As he said goodnight, he gave Tessa a bear hug and added, "Tessa, you know I love you and I've been worried about you. I just don't want you to make a mistake and regret it...but for your sake I will give Wayne the benefit of the doubt and talk to him tomorrow." Tessa nodded but did not say what she was thinking. *It's too late, I already made a mistake.*

*****

Jeremiah never got his opportunity to speak to Wayne the next day, or the day after that. Aunt Rina had told them that Wayne had called and asked off work for a few days to take care of some personal business. Tessa felt a wave of anxiety sweep over her at the news. She desperately needed to see Wayne and know that he was in fact more in love with her than before. Now the inner questions started tormenting Tessa.

Could he not stand to see her? Had he changed his mind about her? Maybe he didn't love her...maybe he didn't even like her! She hated feeling so emotionally vulnerable and realized that this felt like the worst kind of rejection. Now that she had given all of herself to him, could it be true that he didn't want anything more to do with her? The worst part of all was, not knowing! Yes, today she needed to see him more than ever, and she kept gazing up the driveway in the hopes of seeing his truck; but the sun rose and set without a word from him.

She tried to go through the motions of showing Jeremiah around the farm. She tried to enjoy his company and she tried to force herself not to think about Wayne. Her thoughts felt disjointed and scattered. One minute she would want to cry and the next she was sure that he would turn up soon and nothing would have changed between them. What if he had taken time off to go into the jewelry store in the city to buy her an engagement ring? *Yes*, she chided herself, *I have to stop being so negative.* It's all going to be OK.

The weekend seemed to drag by as if time stood still as she waited for any sign of Wayne, yet Monday still came too quickly to say goodbye to Jeremiah. Aunt Rina had bought him a bus ticket back to the base and Tessa was glad that he would not have to hitchhike.

They had not spoken anymore about Wayne or Blake for that matter, but now Jeremiah said, "Tessa, I don't understand why you haven't heard from Blake but I'm sure you will soon. Don't do anything rash until you have spoken to him." Jeremiah noticed how pale Tessa looked and saw the dark smudges under her eyes. Something was definitely wrong, but he hadn't been able to get Tessa to open up to him about what was bothering her. They had had a good few days together but Jeremiah had felt a wall between them throughout the visit. He was sure that no-good weasel, Wayne, had something to do with it; but

Tessa had not wanted to speak any further on the subject. Now she gave him a weak smile and waved as the bus slowly pulled away from the curb.

Jeremiah felt unsettled and lay his head back in the seat. To everyone else he was closing his eyes to take a nap, but instead, Jeremiah was silently praying for his sister. He wondered when last she had prayed and felt sad that things were as they were. Tessa had always been the strong one spiritually, the one to encourage him to turn to God, and it had often made him hungry for that same kind of intimate friendship with the Father. But now things were different, something had changed...and not for the best either. *And where the devil has Blake gotten to anyway?*

14

Blake sighed as he thought, *It's a good thing I'm not superstitious because this sure would be crummy luck!* It had happened again! He was just looking forward to a weekend off when his division was called up to the border. He was meant to be heading towards the farm to finally see Tessa and here he was, squashed in an army truck with twenty other sweaty guys. His teeth crunched together as his jaw tightened in frustration from the dust that was being hurled up and over the tailgate of the truck, coating every inch of him with a veil of red dust. On top of that, the old army truck's suspension had apparently seen better days, because the boys in uniform at his sides kept losing their balance as the truck bounced them from side to side, causing him to be constantly elbowed in the ribs.

Blake felt like he could scream with frustration but put his head down instead and whispered a prayer, "God, please give me patience and grace for this season. Protect me from the enemy's bullets and keep your hand upon Tessa. Help me find a way to get back to her…"

Blake kept up the silent vigil until he finally dozed off into a restless dream where a black panther was following Tessa into a dark cave. He tried to call out to her, to warn her, but no sound came out of his open mouth. Then the panther turned on him and sank his sharp teeth into his side. The pain was excruciating and Blake cried out in agony.

He woke with a start and realized that the pain in his side was actually another sharp elbow whose owner was now hissing, "What's wrong with you! Can't you sit still for a second?" Just then the truck came to a grinding halt, signaling that they had finally arrived at their destination. Blake had never been so happy to get out of a vehicle and immediately stumbled as far away from the other soldiers as he could get. He had to spend some time praying for Tessa, because something was wrong…he felt it in his bones and he could still see the panther's sharp fangs.

*****

Tessa knew she was not meant to go down to Sinethemba's hut, but nevertheless, she found herself ambling down the winding pathway anyway. She had not set eyes on Wayne in a solid week and as each day passed, her restlessness grew. Thoughts swirled round and round in her head until she wanted to scream with confusion. Scenes flashed before her eyes like a movie screen…Blake in the sea scented mist. Jeremiah's angry glare as he watched Wayne that night, not too long ago…and then pictures of Wayne , always unreadable, always vague and handsome-roguish. It all added up to heartache and tears, threatening to spill over sad eyes.

Tessa looked down at Bullet who trotted next to her and thought about the last time she was on this path, carrying him, broken and bleeding in the rain. That memory reminded her to try and concentrate on what she was grateful for, instead of all the things that were wrong in her life. Somehow she had to snap out of this heaviness but just couldn't seem to find the key that would unlock the door to the dark cave she was in. Rounding the final bend in the path Tessa again came upon the circle of huts, and it felt like history was repeating itself. The same children rushed up to her with open hands, waiting for something from her and again she had nothing to give. It felt to Tessa that most of the time lately she had nothing to give. The same fires burned in the round metal bins and the smoke hung thick in the air as before.

As soon as Tessa stepped into Sinethemba's hut, she knew that something was different. A change had taken place since the last time she was here.

The bed that had been on bricks to prevent the tokolosie from biting off toes in the night, was now on the floor. Sinethemba's husband was no longer laying feverish in the bed, but sat at the little wooden table eating a bowl of cornmeal. The bandages around his hand had been removed and the wound had healed nicely. Sinethemba smiled at Tessa and said, "Jesus heal and tokolosie scared now!" Sinethemba threw back her head and laughed loudly, baring her shiny toothless gums. "Weze happy now."

Tessa was amazed at the joy and peace that flooded out of Sinethemba.

"Here, look…" Sinethemba placed a worn Bible in Tessa's hand. As the tattered thin pages flipped open Tessa was surprised to see that the Bible was written in Zulu.

"Where did you get this?"she asked.

"Ole preacher man, he give. We happy now, no more evil tokolosie, he scare of Jesus power."

Sinethemba took the book back and held it against her chest as if it were her shield from the evil tokolosie.

Tessa smiled as she realized that that was exactly what it was, a sword and a shield. It was the key to unlock the dark places. These new converts were teaching her again that it was all so simple. Like little children, they trusted fully in what the Word said. When had she started making things so complicated? Seeing through their fresh eyes of faith, Tessa realized that all she had to do was go to the Father and ask him to forgive her of her sin. He would help her; he promised to place her sins into the sea of forgetfulness…to make her as white as snow. All she had to do was stop running from him and trust him.

Tessa was still pondering on this when she arrived back at the farm and heard Charmaine calling her name.

"Come on, Tessa, I won't take no for an answer!" Charmaine firmly stated as she took Tessa's hand and tried to drag her down the hallway. "I don't know what has gotten into you but you are coming to town with me to buy a dress for the spring dance. It will be so much fun! I'm tired of seeing you moping around here!"

Tessa surprised Charmaine by saying, "OK. I'll come."

She was tired of moping too. Maybe if she kept busy she would stop thinking about her dilemma. She still had not heard a single word from Wayne and vacillated between desperately wanting to see him and hating him for his silence. Again she thought that it felt like the very worst kind of rejection, and the wound ran deep. But wasn't that the way of all sin in the end. Sin had a way of eroding the soul by the pain and hurt it caused.

"Well hurry up then and get ready," Charmaine said as she twisted her long blond hair into a fashionable bun and smiled at herself in the mirror.

*****

It did feel good to be out and about, and Tessa was pleased that she had agreed to shop with Charmaine, even though Charmaine's constant chatter could really work on her nerves. Charmaine held another dress up to Tessa's neck and said, "Oh, this is stunning!"

Tessa looked down at the frilly mint green dress and grimaced. "Maybe..." Tessa mumbled as she hung the gaudy green dress back on the rack.

By late afternoon they had visited every store in town and Tessa's feet ached. Charmaine grabbed her hand and pulled her along the busy sidewalk, "Come on, slow poke! Let's reward ourselves for a job well done! We both found beautiful dresses. Let's get a big slice of chocolate cake and a coffee!"

Tessa hadn't had an appetite, but now she had to admit that the chocolate cake was a good idea. It was moist and melted in her mouth. As she took the last sip of pecan-flavored coffee, she sighed contentedly. Tessa pulled her dress out of the bag and looked at it again. Charmaine had been right; they had both found beautiful dresses.

I wonder if Wayne will like it? Will he even be at the dance? What will I say to him? Should I say anything at all...or should I ignore him completely?

The contentment she had felt a moment ago fled as these thoughts bombarded Tessa's mind. She stuffed the dress back into the bag and said, "I really want to go home now."

Charmaine pulled a face and groaned, "You're such a party-pooper! I still wanted to go to the shoe store down the road."

"Then let's just meet back at the farm, I'm really tired..." Tessa replied, and realized that she had spoken the truth. She had not been sleeping well at all, and the constant internal dialogue over Wayne was exhausting her emotionally. Or was it the guilt of what they had done? Or the memory of Jeremiah's accusing eyes as he had looked at her and Wayne. Or worst of all…was it the unbearable thought that she had completely lost Blake, her actions finally severing what perhaps could still have been.

Tessa weaved her way through the people on the sidewalks, hoping to get to the edge of town where she could catch the 4.30 p.m. bus out to the farmlands. She would have to hurry or she would miss the bus. Picking up her step, Tessa hastily rounded a corner and collided into a man who was standing in a group of people. When she looked up she was horrified to see Wayne's mocking eyes looking down at her. In fact, she was mortified to see *everyone* looking at her!

Tessa was speechless as Wayne drawled, "Hey baby, where did you come from?" he smiled crookedly and added "You following me?"

Tessa tried to take a step backwards but he had hold of her arm and pulled her towards him.

"I've missed you," he whispered, and Tessa was sure she smelled alcohol on his breath. He turned to his companions and said, "Have I told you that this is my best girl?" Tessa felt sick to her stomach and wondered if she was going to throw up on the sidewalk in front of all these people.

What did he mean…his best girl? How many girls were there?

Then he turned back to Tessa and in a sincere voice asked, "You are coming to the Spring dance aren't you? I really want you there."

Tessa looked into his serious pleading eyes and thought that he looked genuinely desperate.

She pulled away from him and said, "I have to go, I'm going to be late for the bus." She hurried past the group and was conscious of her heels clicking along the sidewalk. She heard Wayne shout after her, "You have to come to the dance…we will talk about it tomorrow at work!"

Tessa leaned her head against the cold window pane of the swaying bus. Her head was throbbing terribly. How was it possible for Wayne to cause her so much confusion? One minute she was sure he was toying with her, and the very next he looked like he would cry if she didn't go the dance. And what did he mean by 'my *best* girl'? Was that just an endearing expression or were there other girls? Tessa willed her mind to be still and found comfort in the fact that he had seemed pleased to see her and had not totally ignored her. Perhaps tomorrow she would have more clarity when Wayne was back on the farm…

15

Tessa's first thought as her eyes popped open was that today was the day she would be able to talk to Wayne and finally feel settled, but, by lunch time she realized that this day would be no different from any of the other days. Wayne was nowhere to be seen. *I can't go through another day and sleepless night worrying about this. If he won't come to me...I will have to go to him!*

After lunch Tessa quietly hurried down the pathway and onto the road that led to Wayne's house. Standing on the back porch she pondered what she would say to him when she saw him, and her earlier bravado fled. She stood there a full minute taking in deep, long breaths to steady her nerves, and then knocked on the door. After another minute she knocked again, but the door stayed firmly shut. Tessa thought it a likely analogy because Wayne's heart seemed tightly shut too. Tessa turned to leave but as she stepped off the porch she found an anger building inside of her. How dare he take advantage of her and then not even have the decency to talk to her about it. *He was a coward!*

Tessa marched back up the steps and turned the knob to see if the stubborn door would open. The old wooden door creaked as she swung it open and stepped inside. She wasn't sure what exactly she was looking for but she browsed through the empty house and allowed her fingers to trail over old pictures and dusty ornaments. Maybe just being amongst his things would give her more insight into Wayne's complex behavior.

Eventually Tessa found herself standing in Wayne's bedroom. How little she knew about this man that she had so carelessly given herself too. His bed was unmade and clothes were piled on a chair in the corner. She breathed in his familiar musky aftershave that hung in the room. Tessa walked to the closet and peaked inside. Besides the usual clothes and shoes, there was a hunting rifle and a sjambok, a whip that most farm owners had.

But then she noticed it. The sjambok was covered in old dry blood! Tessa took a step back and almost tripped over a boot that had been carelessly flung onto the floor. She sat down on the bed to stop the wave of dizziness that hit her. She closed her eyes and saw the wounds on Bullet's back. Yes, a sjambok could definitely have inflicted those wounds. But could it possibly have been Wayne? She knew he wasn't fond of the dog but could he have been so cruel to an animal that she loved? No, her mind was playing tricks with her.

"I'm just tired," she whispered to herself. Then she remembered how strange Sinethemba had always acted around Wayne. Did she know something that Tessa didn't? Was she afraid to say? Or had Tessa just not wanted to listen?

All of a sudden Tessa had to get out of this room and out of sight of the bloody weapon. She ran down the hall and wondered what she would do if she saw Wayne coming up the drive. She was an unwelcome intruder in a strange house. Tessa hurried out the house and down the road, arguing with herself.

Could it be true?....No, it was ridiculous to think that Wayne was capable of such a crime...but maybe it was true?...No, it just absolutely could not be...

If she had hoped for a better night sleep, she was worse off than before. She tossed and turned and the little sleep she got was filled with ghost-like beings that watched her from the hallways of a strange house from which she could not escape. In the dream she felt something on her bed, moving, jumping, torturing her; and then she jerked awake to see Charmaine bouncing on her bed.

"Wake up, sleepy head! The big dance is tonight and I am so excited I couldn't sleep anymore."

Tessa groaned and pulled the pillow over her aching head. The sliver of light that came in through the window hurt her eyes and she did not want to think about anything at all, especially not about the dance.

All day the headache clung to her temples and Tessa tried to use it as an excuse to not go to the dance with Charmaine.

"Are you crazy?" Charmaine looked at her incredulously. "The tickets are bought, and our new dresses are pressed and ready! You have to go!"

Two hours later they walked through the doors of the dance hall. The music was blaring and the ironic words of the song caught Tessa's attention immediately, "Forever and ever and ever and ever..."

What lasted forever? Everything changed and nothing was forever. Nothing at all...

Beautiful spring flowers decorated the dance hall, and little twinkling lights crept up the wooden pillars making the room look enchanting. Couples were already sprinkled around the dance floor and Tessa wished she was here under different circumstances. Her soul was raw and she felt vulnerable. Just then she saw him.

Why does he have to be so breathtakingly handsome?

Wayne wore a long sleeve red shirt with the sleeves slightly rolled up, giving him a sleek polished look. His golden hair just touched the collar of his shirt and he was floating around the dance floor with Sharon in his arms, and as usual she was laughing loudly. Tessa remembered how that had worked on her nerves when they had eaten out after church that one time, which now seemed like such a long time ago.

She recognized the Afrikaans boy's thick accent as he greeted her and held out a cup of punch. Hendrik wore a shy smile and slightly reddening cheeks. The contrast between his humble sincerity and Wayne's arrogant smirks was noticeable tonight.

"Would you like to dance?" he said in his thick accent as his cheeks reddened even further. Tessa did not feel like dancing but knew that the boy had been courageous by asking and didn't want to embarrass him by rejecting his timid offer. She nodded her head and they walked onto the dance floor. Unfortunately, at that moment the music turned to a slow love song. Awkwardly they tried to sway to the mournful music but Tessa felt as uncomfortable as Hendrik looked. She tried to give him a reassuring smile but thought; *I knew coming here tonight was going to be a disaster.*

The humiliation didn't last long because suddenly she felt Hendrik step away from her. *Thank goodness, it seems he has changed his mind too.* But instead, when Tessa looked up, she saw Wayne standing beside them.

"I thought I would finish this dance with you," he said to her while he glared at Hendrik. He did not wait for an answer but pushed in and possessively put an arm around Tessa's waist. He pulled her close and started swaying to the music. Tessa tried to push away a little but he tightened his hold and whispered in her ear.

"You look exquisite tonight! I've missed you, my little pigeon."

Tessa closed her eyes and wondered how those words could still thrill her like they did. How was it possible that she would still want to hear it after Wayne's behavior? What was wrong with her?

Wayne had all but ignored her since *that* day. She had worried and had sleepless nights over it, and here she was eating up his every word...again. As the song came to an end, Tessa opened her eyes and caught Sharon staring at them from across the room. Tessa realized that the poor girl was probably in exactly the same position she was.

Waiting, wondering, hurting, but mostly... confused.

The realization made Tessa angry again and the spell was broken. She hissed at Wayne, "We have to talk. Now!"

She grabbed his hand and dragged him into the quiet foyer outside.

"What's this all about?" Wayne looked genuinely concerned and his brilliant blue eyes penetrated her heart. Tessa didn't know where to start explaining the mess her soul was in because of *him*. She decided to start with Bullet and the bloodied sjambok she had discovered in his room. She hoped he wouldn't get mad when she mentioned she had entered his house and gone into his room. But she simply had to know. She watched him closely as she explained what she had done and how the thought had crossed her mind that perhaps it was a sjambok that had inflicted those terrible wounds on Bullet.

Wayne did not flinch or look away. He didn't seem angry or perturbed at all. Taking her hand, he smiled, "How silly girls can be when they start imagining things. That is simply ridiculous."

He lifted her chin and looked deeply into her eyes.

She tried to explain again, "But the blood on the sjambok made me think…"

Wayne interrupted her with a kiss. Then he added, "That's the trouble, you shouldn't worry your pretty little head with *thinking*. Besides, I haven't even used that sjambok. My uncle gave it to me a while back and I haven't gotten to clean it. We don't even know if that was blood. It may just be mud or something."

Wayne pulled away and looked genuinely sad as he said, "I'm hurt that you would think of me that way though…"

He looked so vulnerable and handsome as he stood there leaning against the wall. His musky scent hung in the air around them and Tessa longed for things to be right between them. She was pleased that he would care so much about what she thought of him. Surely if he didn't care about her, what she thought of him wouldn't matter.

"I'm sorry," she heard herself say, "I guess it was silly of me."

He pulled her close again and kissed her but this time the kiss was passionate and hungry. "I'll forgive you if you leave with me. Let's go somewhere quiet."

Tessa still wanted to talk to him about why he hadn't come to see her. She didn't understand why he had been so distant if he cared for her as much as his eyes confessed he did. Maybe it would be a good idea to go somewhere quiet and talk some more since the foyer still had late comers drifting in. Wayne ran his hand through her dark hair and whispered, "You're so beautiful...come away with me."

Tessa felt warm all over as she began to rest in the knowledge that Wayne did want to be with her. There was obviously a very good reason that he had stayed away. She smiled up at him as he took her hand and led her to the door.

"Oh there you are!" Sharon's overly loud voice cracked like thunder through the quiet foyer. "I've been looking all over for you!"

She sashayed over and put her hand possessively on Wayne's arm. She laughed again but this time it sounded forced and it grated on Tessa's nerves. Only then did Sharon turn her gaze toward Tessa. She continued to smile, but her eyes bored threateningly into Tessa as she spoke, "So, did Wayne tell you our news?"

Tessa glanced up at Wayne who looked back at her with expressionless eyes. Gone was the intense loving gaze that had lingered upon her only moments ago. Without waiting for an answer Sharon blurted out, "We're going to have a baby! Can you believe it? I'm so excited! And once Wayne has saved some money we will have a nice outdoor wedding, next to the pond at his house. He has a favorite spot out there," she said as she punched Wayne playfully on the arm and winked at him, "but that's our secret." She looked back at Tessa and continued to prattle on, but Tessa was not hearing a single word. She felt dizzy and nauseated. Was this a joke? She looked at Wayne and willed him to contradict this silly girl's fairy tale. But Wayne stood leaning casually against the wall as if they had been discussing the weather. She looked at Sharon's hand that still hung possessively over Wayne's arm and wondered why he hadn't yet pulled away as a sign of adamant denial! But here he stood, quietly, calmly, saying nothing. His mouth said nothing, his eyes said nothing, and his body said nothing.

Tessa heard Sharon's bubbly voice through a muffled tunnel and shook her head. She had to remind herself to breathe.

"Well cheerio, I have to get back inside and help serve the punch," Sharon's heels clicked hurriedly on the tiled floor as she sashayed away.

"Don't be long now, my honey bunch," she said as she turned and blew Wayne a kiss.

Tessa didn't know if she should laugh or sit down on the floor and cry. She wanted Wayne to kiss her again, but she also felt like slapping him across that handsome face.

She finally ground out, "Say something!" but Wayne just stuffed his hands in his pockets and shrugged his shoulders.

"So it was all a lie? You never cared for me? You cheated on me!"

"How could I cheat on you when we were not an exclusive couple? I never told you I wasn't seeing anyone else," Wayne casually leaned against the wall again and crossed his arms. His laid-back attitude infuriated Tessa.

"I didn't think I needed to *ask* you if you were seeing anyone else. I assumed by the things you said and did that you cared for me…maybe even loved me?" Tessa hated how desperate and whiny her own voice sounded in her ears.

"Well I'm sorry…I didn't plan to have this brat with Sharon. I just should have been more careful. I haven't worked out how I'm going to get out of this yet, but believe me, I will. I am not ready for this."

Tessa's heart skipped a beat as the thought penetrated her mind. How had she not thought about this before? *What if I am pregnant too?* What had she done?

She looked at Wayne and for the first time saw past his handsome face. He was a selfish man who only cared about himself. He didn't know what true love was and he took whatever he wanted from whomever he wanted. He was so different from ...*Blake.* Tessa groaned as she thought about what Blake would think of her now.

Tessa placed her hand on the wall to steady herself as the room began to spin. The words swirled around and around in her mind. *What if I'm pregnant? What if I'm pregnant?*

Suddenly she realized what she had to do. She had to get as far away from Wayne as possible! She gave him a piercing stare and said, "Shame on me for having allowed you into my life. I never want to see you again."

Tessa turned to walk away but Wayne roughly grabbed her arm and jerked her around.

"No one walks away from me! I will tell *you* when I am finished with you." Tessa's arm ached as his finger's bit into her flesh, "And I'm not finished with you yet!" he hissed.

"Wayne, I deserve more than this, and I will never see you again as long as I live." Tessa yanked her arm free and walked out the doors and down the cement steps into the cool night air.

"Well, good riddance to you and that stupid dog of yours," she heard Wayne shout as she crossed the parking lot. Tessa's blood froze and she stopped dead. She turned slowly and looked at Wayne who now stood on the bottom step. His anger bore holes into her as he glared through narrowed eyes.

"So it was you? Another lie. You *were* the one that hurt Bullet..." Tessa's voice trailed off as the truth began to sink in.

"He needed to be taught a lesson! He got what he deserved."

Wayne spat on the floor. She had never seen him do that, but then again, Tessa realized she did not know this man at all. She turned to walk away...there was nothing left to be said. She started crossing the parking lot, but before she got to the corner she heard Wayne shout, "You are wrong again. You *will* see me again. I promise you that."

Tessa did not look back but turned the corner and headed towards the bus station.

The farmhouse was dark and quiet as Tessa entered the kitchen and walked down the creaky hallway. The candle she had lit flickered and died as she entered her room. Once again Tessa found herself in pitch darkness, just like the very first night on arriving at this farm. She patted all around the bedside table until her hand found the box of matches and relit the candle. Tessa was miserable as she sat and glanced around the room. This room was not hers, she didn't belong here anymore. She had thought that Wayne was her friend, and then for a while she had imagined that she had feelings for him, but the truth was that she had never loved him. Her loneliness had caused her to allow him to become her companion and it had brought nothing but pain and confusion into her life. She would have been better off being a little lonely until God brought her a companion. Tessa was angry with herself for having been fooled by Wayne. She tried to think but that dreaded thought took up all the space in her head. *What if I am pregnant? What if I am pregnant?*

The shame of it brought Tessa to her knees on the hard wooden floor. She laid her head down and wept. After her tears were spent Tessa continued to lie on the floor and a plan formulated in her mind. It was as if the cleansing tears had brought clarity to her heavy heart. *I need to get back to the ocean and start a new life. It's time to pack.*

She opened her swollen eyes and started to pick herself up when something behind her headboard caught her eye. A tiny piece of white paper stuck out and when Tessa pulled on it, she found it was an envelope. She sat up on the floor and pulled the candle closer. The handwriting was familiar and then she recognized the spidery scrawl. Her hand started to shake. *It's a letter from Blake.* How long had it been laying there under her bed while she had wondered why he hadn't written? Maybe this one letter held the answers. Maybe it would inform her that he had found someone else and that was why he couldn't write. Maybe it would simply say that he didn't care for her. She had to know but was terrified to read the words that lay inside the white envelope. Tessa trembled as she opened the letter and read:

Dear Tessa,

I only have a few minutes to write as our sergeant is determined to keep us running from morning until night. I actually have the blisters to prove it. We are heading into heated combat territory within the week, but I am not allowed to say more than that.

However, there is something I must say before I leave. I regret not speaking to you about this before I left and have kicked myself for it since! I should've told you then and I pray that I am not too late in saying it now, but ...I love you.

I've loved you for a long time. I've imagined us sharing life together and there is nothing I want more than that. I know this is not the most traditional or romantic way to propose to a girl, but I cannot wait any longer. I'm afraid I have waited too long already. So...Tessa, will you marry me? Please say yes!

I plan to give you a ring as soon as we meet and hope to be married the first chance we get.

Our mail will be forwarded to us and I will be waiting for your reply every day.

I love you. I miss you...

Yours Always,

Blake

Tessa dropped the letter onto the floor as she whispered to an unseen Blake, "It is too late. I have not been faithful to you...you will not want me now."

16

Tessa sat on the bench at the train station and stared down the tracks, willing the train to appear around the corner. She'd been thankful that Charmaine had spent the night at Sharon's house so that she could get up as the rooster crowed to pack her bags. She had quietly escaped into the misty morning air with nothing but the bag she had brought with her and Bullet by her side. Now, she glanced down at Bullet and grudgingly had to admit that Wayne was right. She shuddered as she heard the words he had once spoken, "Isn't he a better behaved dog now?" And he had been right. Bullet was a different dog since the beating. He was horribly obedient all the time! Gone was the playful happy puppy she had known. The former Bullet would have been running and exploring all the way to the train station. But instead he had walked close to Tessa all the way to the station with hardly any interest in the strange sights and sounds.

Usually Tessa would have felt sad about the change in Bullet, but today she was grateful that he was docile and that she didn't have to chase him all over the place. He now sat nervously panting next to her and she patted his head. "It's alright boy, you're going to love the ocean."

Tessa had purchased a ticket on the first train that was heading to the ocean in any direction. It had been like rolling a dice and the dice had landed on Port Elizabeth. In a way Tessa was relieved that the dice had not landed on Cape Town because although it was her home town, it would have been unbearable facing the familiar places without Blake and Jeremiah. A pang of guilt stung her as she thought about the note she had left for Aunt Rina.

Dear Auntie Rina,

Thank you so much for all you have done. However, I feel like it's time for me to head back to my beloved ocean and make a new life for myself. I cannot tell you where I am going yet, but will write when I am settled. Please pass this message on to Jeremiah for me.

Thanks again,

Tessa

The truth was that she could not face Jeremiah. Not until she knew for sure that she was not pregnant. She feared that Jeremiah would take one look at her and her guilt alone would shout it out. She remembered how he had glared at Wayne and wouldn't put it past him to go beat him to a pulp. Not that he didn't deserve it, but she didn't want Jeremiah to get into trouble because of her stupidity. Tessa glanced down the tracks again. The train was already a few minutes late, and she didn't want to run the risk of Aunt Rina finding her note and chasing her down at the train station. She knew that they would already be up at the farm and by now, they would be looking for her.

She wondered if Wayne was there already since he had some spring seeding to do. She tried to imagine what he would have said to her this morning. Would he still have been angry, or would he have given her that crooked smile and said he was sorry?

Either way, the image made Tessa's stomach turn. She had seen the real person that hid behind that handsome grin, and was glad to be rid of him. Sharon could have him.

The train whistled happily as it slowly curled around the corner. White puffy steam encircled it and for a split second Tessa imagined that she was about to embark on an enchanted adventure. But immediately the truth of her situation pulled her down into reality. This would be no enchanted adventure. She was alone. She didn't know what she would do once she arrived in Port Elizabeth. And she only had the money that Jeremiah had given her on his last visit. It was enough for train fare and perhaps two weeks of frugal living. She would have to find a job right away, and she didn't think that milking cows would do anything for her résumé.

But worst of all was the knowledge that Blake was out there somewhere and didn't know the truth about her. He didn't know that she may be carrying another man's child. If only she could rewind the clock. Now everything was ruined, and she would never be able to be with Blake. He would probably find himself another wife as soon as he knew the truth about her. No, this was not a great adventure. It was simply an escape to a place where no one could find her.

The conductor walked over and disrupted her torturous thoughts. "He will have to be kenneled now. It's in the last carriage over there."

He seemed to point in the direction of the last carriage with his long sharp nose. "Can he not stay with me in my compartment? He is very obedient and quiet," Tessa pleaded.

"That's against the rules," the sharp nose lifted slightly in disdain as the conductor looked at Bullet, "All animals in the back."

After getting Bullet tucked into his kennel on the last car, Tessa was finally settled in her compartment. She hoped that she would not share the small space with three more people. Tonight, the four seats would be turned into beds and Tessa couldn't imagine being cooped up in such a confined space with three other strangers.

The only one already in the compartment with her was a little old lady. She wore a pretty striped dress that hung on the thin body. Her gray hair was tied up with a bright blue ribbon that did not match the dress or the purple socks on the woman's small feet. The wrinkles ran like deep rivers across the old woman's face but she had twinkling brown eyes and smiled at Tessa. "My feet are always cold on the train honey. I have an extra pair if you need it."

She handed Tessa a pair of green polka-dot socks which were more bizarre than the purple ones she had been caught staring at for too long. Tessa blushed slightly as she took the socks out of the old crooked hand and put them on her cold feet.

"My name is Ginger," the woman spoke and tapped the big thermos next to her. I brought enough to share. With that, she poured out the warm liquid into two little cups and handed Tessa one of them.

"Mmm, this is delicious!" Tessa smiled at Ginger. She had not eaten yet and her stomach had been growling for hours already. The brown liquid tasted like nothing she had ever had before. It was a sweet, nutty flavored creamy drink. "What is it?" She asked.

"Oh, it's just my special recipe made from coffee and milk powder and some other little secret ingredients."

"Well, it's really good, thank you!" Tessa hoped she wasn't being drugged, but looking into the friendly twinkling eyes, she highly doubted it.

Ginger began to hum a tune as the train started clacking down the tracks. Tessa gazed out of the window as the farmhouses became less frequent and soon there was no human life to see. All that was left to see were miles and miles of semi-desert terrain. She pulled the folded blue blanket out from the shelf against the wall and covered herself, stifling a yawn. Soon her eyes closed and the humming and rocking sent her into a peaceful sleep.

*****

Jeremiah stood on the back steps of the farmhouse and pounded on the door. Tessa would be so surprised by this visit. He wasn't meant to have the weekend off but his sergeant had sprung it on them by saying, "You boys take the weekend off because we are heading into active combat at the front lines next week. Make sure you are back on Monday morning or you will be considered A.W.O.L! So don't get any ideas!"

Now Jeremiah's green eyes sparkled in the early morning light with the anticipation of Tessa's smile. His sister needed time with him and he felt guilty for having left her on the farm all this time. He knew she wasn't altogether happy and he hoped that that snake, Wayne, was not still hanging around! He would certainly put an end to that on this visit. He hadn't had a chance last time because the snake had slithered into a hole and had not come out again while he was visiting. But this time would be different. Yes siree! He would go and find Wayne in his snake hole and drag him out.

Jeremiah pounded on the door again and suddenly Aunt Rina was standing in front of him. But instead of a huge hug and a joyful welcoming, Jeremiah saw a hesitant smile.

"What's wrong Auntie Rina?" were the first words out of his mouth.

"I'm sorry Jeremiah, but Tessa is gone." She walked into the kitchen and Jeremiah followed her.

"What do you mean *gone*?"

Aunt Rina handed him the note and turned away quietly to light the stove.

Dear Auntie Rina,

Thank you so much for all you have done. However, I feel like it's time for me to head back to my beloved ocean and make a new life for myself. I do not belong here on the farm. I cannot tell you where I am going yet, but I will write when I am settled. Please pass this message on to Jeremiah for me.

Thanks again,
Tessa

Jeremiah flipped the note over and then reread the few emotionless words.

"That's it?" he asked Aunt Rina, who shrugged and continued to make the strong black coffee.

"What happened?"

"Sit down, Jeremiah. I will make you some bacon and eggs and we will talk."

Jeremiah sat down with the note in front of him and willed his mind to stop whirling. Where had Tessa gone? Back to Cape Town? Why had she not said where she was going? His emotions twisted round and round from worry to confusion. He felt an anger rise up in him. Was he angry at Tessa for leaving? Or was he angry with Auntie Rina or that snake Wayne? He was sure Wayne had something to do with it! Or maybe he was angry with himself for not taking better care of his sister. Round and round his mind spiraled, and he couldn't wait for bacon and eggs to get his answers.

"Aunt Rina, what happened? Where did she go?"

Aunt Rina placed a steaming mug of coffee in front of Jeremiah and patted his cold hand. His questions came through piercing green eyes. Was it an accusation she saw there? Or was it suspicion? Maybe she should have taken more time to talk with Tessa and see how she was doing. But she had left that up to the young ones, Charmaine and Wayne.

"I honestly don't know the answer to your question Jeremiah," Aunt Rina sighed as she sat down heavily on the wooden bench.

"I'm sorry. All I can say is that Tessa seemed happy enough here on the farm. I know she had grown close to Wayne, who works for us, but I don't know why she left. Charmaine seemed to think that she had a good time at the dance the other night. She didn't discuss anything with us though. She kept her thoughts to herself most of the time. I wish she had spoken to me, but she didn't. The note is all she left. I have no idea where she has gone. I had hoped that you would have some idea."

"No, she really doesn't have any family besides me. But I sure know who I am going to ask! Where does Wayne live?"

Aunt Rina didn't like the murderous look that stared back at her and she was glad she could say, "Actually, Wayne has taken some of his doves to Cape Town for a big sale. He won't be back for weeks. Besides, I don't know if he would be able to tell you anything." Aunt Rina stood and turned the frying bacon one more time. Jeremiah watched as she cracked the big farm eggs, one by one, and slid them into the hot oil. He wondered what Tessa was eating this morning

17

Where am I? Why is my bed rocking? Tessa struggled to focus. She opened one eye and looked around the semi-dark room. The shapes looked odd and she shook her head. The sudden movement caused her head to spin with dizziness. Closing her eyes again she sat quietly for a moment and remembered that she was on the train to Port Elizabeth. She stretched and yawned, realizing that she must have been sleeping for most of the day! Lifting the blind she looked out of the window at the twilight sunset. The sun was almost completely gone, but it had left behind the famous African sunset of molten red, orange, and purple in a sky close enough to touch. Tessa was sure that a more beautiful sunset could never have been seen anywhere else on earth but here in the semi-desert of Africa. She watched the last beautiful ray disappear as the train gently rocked peace into her very bones.

It was here that Tessa thought about God, here in this moment of silence when the octopus arms of color and light drew back into a dark stillness. She sensed the wall her sin had put up between herself and God. She was tired of saying sorry to him for her mistakes and sin, and she was sure he was tired of hearing it too. But here, now, in the perfect moment she whispered to her long lost friend, "Thank you, Lord, for this moment of beauty and peace." She continued to stand against the window until the sky turned black and all she could see was her reflection in the glass. Her long dark hair had come out of the pony tail and hung haphazardly around her shoulders. Her face was thin and pale.

She finally pulled down the shade and was aware of her loudly-grumbling stomach. All Tessa had had all day was the tasty potion from Ginger's thermos Tessa now believed that perhaps it was the secret potion that had put her into a deep sleep all day.

She combed her hair, put on a light layer of pink lipstick, and walked down the long rocking corridor to the dining car.

"There you are at last!" Ginger called out, causing all the passengers to look up as Tessa walked through the car.

"I've been waiting for you, dear. My concoction worked really well, you look much better! Now sit down, and let's eat. I've had three sundowners while waiting on you to get up." Ginger threw her head back and laughed unrestrainedly. She wore a straw hat with plastic flowers and fruit stuck on it and the cherries and grapes wobbled up and down as she laughed. Tessa had to smile at the eccentric old lady and thought that she was beautiful, even though the tears of laughter ran down rivers of wrinkles on her ancient face. Her true beauty shone through the charm of her gentle spirit. Tessa was aware of the other passengers who looked down their nose at Ginger, as though they were afraid of her weirdness. She recognized those snobby looks of judgment and she suddenly felt very protective of her new friend. In a moment of impulse she asked Ginger "May I wear your beautiful hat?"

"Sure, honey!" Ginger said as she gently placed it on Tessa's head as though it were a crown. "There now, it suits you."

Tessa grinned at Ginger and felt some of the carefree joy that Ginger carried, float through her. "Ginger, I hope I look as beautiful as you do when I am your age, and I wish that I will be as happy as you are."

Ginger reached out and touched Tessa's hand with orange nail-polished fingers.

"Well honey, you are beautiful. And as for happiness, that is something you must choose every day. If you wait for everything to be perfect, you will never be happy. Life is messy sometimes, so you have to choose to be happy in the day you have been given. It cannot be exchanged, replaced, or refunded. You only have those 1440 minutes that a single day gives you."

Ginger winked at Tessa as if she already knew everything Tessa was going through. "Are you ready to order yet?" A waiter with a stiff white jacket asked. His big brass buttons shimmered in the low light.

"Oh, yes honey, we are famished! Bring me the Roasted Chicken breast with Kipfier potatoes, chorizo, spinach in paprika oil....and another pot of tea." Ginger replied and then gave the waiter a familiar pat on the arm. "Thanks, Adam."

Turning to Tessa the waiter smiled, showing off his pearly white teeth that shone out of the dark shiny face. "And you madam?"

"Ummm…" Tessa flipped the pages of the menu. She looked up at Ginger and said, "Sorry, I don't know what to eat, there are so many choices!"

"Well, honey, I know this menu back to front! Let me help you. Do you like curry?"

"Curry sounds great," Tessa replied as her stomach growled loudly.

Ginger turned to the waiter and without opening the menu, ordered for Tessa.

"She will have the Madras Beef Curry with Rito bread, Steamed rice and Yoghurt Riata."

The waiter's large white teeth sparkled in the newly lit candle light, "That is a good choice madam. I will be right back."

Tessa looked at Ginger in amazement, "How do you know the menu off by heart?"

"Well, I have traveled on this train every year for ten years. I am also usually alone and have a lot of free time in the dining car to study it. That's the secret you know, you have to look busy when you dine alone." Ginger winked at Tessa.

"If I may ask," Tessa took a long sip of water and continued, "Where does this train take you every year?"

"Oh honey, I go and visit my husband."

Tessa sat quietly and wondered why Ginger was not with her husband. Was he in a home somewhere, or were they divorced? If so, why would she visit him every year? It was all very strange but she didn't want to be rude by asking any more questions.

"And where is this train taking you, honey?" Ginger queried.

"Oh, just to the ocean," Tessa replied. They sat in silence for a moment as they both recognized the unanswered questions that lay between them. Finally Ginger said, "I was married to my husband for fifty years, you know?"

"That is a long time," Tessa said for lack of knowing what else to say.

"Yes, and I loved that man, but marriage is terribly hard work sometimes. There are waves that come with marriage, you know," Ginger said, and then was silent as though that explained it all.

"What do you mean?" Tessa leaned forward in her chair.

"Well honey, it's like the waves of the ocean, you understand?"

Tessa shook her head slightly and the grapes on the hat wobbled, causing her to remember the uncharacteristically carefree moment when she had put the flamboyant hat on her head. Now she felt self-conscious as other passengers entered the dining car and looked at her for a second longer than what was considered polite. She took the hat off and handed it back to Ginger who plopped it unceremoniously back onto her gray head. The plump purple grapes now jiggled wildly.

"You see dear, the ocean changes all the time. Some days it is quiet and smooth and other days it throws itself around in horrible turmoil. The waves seem to be fighting with each other. Then there are times when the water is hot, and other times it freezes your toes off. Oh the ocean has such playfulness and passion don't you think? But it has its dark side too and it even changes color sometimes. Don't you just love that turquoise blue? That is my favorite color of the ocean."

The white-toothed waiter appeared bearing plates laden with aromatic foods. The steam swirled around as he placed the plates down and said, "Enjoy your meal, my ladies."

Ginger skipped over all three forks and picked up a spoon, which she pointed at Tessa then said, "So you see, marriage is like the ocean!"

Tessa ate her spicy curry and picked out the flavor-enhancing bay leaves while she thought about the analogy of the ocean being like a marriage.

Ginger had poured a cup of English black tea and was now adding a splash of milk to it. She would take a tiny sip between her little bites of food. "Isn't hot tea just the most beautiful thing on God's green earth?"

Tessa nodded distractedly and said, "Ginger, what made you stay with your husband during the hard times?"

"Oh honey, when you love the ocean you have to love it in all its forms. During a writhing storm you just have to wait 'til the sun shines again and the waters get calm. And it always changes. It never stays the same. This is the mistake that young people make. They think because the waves are this way today...they will be that way forever. You have to trust that things can change. They always do."

Tessa thought about Blake. Could this apply to her? Could she tell him the truth and believe that things could still work out for the best even if the truth caused a storm between them for a little while. Surely it was worth giving it a try. Look, here was Ginger, still going to visit her husband after fifty years of marriage waves. Tessa felt lighthearted and suddenly excited. Even if she was pregnant, perhaps Blake would even allow his heart to be opened to this child?

She sipped her tea and smiled at Ginger who now sat back against the seat holding her stomach. "Oh honey, my eyes were too big for my stomach and now I need my bed."

Tessa noticed that most of the food was still on Ginger's plate. She looked at Ginger's bony shoulders and asked, "Are you sure you ate enough?"

"Oh yes, honey! One must never overeat though. It's very bad for the digestion."

*****

Within thirty minutes Ginger was tucked into her bed and was fast asleep.

Tessa lay in the bed and wondered how she would sleep after sleeping all day and then drinking pots of tea right before bedtime. She lay in the dark for a long time thinking about all that Ginger had said. The words had given her hope. Now all she needed was courage. After another hour passed of staring into the darkness, Tessa sat up and switched on the little light above her bed. She would do it! She would write a letter to Blake right now and explain it all. She would leave nothing out. She would give him time for the waves to pound and crash and then he would contact her and declare his undying love. It would all be fine.

Tessa finished the letter in the middle of the night and now lay in the pitch darkness, listening to the monotonous clackety clack of the wheels on the metal track, before finally giving in to the rhythmic swaying of the train. For the first night in a long time, Tessa slept the restful sleep that belonged to the unburdened ones.

18

Blake wondered why he had to be a part of the Angolan Bush War instead of being at home in Cape Town and snorkeling in the blue ocean. It was hot and dry and the thorny trees gave off no shade at all. The red dust lifted in tiny puffs around his army boots as he patrolled the border between Southwest Africa and Angola. All he could think about was Tessa. He was sure that she would have gotten the letter by now. Every day he held his breath as the life-giving letters were passed around, but so far he had not received a letter back. Maybe today would be the day. He swatted at a mosquito that buzzed around his sunburned neck and wished for the long day to end. Here one not only had to look out for unexpected enemy fire, but there were snakes that slithered underfoot and bugs of all kinds. His skin crawled, just thinking about some of the weird reptiles he had seen near his sleeping bag at night. He always made sure to shake out the bedding before getting into it at night. Besides that, there were wild animals ...'*that roamed around seeking whom they could devour*'. Blake smiled at the words of the scripture that came to mind. He squashed another fat mosquito that sat boldly on his hand, sucking his blood. All he needed was a dose of malaria to add to his troubles.

One thing was for sure though. He had never seen as many twinkling stars as what he did in the pitch darkness at night. The sky was strewn with billions of bright stars, and the nights were perfect after the late-afternoon torrential downpours which occurred every day without fail. Blake didn't mind the rain because it cooled everything off a little and gave him some respite from the grueling heat that clung to his heavy brown uniform.

After his patrol returned to the make-shift barracks that evening, Blake hurried to the mess hall, where he had some form of mystery stew sloshed into his tin plate. He ate quickly but picked out the peas and wrapped them in a serviette. He stuck an apple into his pocket before rushing back to his bed where his eyes hastily scanned the room for his friend. The room was getting dark already and he didn't see him at first, causing Blake to worry that his friend had wandered off. Then Champ jumped out from behind the bed and flung himself onto Blake's neck. His long tail wrapped around Blake's shoulder, and he jumped up and down hitting Blake on the head in greeting.

"Hello boy, did you miss me today?" Blake laughed as he scratched the blue velvet monkey between his tiny ears. Blake had found the orphan monkey the day after he arrived at the border. The little thing had been dehydrated and starved so Blake had assumed that the mother had probably become a meal herself. The monkey kept patting Blake on the head while making weird little sounds.

"OK you rascal. I know you are hungry. Here's your dinner, you spoilt monkey."

Blake unwrapped the serviette and poured the peas into Champs plate. He cut the apple into little pieces and added it to the peas. Champ hurried to his little buckled-tin plate and picked the peas up one by one with his tiny brown fingers and popped them in his mouth.

"Now Champ, I'm going to shower. Do not throw your food on my bed again!"

Blake couldn't count the times the monkey had thrown bits of uneaten fruit and vegetables all over the bed. Like the one night Blake had crept into the sleeping bag and got stuck by a bunch of seeds that Champ had decided to store for a middle of the night treat. Blake turned at the door and pointed his finger at Champ, "I mean it!"

Champ pulled his face and a piece of apple dropped out of his mouth, which he immediately scooped up from the dusty floor and popped back into his mouth. Blake shook his head and headed for the showers. He didn't want to admit it, but he was getting far too attached to that little menace.

*****

Tessa awoke to the sound of much chaos outside of the now stationary train. She yawned widely and stretched like a warm cat. Outside she heard dogs barking and people laughing and talking on the platform of the train station. A whistle blew in the far distance and Tessa wondered what had become of Ginger who was nowhere in sight. Tessa looked over and her eyes fell on the letter she had written to Blake last night. She hurriedly jumped out of bed and threw some clothes on. After splashing water on her face, she quickly ran a brush through her tangled hair. Hurrying off the train she bumped into the conductor with the sharp nose, almost unbalancing him.

"Oh sorry! I just wanted to mail this letter before the train left."

"No need to hurry so," the conductor said irritably, "this is an hour stop."

"Can I check on my dog while we are stopped?" "No need to do that," the conductor scowled.

"We have people that feed and water them."

With that, the conductor turned away as if Tessa was truly a nuisance. She watched his stiff back as he strode through the crowd and wondered why some people were able to make her feel like a nuisance while others, like Ginger, made her feel special and loved. This thought again brought her back to the difference between Wayne and Blake and the letter burned in her hand. She just had to mail it, today, now. She hurried through the big station archway and out onto the street.

The weather was perfect and Tessa was glad to be stretching her legs as she walked down the cobbled road that led to a few small shops. She went into the pharmacy on the corner and left with two things, stamps and... a pregnancy test. Even though she had told Blake everything in the letter, she had not mentioned this part. This was the part that could change everything forever. She needed to know the test result before she mailed the letter.

Tessa walked further down the road and found a coffee shop where she went in and ordered a cup of coffee.

"We've just put a fresh pot on to brew. It will be ready in about five minutes," the young man said as he set a plate of bacon and eggs in front of the woman sitting on the stool at the bar. *That's all the time I need. It may as well be now.*

Tessa sat in the bathroom of the nameless coffee shop, in the nameless town, and held her breath. She really didn't even know where they had stopped and she hadn't read the name of the coffee shop. In some way she truly had disappeared from the planet. Did anyone in the world even care? Would anyone miss her if she just sat here in this bathroom forever?

Perhaps Blake would care. But the difference between one blue line or two, would play a big part in their future. The pregnancy test had read "Quick two-minute test."

Who knew that two minutes could pass so slowly! Tessa took a shaky breath and waited. There was nothing quick about the wait and the minutes passed by at an agonizing pace. She looked at the results and waited an extra three minutes, to be sure.

Tessa walked over to the sink and splashed water on her face. She looked into the mirror and saw evidence in her eyes of the relief that had flooded her soul a few minutes ago. The test was negative. She was not pregnant! She would never have to deal with Wayne again. She could forget about him and everything that had happened. She would marry Blake and they would live happily ever after.

Tessa sipped her coffee slowly and breathed deeply. Everything was going to be all right after all! Looking at the clock on the wall, she decided to head back to the train and hopefully still catch Ginger in the breakfast car. She already felt attached to the old woman and hoped they would be able to see each other in Port Elizabeth once they had settled, although Tessa still had no idea where she would go once the train stopped there. But today was a good day and she was going to celebrate it and not worry about the future. Before dropping the letter into the mailbox outside of the coffee shop, Tessa applied a layer of red lipstick and pressed her lips against the white envelope. She smiled as she envisioned Blake receiving her declaration of undying love. She hoped the guys wouldn't tease him too much when they saw the cherry-lipped envelope. But mostly, she hoped that the confession in the envelope would not ruin what she wished to have with Blake.

The walk back to the train station was pleasant, and Tessa even smiled at the long- nosed conductor who pretended not to see her as she passed him by.

*****

Blake woke up with Champ jumping up and down on the bed.

"Quit it, Champ!" He rolled over and pulled the covers over his head. The next minute he heard the tin plate roll around the floor and Blake sighed knowing there would be no more sleep for him. He opened his bleary eyes and called Champ who jumped back on the bed and started picking at Blake's hair as if he were looking for fleas. Blake's eyes grew heavy as the monkey's long fingers picked through his hair, but he jolted awake when Champ screeched and leapt off the bed. "What the devil are you doing?"

Champ ignored Blake's yelling as he chased the grasshopper that had caught his eye. Blake knew that chasing grasshoppers was his favorite game, and although Champ was mostly vegetarian, every now and then he enjoyed crunching on a fat green grasshopper.

After stumbling to the make-shift bathroom, Blake got dressed and picked up his rifle. Champ was eating the grasshopper but watched Blake's every move.

"I will be back later. Don't make a mess while I am gone!"

"Kek-kek-kek," Champ continued making the loud chattering sound as Blake walked away.

"Kek-kek-kek."

Blake had learned from the natives that lived in the area that this was the way that monkeys declared their territory. Turning as he walked, Blake shouted at the monkey who was now peaking out of the door, "No, it's not your house, it's mine! Now be good."

The cheeky monkey shouted all the louder "kek-kek-kek," and Blake smiled as he hurried to meet his troop leader.

The little monkey had crept into his heart, and Blake had already decided that he would take Champ home with him when he left. Somehow he had to hide the little bugger. He wondered how Tessa would like him, though he was sure they would get on well because Tessa loved all animals. Wouldn't she be surprised when he pulled Champ out of his bag along with the shiny diamond ring? Maybe he could teach Champ to go down on one knee with him and give Tessa the ring. That would definitely endear him to her. He wasn't sure if Champ would do it though, because it would completely depend on his mood, and who knew what his mood would be that day? Nevertheless, the thought of it made Blake start whistling and he whistled all the way to his post.

19

Tessa looked forward to breakfast with Ginger after the wonderful dinner they had shared last night. It was good to not be alone. She found herself breathing a quick prayer, "Thank you Lord for giving me Ginger for company on this trip."

Her stomach rumbled loudly as she hurried to the bathroom to freshen up before going to the dining car. As Tessa got back to the compartment she ran the brush through her long hair one more time before turning to the door. She noticed that the train was slowing down again to stop at a tiny little platform in the middle of what seemed like nowhere land. Tessa watched through the window as the lazy breeze flattened the long dry grass, but there was nothing much else to see here. As she turned away her eye caught something on the platform and Tessa did a double take.

Was that Ginger? It couldn't be! But sure enough Ginger was walking down the platform in red high-heel shoes, a bright pink scarf hung around her thin neck. The crazy hat from last night was perched sideways on top of her head and the grapes were bouncing up and down as Ginger walked. What was even more ludicrous was that Ginger could not see over the enormous bouquet of flowers she was carrying and walked as if she were drunk, two steps to the left and then four steps to the right. Tessa hoped that no one else was watching this spectacle take place.

Tessa flung the compartment window open, "Ginger! Ginger!"

Ginger peeped though the stems of flowers.

"Oh, hi there honey!" she called back to Tessa. "I wanted to say goodbye, but I couldn't find you."

"Ginger, where are you going? I thought you were travelling to see your husband in Port Elizabeth."

"Oh no, honey! My husband is here and I'm going to see him now. Aren't these flowers beautiful? He loves flowers."

Tessa leaned further out of the window as Ginger came closer to show her the bouquet. "Yes, Ginger they are beautiful," Tessa responded absentmindedly while looking up and down the platform.

"Is your husband going to meet you here?"

"Oh no, honey, don't be ridiculous!"

Ginger smiled broadly and shook her head. "I'm taking these to him."

Tessa looked at the forlorn platform and shivered at the thought of Ginger being left alone on the platform once the dust settled from the departing train.

"How far do you have to go?" she asked Ginger.

"Oh honey, it's just up that little hill," Ginger pointed with her chin, "he's buried right underneath that big tree over there."

Buried? Under a tree in the middle of nowhere?

Now Tessa started doubting Gingers soundness of mind. What if she wandered off into the hills and was eaten by a lion or something? What if this was all just part of a wild imagination. She couldn't just *leave* her here! But the train would only be here another few minutes and Tessa felt quite panicked. She didn't know what to do.

"Ginger, you said you have been doing this trip for ten years? Do you come all this way to put flowers on your husband's grave?"

"Oh yes, honey. Ten years now."

"But…" Tessa didn't know how to word her thoughts without sounding rude, but time was running out. She knew that Pinocchio, the sharp nosed conductor, was getting ready to blow his shrill whistle.

So Tessa said the only thing she could think of saying, "But why, Ginger?" She just had to understand.

"Because I love to give him these flowers that he always loved. He always spent so much time in our garden between the flower beds; I just have to bring him some flowers on our anniversary. And then I sit at the grave and think about the ocean and how calm the waves were between us in our last years together. And I pray and thank God for giving me these wonderful memories and for helping us not to give up during the difficult storms in our first years of marriage. Just imagine if we had given up? What a terrible mistake it would have been."

With that, Ginger stepped up close to the train's window and whispered, "Now honey, don't you give up on life or love….remember the ocean waves that change from day to day and season to season." The train jumped forward as it started moving and Tessa leaned as far as she could out of the window and said, "I won't forget the ocean and I won't forget you!" She waved and watched as the little wrinkled lady eventually became just a colorful dot on the platform.

Tessa sat down and wiped the tears that ran down her cheeks with the back of her hand. Why did everyone always have to leave?

After drying her eyes, Tessa walked down to the dining car and sat in the same seat she had been in last night. It was hard to believe that she had only known Ginger for such a short time, and yet she missed the woman's quirky presence.

She ordered bacon and eggs with toast and a pot of tea. Tessa looked out of the window as the miles flew by. She put grape jelly on her toast and poured herself another cup of tea, watching as the terrain changed. Gone was the dry flat ground from before, and in its place were little hills and valleys with green shrubbery dotted here and there. Tessa sat back against the seat and stared out at the scenery as she thought about Ginger. She wondered how long she would stay at the grave. She wondered where she would spend the night. She wondered if she would be safe out there all alone.

Suddenly Tessa felt, rather than saw, a waiter standing beside her table. She looked up to see the waiter from the previous night. Hadn't Ginger known him by name? It was either Allen or Andrew ...or something like that.

"Sorry, I've forgotten your name," Tessa said.

"I am Adam," he retorted as he topped up the cup of tea that sat in front of Tessa.

"Do you need anything else?"

"No thank you, I am fine," Tessa said as he turned to walk away.

"Adam?" She called after watching the stiff white jacket walk down the dining car. He turned and came back to the table.

"Yes, madam?"

"Adam, do you remember that elderly lady I dined with last night?"

"Yes, madam."

"Well, I was just wondering if you've met her before?"

"Yes, madam."

Tessa tried to be patient with the *yes madam* answers. It was like pulling teeth. She waited for an explanation that would usually follow, but Adam stood quietly beside the table.

"Adam, can you tell me what you know about Miss Ginger?"

"Yes, Madam."

This was exasperating. Tessa was about to say, "Well can you tell me about her right now," when Adam said, "She takes this train at the same time every year. She always brings me a new blanket to take home to my family."

That sounds just like Ginger.

"And on her way back she always brings me a beautiful stone from under that tree where she sits."

"On her way home? You mean she catches this train?" Tessa didn't understand what the stone was all about, but Ginger probably had some peculiar reason for that too.

"Yes, madam. In two days we pick her up."

"Two days? But where does she stay for two days?" Tessa pictured Ginger living under the tree in the middle of no-man's land for two days and nights. A vision flashed before her eyes of the old woman doing a war dance around a raging fire at night. Tessa shook her head, annoyed with herself for the silly thought. Ginger was eccentric for sure, but not crazy.

She heard Adam say, "There is a nice cabin in those hills. Madam Ginger has friends there and they get good honey from the bees. Miss Ginger brings me honey every year that I take home."

Tessa felt relieved that some of her questions had been answered, although most of it sounded like a farfetched adventure out of a children's book.

Flowers on a grave in the middle of nowhere, stones as gifts, a cabin on a hill, bees and honey?

Tessa glanced up at Adam to make sure that this was not all a joke, but there was no sign of jesting on his brown serious face.

"Adam, do you have a pen?"

"Yes, madam." *Ugh, here we go again with the yes madam.*

"May I use your pen?"

"Yes, madam." Adam replied and this time he pulled the pen out of his pocket.

Tessa scribbled a note on the paper serviette that lay on the table.

Dear Ginger,

It was wonderful meeting you. Please write to me at Van Staden's River Mouth Resort in Port Elizabeth so that we can keep in touch.

Thank you for everything,

Tessa

"Please give this to Miss Ginger when you see her," she handed the note to Adam who nodded, and then stuffed it into his crisp jacket pocket. He bowed slightly and was gone.

In a split second Tessa had made a decision that she would go to the place she remembered as a child, where she and Jeremiah had played and fished for hours. Van Staden's Resort held such warm memories for Tessa even though they had not visited there often. In those days her mother, although stern, had allowed a smile to play on her lips when she saw the giant sandcastles her children had made in the sand. It was one of the few times Tessa had felt her mother's pride as she inspected the ornate castle that stood tall in the shimmering sand.

Yes, that is where she was meant to go. She had no idea what she would do once she arrived there, but after meeting Ginger she realized that life should not be lived in fear. Every day was an adventure and there was always something to celebrate, something new to do or see. Tessa pondered how crossing paths with one random person could touch one's life and alter one's direction with a mere perspective change. Ginger had done that for Tessa in a few short hours. Now Tessa felt free and ready to enjoy her journey. She looked out of new eyes and felt more positive about life than what she had in a long time. She thought about Blake and hoped that he would get *the* letter soon, the letter that confessed it all, the letter in which he would see how upset she was about her mistakes and how much she really loved him. Tessa rubbed her empty ring finger. She looked down at her hands and wondered what sort of ring he'd get for her. It really didn't matter though. All she knew was that she would finally be Blake's wife!

Now that she knew where she was going, she quickly wrote a short note to Blake giving him her new address. She would pop this one in the mail at the Port Elizabeth station and also call Jeremiah to tell him where she was. She knew that he had probably been worrying about her and felt a stab of guilt for having left him without any information of where she was going. Knowing her brother, he was probably quite angry with her. He usually got angry when he worried. But in all fairness…she hadn't known exactly where she was going until a moment ago.

*****

Blake was still whistling as he fell in behind the soldier in front of him. He really hoped his little monkey would be good today and not get in to mischief. He was never quite sure of what he would find in his barracks when he got back. But today it really didn't matter because he would get a letter from Tessa. He just felt it in his bones! Today was the day. He couldn't wait to see her again, those green eyes captivated him. She was so beautiful. Even the scar on her cheek enhanced her striking features and he couldn't wait to run his fingers through that long shiny hair. Why had he been such a procrastinator? He was just lucky that no other man had stolen her heart while he had wasted the time away. Blake stopped whistling as the thought of another man holding Tessa, kissing her, crossed his imagination. He felt a deep jealousy and an intense anger rising up. No, Tessa was always his and always would be. No other man had, or would, ever lay a finger on her. Of that he was sure.

The day was crisp and clear. Although they were meant to be in a combat area, there wasn't a sign of movement anywhere as they patrolled the area that lay close to the borderline. The usually straight line of soldiers now became a little zigzagged, and the firm grip on rifles relaxed as the day wore on and the African sun beat down on brown camouflaged uniforms. Each man seemed lost in his own thoughts of faraway homes and loved ones.

There was no warning. No time to think. No time to run. The buried mine had been set off by a careless boot somewhere up front and the explosion rocked the earth. The noise was deafening, shrapnel flew through the air as men screamed. Blake saw only a bright white light as the pain in his head overtook him, then everything went black.

20

The smell of the ocean almost brought tears of joy to Tessa's eyes which fed on the green hills and valleys, hungry to finally spot the blue waves. The train lurched forward as if it, too, was in a hurry to arrive at its destination. Tessa was standing at the doors before the train even came to a halt and hopped off as soon as they opened. She had to contain herself on the bustling station from breaking out into a run. When she got to the last compartment she heard the familiar whine and saw a cage that had already been set on the station floor. She ran to Bullet, flung open the cage door, and was almost knocked to the ground as he jumped up to greet her. His tail wagged crazily and he cried loudly as he tried to lick Tessa's face. Having been such a timid dog since his beating, Tessa had not noticed how big he had grown in the past months.

"Hello, boy!" Tessa laughed, "I missed you, too!"

The Pinocchio conductor looked at the display of affection between beast and human with a disapproving, grinch-like stare, but this time Tessa didn't care.

It was the first time in a long while that the dog seemed energetic and Tessa noticed the naughty twinkle in his eye that he'd had as a puppy. It was almost as if he knew that they had left danger behind. Tessa shivered at the remembrance of Wayne's icy eyes when he had looked at Bullet. She watched the dog's attention wander to the pigeons that waltzed across the station's floor, and she hurried to put on his chain.

"Come on boy, leave the pigeons and let me show you the beach! You're going to love it!"

The taxi driver had not wanted a dog in his car so Tessa had to pay him extra to allow Bullet onto the back seat. She parted with the extra 30 rand very grudgingly as her wallet was quickly growing thinner and thinner. The stop at the grocery store had cost her a small fortune, and she ran through the list in her head to try and add it up. Bread, cheese, milk, eggs, bananas, peanut butter, toilet paper, a frozen chicken, a can of peas....rice and dog food. She had had to run back in for the most important thing, *teabags*!

Tessa frowned as she worked out how long her money would last. She had to find work, and quickly. Bullet barked loudly at some tribal women who were sitting at a stand on the side of the road selling colorful beaded necklaces and earrings. Their own ears had been stretched by ever widening sticks until the earlobes hung down on their shoulders. They wore bright clothes and bangles that wound like snakes up their arms.

"Shut that dog up or I will put him out on the side of the road," the taxi driver with the frizzy hair shouted. This made Bullet bark all the louder. "I said, shut that bloody dog up!"

Tessa definitely did not want to be let out on the side of the road. They were deep into the country already, and all that surrounded them now was empty stretches of fields without a human in sight.

"Bullet, be quiet!" Tessa said, but Bullet was restless now after being cooped up so long and he wouldn't sit down or stop barking. Tessa suddenly had an idea. She tore the bag of dog food that lay at her feet and pulled out a handful of pellets.

"Here, boy!"

The handful was gone in three quick crunches, after two more handfuls Tessa wondered if Bullet had actually been fed anything on the train. Tessa continued to feed him because while he ate he didn't bark. The road wound like a long snake, up and over new hills and then down and round into valleys. Then suddenly, there it was. They had crested the final hill and the sight took Tessa's breath away. Even Bullet stopped his exceptionally loud crunching and looked out of the window.

Down below, nestled between a hill and the ocean, lay Van Staden's resort. Here, hidden from the world, lay this magical place. Where the wide lagoon kissed the ocean, the waters swelled and rippled. The ocean itself looked fierce and menacing with the fiery waves that smashed onto the sand with a deafening thud.

Round thatched bungalows dotted the higher grasslands, and Tessa smiled as she remembered the bungalow she had stayed in as a child. It had been the very highest one and from there she had sat and looked out onto the splendid ocean waves. Her mother had complained about the steps that she had to climb and even in those days her cane had melodiously tapped its way up and down the winding stone steps. It was only later that the tapping had become angry and was used as a demand for something or another.

The taxi driver turfed Tessa's baggage and groceries out as quickly as he could and sped off into the late afternoon sunset. Tessa tied Bullet around the nearest pole and hoped that he would serve as a guard dog for their belongings.

"Bullet, watch our stuff!" Tessa said as she turned and walked into the manager's office. An old man stumbled from the dusty back office and smiled at Tessa.

"How can I help you?"

"I need to rent a bungalow please, and I was wondering if that top corner one was open."

"They are almost all open. Peak season only really starts in summer. We are still a few months away. There are only a handful of guests here now." The old man seemed kind and Tessa wondered how he would like Ginger.

He looked at Tessa, "It can get kind of lonely out here if you are by yourself," he said with a raised eyebrow.

"Well, I'm not technically by myself, I have a dog. I hope that is not a problem?"

The old man gazed at Tessa for what felt like forever, and now she feared that she had come all this way to be turned back. What if he would not let Bullet stay? Eventually he nodded and said, "Well, I have heard that a dog is a man's best friend."

"Yes, sometimes that is all you have," Tessa said as she took the key he held out to her.

"Sometimes, that is enough," the old man winked at Tessa as he took the payment for a two-week stay. Tessa looked at the money she had left. There would be enough for one more week's groceries. She had to find a job in the next few days.

It took Tessa three trips up the flight of stone stairs to get all of her belongings into the Bungalow. Though exhausted when she finally closed the door, Tessa knew that she would not be able to rest until she had made this little thatched bungalow feel like home. She quickly unpacked the few groceries into the little white cabinet in the kitchen. Glancing at the ancient stove, she hoped it would actually work. Then she hurried into the bedroom and was glad to see that the bed had clean linen on it. There was also a thick rug on the floor which she pulled over and set next to the bed.

"This is your bed, Bullet. You're going to be an inside dog from now on, and I promise that you will never have to stay outside in the cold again."

Apparently Bullet did not need to rest yet because he sniffed the rug then continued to circle the bungalow, inspecting every nook and cranny. When everything was in its place, Tessa looked out the window and saw that the sun was now hovering just above the water. She knew it would be dark soon but if they hurried, they could catch the sunset on the beach.

Just as Tessa had hoped, the sunset was truly spectacular. Red and yellow streaks wound together in the sky, creating an orange halo around the sun. It shone down on the beach causing the sand between Tessa's toes to shimmer like tiny golden nuggets. There was not another person on the beach and Tessa put her head back and soaked up the last rays of the sun that shone down for her alone. She closed her eyes and breathed deeply as peace filled her being. There was nothing else here but the sound of the waves and the stroking of the sun

Where is Bullet? Tessa's head snapped back up and she quickly scanned the beach. Where had that dog disappeared to? He had been beside her just a few moments ago…

"Bullet!" Tessa shouted.

How on earth could one lose the same dog so many times? Tessa's mind started racing. Bullet didn't know the area and wouldn't find his way back to her. She really needed to get him a collar with a tag as soon as possible.

"Bullet!" Tessa shouted again.

The sun now dipped into the sea and the gold sand immediately vanished, leaving Tessa with cold toes and a slight shiver. Tessa started to feel desperation overwhelm her. How could she go back to the lonely bungalow without Bullet? Now that the sun had set, it was almost dark. Soon she would not be able to see anything out here on the beach. The darker it got, the louder the waves seemed to smash against the shore.

"Bullet!" Tessa shouted out through a throat that was choking up with unshed tears. Then, in the dim twilight, Tessa saw two dogs come over the high sand dune to the right of her. At first she stiffened with fear. The dogs could be ferocious, and she didn't see the owner anywhere. But as they charged down the sand dune and headed directly for her she recognized Bullet's playful bounce.

"Bullet!" Tessa laughed now as he jumped up against her. "You are such a naughty boy! You are not allowed to run off like that!" Tessa tried to scold Bullet, but he paid her no attention as he wrestled with his new playmate.

"I figured you had lost your friend," a voice said from behind, causing her to whip around in fright. She immediately relaxed when she saw that the voice belonged to the old man from the manager's office. She could just make out his kind smile in the darkness that pressed in all around them.

"Yes, I'm sorry that he bothered you. He just vanished! Thank you for bringing him back ...I was so worried."

"No bother at all, in fact my 'Pepsi' here has finally made a friend. She has been so lonely since our 'Popeye' passed last year, bless his soul."

Pepsi...Popeye. Tessa tried to suppress the inappropriate smile that played on her lips at the dogs' funny names, although they seemed to suit the quaint old man.

Tessa extended her hand and said, "Well, my name is Tessa and his name is Bullet."

"Well that's a funny name for a dog, isn't it?" The old man grinned knowingly as he shook Tessa's hand, "Just call me Pops, like everyone else around here." He turned and gave a sharp whistle which brought Pepsi up to his side immediately. "Let's go home."

Tessa and Bullet walked back with them to the lighted area of the bungalows and then went their separate ways, but not before Pops said, "Let's have the friends play together soon."

"Bullet would love that. Thank you."

Back inside the bungalow, Tessa felt happy. It had been so good to be on the shimmering sand again, and she could hear the smashing waves from inside the hut. Besides that, chatting with Pops on the walk home had done her heart good. He made her feel safe and she thought his name was perfect for him. Not only had Bullet made a new friend, but she had too.

Tessa hummed as she put the kettle on. Her stomach growled, and she was glad that she had remembered to buy the teabags because a hot cup of tea and a few slices of toast would have to do for supper. Tomorrow she would cook something in her own little home.

Bullet gobbled his pellets and drank some water but was lying down on the rug before Tessa even got into the bed. After the lights had been switched off, the bungalow was thrown into pitch darkness, reminding Tessa of her first lonely, cold night on the farm. But here in this little bungalow, listening to the waves on the shore, Tessa sighed contently and drifted off into a peaceful sleep.

A few days later Tessa stood at the pay phone and dialed the number to Jeremiah's military camp. It was time to let her brother know where she was, although Tessa steeled herself against the anger she was sure to hear. Minutes later, Tessa hung up the phone and felt relieved but disappointed at the same time. She replayed the voice of the soldier on the other end of the line...*No, Jeremiah was not there, he had been sent to the border a week ago....No, he couldn't give out that information; the only way was for her to write and they would forward the letter on to him, however, the mail going out was slow and it would take some time....She shouldn't be in a hurry for a response...No, he couldn't take her name and number and pass it on to Jeremiah....* Everything had been no, no, no.

Tessa hurried back to the bungalow and wrote a letter to Jeremiah explaining where she was and that she hoped he would bump into Blake, who by now should have received her last letter and passed on the information of her whereabouts.

21

Jeremiah sat next to Blake's bed with his beret between his hands, which he twirled around and around. He had to do something with his hands to keep from clenching them in fear. He had only been on the border a few days when he had found out that Blake was here, but he had not been prepared to see him in this state. Blake lay as if dead, his head was bandaged and his leg had been operated on from the shrapnel that had almost sliced it off. Dark rings lay under his eyes and a blue bruise ran down the side of his cheek.

"Coma," the doctors had said. And then the dreaded words, "Not sure about brain damage yet…or amnesia. We will have to see if, and when, he wakes up."

Jeremiah squeezed the beret in frustration and leaned back in the uncomfortable chair.

How was this possible? His friend did not deserve this. Besides, Jeremiah had hoped Blake would have been able to tell him of Tessa's whereabouts. Surely, she had written to Blake. Did she know about the ring that Blake had already purchased for her? There was no way of getting answers to the many questions swirling around in his head, unless Blake woke up. Jeremiah shuddered at his next thought...and even then, what if Blake didn't remember him or Tessa? What if he had brain damage?

Jeremiah had to get back to his platoon but he bowed his head and prayed to God. He pleaded with God to heal Blake and wake him up. He also begged God to keep Tessa safe wherever she was. And as an afterthought he added, "And help me not to kill Wayne if I find out he has something to do with her disappearance!"

*****

Tessa sat on the steep sand dune and let her eyes feast on the heavenly scene in front of her. Surely even heaven could not be more beautiful. The summer morning was crystal clear and the ocean was a deep, sparkling blue. The waves pushed up through the channel of the lagoon causing the waters to mingle and swirl together. Tessa glanced further up the lagoon and saw how the waters stilled as it slowed round the corner. There the water looked like glass. The only ripple on the top of the water was from the eel that slithered across the lagoon, from one side to another. The universe was so quiet that it almost made Tessa's ears hurt. Digging her toes into the sand, she realized that she felt closer to God here than she had in a long time, and for the next two hours Tessa spoke to him openly, as one friend to another. She told him all about Wayne and asked for his complete forgiveness over her disobedience and sin. She had put off bringing it all to the light because her guilt had weighed on her heavily. She not only felt tainted, but she had betrayed Blake - who surely believed that she had been faithful to him, even though it had been an unspoken agreement.

No matter how much longer she prayed, the burden pressed against her chest until Tessa fell silent. And in the silence, the still small voice came to her, "'I have removed your sins as far as the East is from the West and I will remember your sins no more. I will cast them into the sea of forgetfulness!'"

Tessa looked at the crashing waves on the shore and imagined her sins being cast into the rolling sea, to be washed away forever! They truly were gone! Her heart suddenly felt light, and when Tessa descended the sand dune, she realized that she was no longer the same. She was no longer tainted, and her heart had been made as white as snow. She could finally face Blake and Jeremiah and not feel ashamed. She had even forgiven Wayne up there on the sand dune, and although she never wanted to see him again, she had released him to God. Yes, today was a good day! A new day!

*****

Two months had passed with every day being exactly the same at the stinking border. The only thing that had changed for Jeremiah was the weather. Every day was hotter than the day before, and the sweat poured into his eyes as he plodded along the patrol area. Red dust rose as the boots marched along, and Jeremiah was sure that it would be harder to spot any covered mines. He sat at Blake's bed for a little while everyday and saw firsthand what the exploding mines could do. The hospital beds were full of armless, legless, and sometimes eyeless men. How would he be able to scuba dive and swim in the ocean without arms or legs? It would surely be worse than dying and he was glad that Blake's leg was healing so well. At least he still had two arms and two legs. Although his face had healed and the bandages around his head had been removed, he was still in a coma.

Jeremiah wiped the sweat from his brow and sipped from his canteen. The water was warm and stale but it wet his dry mouth, and he appreciated the little shade that the thorn tree provided as he sat and rested for a few minutes. As he sat under the tree, an idea came to him and he wondered why he had not thought of it before! He would go to Blake's bungalow and see if there was any mail waiting for him there. If Tessa had written to Blake then he would be able to find her. He missed his sister and worried about her every day. He felt responsible for leaving her at the farm. She must have been terribly unhappy there to have disappeared like that. But what else could he have done? They had no other family and he didn't choose to leave for the army! Perhaps tonight he would find an answer.

After showering and then having dinner in the mess hall, which consisted of meatballs and mashed potatoes, Jeremiah walked down to Blake's barracks. This division had set up partitions made from army blankets between their beds, so that each soldier had a semi-private place. Jeremiah was pleased that he didn't have to explain to anyone what he was doing rifling through Blake's belongings. Sure enough, there were a couple of letters on the make-shift side table and Jeremiah hurried over to them. His heart was beating fast at the anticipation of seeing his sister's handwriting. As he sat down on the bed with the letters in his hand, a rotten apple suddenly spattered against the side of his head. Jeremiah jumped up in fright with his fists balled, the letters flying in every direction. Wiping the side of his face with his sleeve, he grit his teeth. He was going to flatten the guy who had thrown the fruit. He was going to put him in the hospital. The man would regret this day for a long time to come. Jeremiah felt all the frustrations he had been feeling rise up in a ball of anger. This was the perfect time to decompress, and it wouldn't be his fault. He flung the blanket- curtain aside, sure now that it must have been the guy in the next bunk playing a prank. But there was no one there. Jeremiah was confused because an apple could not have been thrown by an invisible person! He wiped his face again and stooped to pick up the scattered letters, then sat down on the bed and started scanning them. Just then a handful of nuts flew through the air and landed on his head, scattering in all directions.

"That's it!" Jeremiah's large body jumped off the bed and he hurled himself in the direction that the nuts had come from. Again, there was no one to be seen, and now Jeremiah started wondering if there was perhaps some paranormal activity going on. He had heard about the spells that the witch doctors cast upon their enemies, but he had never paid much attention to that kind of thing. Although, he had to be honest, this was freaking him out. Perhaps he should just grab the letters and run.

As Jeremiah stooped down to pick up a letter that had slid under the bed, he jumped back when he saw a snake slither underneath the bed. Jeremiah hated snakes and his skin crawled. He backed away from the bed and then leaned down to get a better look at the snake. Surprisingly, it wasn't a snake after all but a long tail! What on earth was hiding under the bed? He jumped up and took a step backwards, thinking he was really more comfortable with facing sea creatures than some of these odd looking things here on the border. Just then the soldier that belonged to the next bed came plodding in from his watch. He flopped onto his bed and said, "That's Champ."

"What is it?" Jeremiah asked.

"Well it was Blake's pet monkey, but it has gone kind of crazy since Blake didn't come back. I leave fruit and nuts out for the thing but he doesn't eat much and has become anti-social. If I could catch him I would go and throw the little buggar into the bush where he belongs, hey?" The soldier yawned loudly and as an afterthought added, "Who are you, anyway?"

"I'm a friend of Blake's from back home. I'm…just picking up his mail."

"Well take the little buggar with you too, hey." With that the soldier turned on his side and covered his head with his grey army blanket.

"What am I supposed to do with a monkey?" Jeremiah mumbled to himself.

Jeremiah tried coaxing Champ out from under the bed for over an hour. After leaving a trail of fruit that didn't budge the stubborn monkey, he broke off a piece of chocolate that he had stuffed in his pocket earlier in the day.

"I don't know if monkeys like chocolate," he whispered to Champ, whose inquisitive button eyes bounced between the chocolate and Jeremiah's eyes, "but you should try a piece. It's really sweet. Look here….umm it's so good." Jeremiah bit off a corner of the rich chocolate. The bar of chocolate was almost finished and the monkey had not budged at all. Every now and then, Champ would jump up and down and scream, but he had not ventured forward an inch.

Jeremiah finally sat on the floor and leaned against the bed. His back ached from bending over and peaking at the stupid monkey. The soldier in the next bed kept snoring loudly and Jeremiah wondered how he could sleep through all the screeching. He pulled the letter out of his pocket and while sitting on the floor, he slipped open the envelope. He knew that the letter was not addressed to him and a twinge of guilt swept through him as he saw Tessa's handwriting sprawled across the white page. *Well, it can't be helped! Blake can't read it now and I have to know where Tessa has gone.*

My dearest Blake,

This is a hard letter to write. I will not make small talk but get right to the point before I lose my nerve completely. The letter you wrote to me declaring your love held the words I had longed to hear for so long. I cried and cried. My tears were not tears of joy, but tears of shame and regret. Let me explain...

Someone at the farm had delivered the letter to my room when I was not there, and it had somehow landed underneath the bed. Ironically, I lay awake for hours at night longing for you and wondering why you had not written to me. As the weeks passed, I began to believe that you did not care for me at all and that our time together had just been a figment of my imagination. I was terribly lonely and sad. That is no excuse for what happened, but I am hoping you will understand. Wayne, a neighbor and helper on Aunt Rina's farm, befriended me and we worked together.

We spent time together and one thing led to another. I tried to block you out of my mind and thought I was falling in love with Wayne. I later found out that he was quite a scoundrel, but unfortunately not before...I gave myself to him. It was a terrible mistake and I cannot imagine how this must make you feel, after your beautiful letter and proposal. I can only hope that you will find it in your heart to forgive me. I want nothing more than to be your wife as soon as possible. Please tell me that the offer still stands...I am so sorry.

I love you. I love you. I love you.

I will be seeing you soon then?

Tessa

P.S. Excuse my handwriting, I am on a rocking train as I write this. I will send another letter soon telling you where I have settled.

Jeremiah crumpled the letter into a tiny ball and then smashed it with his balled fist into his hand. He had known that Wayne was a bad apple when he saw him at the farm.

As rotten as the apple that was just thrown at his head. He should have taken Wayne outside the night he met him. Confronted him! Warned him! Plowed him into the ground! He should have done something.

He hung his head in his hands and thought about Tessa. Conflicting emotions wrestled inside of him. He felt sorry for her although he was angry with her, too. Angry because she should have known better, angry that she had left the farm without speaking to him, angry that Blake would be crushed when he read this letter.

No, if Blake ever opened his eyes again, it would be best for him to never see these words. Maybe they could still just pick up where they had left off. Now all that was left to do was to wait for Tessa's next letter revealing her whereabouts. She never needed to know that he had read this letter, and that Blake had not. All of this would be in the past and they could all go on as before.

Everything will be just fine, as soon as Blake comes out of the coma. Jeremiah felt his spirits lifting...*yes, everything is going to be just fine.* He lifted his head out of his hands and opened his eyes to see the little monkey sitting next to him on the floor. The bright eyes watched him curiously.

"Hey, little fellow. Are we friends now?" The long tail hesitantly curled around Jeremiahs arm in response to the question.

After sitting together for a while longer, Champ jumped up onto Jeremiah's shoulder and screeched 'kek-kek-kek' while bouncing up and down.

"I guess that's a yes," Jeremiah stood up carefully, hoping that the monkey would not jump off and scurry under the bed again.

"You want to live with me?" Now the monkey sat behind Jeremiahs neck and curled his little hands around Jeremiah's head, covering his eyes.

Jeremiah laughed out loud, "Well, I have to see where I am going!"

Before walking out of the room, Jeremiah bent down and picked up the crumpled letter. He carried the monkey and the letter out of the barracks and into the sunset. Passing by a burning barrel of wood, he tossed the letter into the fire without missing a stride. It was gone, the past was gone. He strode determinedly into the future with the blue velvet monkey jumping on his back.

22

Six weeks had passed since Tessa had arrived at the ocean, and she had fallen into an easy rhythm. In the mornings she worked at the resort's café. She sold simple fare like coffee, bread, eggs, and sugar for the regulars who ran out of these things, or to the vacationers that had simply forgotten to pack something in their already too-full RVs. The café had become really busy since the Christmas holidays were almost upon them. The summer sun baked down on the perfect beach while the Beach Boys blared from the radio nearby giving the resort a happy holiday atmosphere. The scent of watermelon and sunscreen wafted into the café on gusts of salty sea air, and Christmas trees decorated the office and café. Tessa had even bought a little tree for her bungalow that she would decorate in the next week.

Her afternoons were spent exploring for a good fishing spot along the beach or river. More than once in the last week, Tessa had fried up some fish that she had caught in the late afternoon on the beach. The only problem was that she had no one to share the experience with. She wondered time and again why she had not heard from Blake. Had he decided that he did not want her after all? And what about Jeremiah? Surely he had received the letter of her whereabouts by now?

While she pondered these questions, Tessa and Bullet took their usual route around the back side of the resort that led to a rocky area on the beach. The vacationers seemed to stay on the main beach, and Tessa tried to keep Bullet away from the crowds. Sitting on a big rock and soaking up the last rays of the sun, Tessa looked over the foaming waves and felt God's presence. She had often spent time with God out here on this rock and had felt his cleansing stream wash over her, making her as white as snow. She lay back on her elbows and watched Bullet chase a seagull. All was serene. All was quiet.

In the stillness Tessa started to pray for Blake, for his protection, for him to find his way back to her side. She prayed for Jeremiah too, that he would not be angry with her and that she would see her beloved brother soon. A new confidence settled over Tessa as she prayed, and she knew without a shadow of a doubt that God heard her prayers and that he was involved in her day-to-day life. Besides that, another good thing had happened since spending time with God. Even when she tried to conjure up an image of Wayne, nothing came to mind. No emotion, no face, nothing. Tessa had truly forgiven him and he was finally out of her mind and life. She felt free as she sat on the rock breathing in the familiar salty sea air.

*****

Blake gingerly opened one eye but winced as the sunlight streaming through the window immediately intensified the severe headache he had woken up with. He lay still for a minute and tried to push down the nausea that rose up. His mind felt jumbled and he struggled to put the pieces of the puzzle together. He knew he was in the hospital but what had happened to him, he wasn't sure. The last thing he remembered was saying goodbye to Champ. *Oh no, what had become of Champ?*

Blake imagined his little friend lying dead from starvation, and this image caused him to force his eyes open. He gritted his teeth together from the pain and felt like he was on the verge of going back into the deep black hole. Another wave of nausea passed through him, but he kept his eyes glued to the white ceiling. After a few minutes he felt a little better and slowly turned his head. Jeremiah was slouched in a chair against the wall and staring at a letter in his hand. It had him so captivated that he hadn't seen the slight movement in the bed. Blake wondered why Jeremiah was sitting there and then started worrying that his injuries were worse than he thought. What if his legs had been amputated? Could he even feel his legs? Blake squirmed in the bed causing another searing jolt of pain to shoot through his head, but he was relieved to find that he still had two legs attached to his body. This time Jeremiah caught the movement and bolted up from the chair.

"Hey, man! Finally! Thank God you're awake!" He grinned at Blake and added, "How are you feeling? Should I get a doctor? Yes, I probably should get a doctor. Wait here!"

He turned to hurry out of the room and then turned back, "Of course you will wait here. Sorry, I'm just excited to see you back in the land of the living." Jeremiah laughed and hurried towards the door.

Blake managed to croak out, "No, wait....What happened? How long have I been here?"

Jeremiah pulled a chair up to the bed and told Blake everything he knew about the explosion.

"How long have I been here?" Blake repeated and then, "What has happened to Champ?" Jeremiah answered all the questions patiently, and Blake actually gave him a half smile when he heard about Champs new antics. He was relieved that the little monkey had not actually starved to death as he had imagined. Then Blake asked the question that had been burning in his mind since he had opened his eyes. And all he said was, "Tessa?"

Jeremiah picked up the letter that had fluttered to the ground when he had jumped up earlier. Aloud he read,

Dear Jeremiah,

I am so sorry that I left the farm without letting you know where I was going, but at the time I didn't know myself. Please forgive me and don't be angry.

I have found myself at our childhood vacation spot and it makes me miss you so much. I am at Van Staden's resort and am working in the café and living in one of the bungalows...in fact I am living in 'our' bungalow, number 7 on top of the hill. Please come and visit me as soon as possible.

Jeremiah felt a twinge of guilt as he left out the next part,

I have written to Blake explaining all that happened at the farm. You know by now that he has asked me to marry him and I cannot wait. I only hope that he will forgive me of my sins, as the Lord has.

Jeremiah continued reading the rest of the letter out loud,

Please tell Blake that I cannot wait to see him and the answer is YES YES YES!

All my love,
Tessa
      P.S. I don't understand why the postman never has a letter for me and I try not to get discouraged. I hope to hear from both of you very soon.

Jeremiah and Blake both sat in silence, lost in their own thoughts. Jeremiah wondered if maybe he shouldn't have thrown Tessa's letter of confession away. Maybe Blake needed to know the truth. But it was too late for regret now. The letter was burnt into ash and best forgotten. As he looked at Blake's joyful expression, he comforted himself with the thought that the letter would only have brought

Blake sadness, and he had suffered enough. *Better to let bygones be bygones…*

Blake tried to sit up but felt the world spin.

"Hey, not so fast, what's the hurry?" Jeremiah said as he steadied Blake.

"I need to get up so I can figure out a way to get leave and go to see Tessa. I cannot wait any longer. So much has kept us apart and I have the ring. It needs to be on her finger!"

"OK cowboy, just lie down and relax. First you have to get well, and then I'm sure you will be discharged. Do you know you had surgery on your leg and almost lost it? The damage was severe but you were lucky. Hopefully you can walk out of here in a couple of weeks on two legs! Let me go and get a doctor now and he can check you out."

Blake lay back on the pillow as he watched Jeremiah leave the room and whispered,

"You better believe I will be walking out of here on two legs… and sooner than you think!" He closed his eyes and pictured those amazing green eyes, looking at him from a porcelain face. Long dark hair flowed around sculptured shoulders, and perfect lips whispered to him…'yes, yes, yes.'

23

Wayne aimed the rifle at the rabbit's head and pulled the trigger. The bullet hit the target and Wayne picked the headless rabbit up by the feet. He swung it as he walked back to the truck leaving a trail of blood on the hot sand. Tossing the dead rabbit carelessly into the back of the truck, he watched it land on his other victims of the day and he frowned. Usually hunting took the edge off, but today it had not helped him feel any better. Who did Tessa think she was, talking to him like that outside of the dance hall? It still burned him when he remembered her walking away, her head held high and regal! Did she think she was better than him? She had been lucky to have him at all! Didn't she see how the girls flocked at his feet? But if it wasn't for that silly Sharon, perhaps Tessa would still be here. Thank God Sharon had lost the brat and now he was off the hook. What a lucky break! He would definitely have to be more careful in the future. As for Sharon…he couldn't stand how pathetic she looked when she saw him around town. Her sad eyes trailed his every move. He hated weak people, and

Sharon was weak. But Tessa on the other hand was another story completely.

It had taken some real guts to pack up and leave like that. His thoughts lingered on Tessa and he lit a cigarette. He had just recently started smoking again, hoping that the habit would calm his taut nerves. He blew out a round ring of blue-grey smoke that hung in the air like a perfect wedding band. Tessa really was a kind and beautiful person, and she made him feel peaceful. He could see himself settling down with her. He may even love her.

He could even learn to put up with that mutt of hers, in order to be with her. Of course, there were always ways and means of making a dog disappear for good. He glanced back at the stiffening creatures in the back of the truck. Flies sat on the coagulating blood as it dripped off the truck bed and soaked into the ground at his feet. Slamming the tail gate, he took another long draw of his cigarette. The problem was, no one knew where Tessa had gone. Or at least, they were not telling *him*.

Wayne punched the steering wheel with his bloody hand, the residue left from his successful hunting day. Who did she think she was…leaving him behind without a single word? He had been sure she would have shown up at his door the next morning after the dance, begging his forgiveness for the scene the night before. He had imagined her swollen eyes from a night of torment at the thought of being separated from him forever. But no, she had not done any of that. She had disappeared into the night and come hell or high water, he would find that girl and drag her back here to marry him! Wayne put the truck into first gear and peeled out onto the gravel road, making the car swerve violently and causing gravel to spray up into the air, leaving a cloud of angry dust trailing behind him.

*****

Tessa sat in her cozy bungalow and stared at the twinkling lights on the Christmas tree. A leg of lamb roasted in the oven while a bottle of sparkling grape juice sat chilling on ice. Today was the 24th of December and she had been determined to celebrate Christmas in her new home. Pops had agreed to come for lunch and then take the dogs for a long lope on the beach. Tessa had grown to see Pops as a kind grandfather and she always felt safe when he was around. She imagined that this must be how people felt towards a good father. She stared at the twinkling lights on the tree as she realized how much she had missed out on, not having had a father or grandfather in her life. But she was excited about not spending Christmas Eve alone and went into the kitchen to sprinkle more rosemary over the lamb.

Just as she closed the oven door, she heard Bullet growl and then bark at the knock on the bungalow door. Before Tessa could open the door, a white folded piece of paper was slid under it. Tessa picked it up and read it. So here she was again, all alone.

Pops had sent her a message that he was down with a cold and was going to spend the rest of the day in bed, trying to shake the chills and sore throat. Tessa looked down at her light summer dress and rubbed her fingers against the lace trim. She had dressed up for Christmas Eve and had even curled her hair and carefully applied mascara and ruby-red lipstick for this celebration lunch. Now she would have no one to share it with. Bullet seemed to sense her melancholy mood and kept nudging her leg and staring into her eyes.

"It's alright boy, at least we have each other for Christmas!" She scratched his head and added, "I even got you a present, but you can't have it until tomorrow morning!"

Bullet whined as Tessa said, "No presents until Christmas morning. That's the rule!"

Tessa ran a hand over Bullet's head and said, "At least I always have you to talk to."

Bullet cocked his head to the side and whined again. She knew this was not a sign of agreement but a request for a walk. Tessa reached for Bullet's leash, "You're right, there is no point moping around here."

Tessa decided to keep Bullet on a leash until they were far enough out on their secluded beach. From time to time the management came by to check on how Pops was running the place, and she would never want Pops to get into trouble over Bullet scaring the summer vacationers.

It was a brilliant day, and Tessa drank in the scenery that she never got tired of. The blue water was magnificent and the sand sparkled like diamonds. Seagulls swirled energetically as if they too knew, it was Christmas Eve. And if that wasn't enough, Tessa saw more shells on the beach than she ever had before. She lifted a big orange shell to her ear and listened to the sound of the ocean inside, a trick her mother had taught her on this very beach when she was a young child. The memory made her miss Jeremiah terribly because they had always competed for the biggest shell on the beach. Where was he today? After picking up a few more shells and watching Bullet run in and out of the waves, Tessa slowly meandered back towards the bungalow. The aroma of lamb met her before she reached the top step, and her stomach growled as she opened the door. "Looks like I am just in time for lunch," a voice said from inside the bungalow. Tessa almost jumped out of her skin with fright. Bullet went berserk as Jeremiah got up from the sofa. Tessa couldn't believe her eyes and fell into his arms as tears poured down her face, all the while Bullet growled and ran in circles around them. After hugging Tessa for a minute, Jeremiah knelt down on the floor and patted his chest.

"Come here, boy!" It didn't take long and Bullet was standing up on his back legs, licking Jeremiah's face. Tessa knelt down next to them and watched in sheer delight at the scene of her beloved brother and Bullet making friends. How different Bullet seemed with Jeremiah compared to how he was with Wayne. Tessa chided herself for not having *known* that Wayne was mistreating Bullet. But today was not a day for regret but a day of celebration!

After Bullet settled down Tessa looked at Jeremiah, "I can't believe you are here! It's like a dream come true. I'm so happy!" She threw her arms around his neck and squeezed him tightly.

"OK, OK, you're going to kill me before I get to eat that delicious smelling lamb. You know, I only travelled all this way for the meal I knew you would have in the oven on Christmas Eve!"

Tessa punched him affectionately, "Yes, I know your unquenchable appetite! Well everything is about ready and I'm starving too, so let me set the table quickly."

Jeremiah followed her to the kitchen and watched her take out two sets of plates and put them on the tiny table.

He leaned against the doorframe and asked, "So I know that is a really small table but is there room for three plates?"

Tessa wondered if Jeremiah assumed she had a guest coming already, "Well we could squeeze a third person in,

but my guest cancelled this morning because he is sick."
She continued chatting excitedly, "I can't wait for you to meet Pops...he is so kind and sweet. You will like him and"

"Tessa, I brought you a Christmas present," Jeremiah interrupted Tessa half sentence, "but I left it on the bottom step because I couldn't carry it up all the stairs. I need your help." Tessa looked up at Jeremiah with a confused expression, "A present that big? I hope it will fit in this tiny bungalow."

Then a frown crossed her face, "Why didn't you say so?...Someone might steal it down there!"

She hurried to the door and spoke over her shoulder, "Come on, let's hurry. It's been a while since I've gotten a gift from my big brother!" Tessa took the stairs down to the bottom road two at a time and she heard Jeremiah laughing behind her, "Slow down, it's not going anywhere!"

Tessa ignored him and hurried along while she imagined what it could be. Perhaps a TV or a piece of furniture? Or maybe it was a box of books? Jeremiah knew how much she loved to read.   She was still musing over these options when she took the last two steps that curved onto the road and stopped abruptly, causing Jeremiah to collide into her from behind. There in front of her stood Blake. Tessa stood frozen in place and stared at him in disbelief.

Dressed in his army uniform he looked even more handsome than Tessa remembered. His shoulders seemed broader than ever, and his short dark hair suited him well. Pure white teeth shone out of a perfect smile that accentuated his olive skin and deep dimples. Tessa felt butterflies in her stomach and self consciously smoothed down her pretty dress. Blake smiled at her as he took the first step forward and said, "Did the cat get your tongue?"

Tessa noticed how self-assured he was. He had left a boy and come back a man. Blake took another step forward and gently took her face in his large hands and kissed her lightly on the cheek. He stepped back and laughed as Tessa stood dead still and stared at him.

"Are you alright, or do you need me to practice the CPR I learned in the army?" he inquired playfully.

Jeremiah bumped Tessa from behind, "Hey, how about a thank you? I had to drag this present with me all the way from the border."

The bump jolted Tessa out of her trance, and she reminded herself to breathe before she passed out. She stepped into Blake's arms and clung to him.

"That's more like it! I was getting worried for a minute there."

Although he was still smiling, Tessa sensed the unasked question in his dark eyes. She took Blake's hands between hers and squeezed them, "I am so glad that you are here. You are all I wanted for Christmas."

With a mock bow Blake replied, "Well then, I'm happy to oblige, madam."

"Oh, and what about me? Am I just chopped liver over here?" Jeremiah chimed in.

"OK, I wanted to see you too," Tessa laughed but whispered to Blake, "but mostly I wanted to see you." Blake winked at Tessa, and she again thought that he was even more striking than before.

Somehow, in her shocked state, Tessa had tuned out Bullet's incessant barking, but now it broke through and she looked down to shush Bullet who was circling Blake's brown army bag. He barked, growled, and backed away, only to gingerly edge towards the bag again and then jump back in fright. Tessa heard herself scream as she saw the long gray snake slither from the partially opened zipper. Bullet responded to the scream by trying to catch the snake in his large teeth. Blake quickly bent down and yanked the bag into his arms. Tessa stepped back, "Watch out, there's a snake!"

"It's OK Tessa, it's not a snake. Look." He unzipped the bag and the 'snake' turned out to be the long tail of a blue velvet monkey. The monkey jumped onto Blake's shoulder and then pounced onto Jeremiah's neck, giving him a little bite.

"See, this is the way they make friends and establish hierarchy. They like to nip. Don't be scared." Tessa felt shaky as Jeremiah brought the monkey over to her. He sniffed her and then jumped onto her head. He immediately started grooming her and Tessa had to smile as she realized that he was probably looking for fleas. Bullet didn't like the monkey sitting on Tessa and jumped up and down yapping constantly.

"What are we going to do about this?" she nervously eyed Blake who was still smiling and didn't look perturbed at all.

"They will make friends before we know it. Come here, Bullet!" he whistled and held up a stick of dried ostrich meat. "Look what I brought a special boy!" Bullet's attention turned away from the monkey and he cautiously approached Blake's outstretched hand. "Come on, let's make friends." Two minutes later Bullet was still being fed strips of ostrich biltong and chewing the dried jerky with pleasure. Blake was kneeling beside him stroking his shiny fur.

Tessa couldn't help thinking about how different Wayne had been towards Bullet and the memory suddenly made her feel anxious. She glanced at Blake again who looked totally happy and normal. Had he read the letter and completely forgiven her? It seemed he had completely forgotten, too, because Tessa didn't see any hint of hurt in his smiling eyes.

I will have to talk to him about it tonight when we are alone. I need to know how he feels before we continue.

The monkey noticed Blake stroking Bullet and leaped from Tessa onto Blake's back, wrapping the long tail around his neck. The dog growled but didn't move away. Blake quietly spoke as he kept running his hand over Bullet's back, "This is Champ. He is your new friend."

Tessa felt a surge of love for Blake as she heard the kindness in his voice and saw the gentleness in his touch. She watched as he stood up and noticed for the first time the grimace on his face as he put pressure on his right leg. Now that the initial shock of seeing him had worn off, she also noticed the limp he had as he took a step towards her.

"You're injured?"

"I'm fine…just need to sit down a while," he replied as he surveyed the many steps leading up to the bungalow at the top of the hill. "This may take a while…"

"Nonsense," Jeremiah stepped forward and hoisted Blake over his shoulder like a sack of potatoes. "I didn't do boot camp for nothing. I've practiced this move hundreds of times!" Turning, he headed up the steps toward the bungalow.

Tessa followed with Blake's bag, smiling at the sight in front of her and wondering what people would think of this picture. A man carrying another man, who had a monkey on his back, and a dog circling at their feet that threatened to have them all tumble down the hill. Tessa's lonely, quiet Christmas was turning into a loud chaotic one, and she loved everything about it.

24

It had been a perfect day. The lamb roast had been delicious and the boys had not left a single bite. Jeremiah had carried Blake down the steps again and they had gone for a slow walk along the beach at sunset. Bullet and Champ were not exactly friends yet, but the barking and screeching had stopped. Jeremiah had claimed sore muscles from carrying a sack of potatoes up and down all day and had retired to his sleeping bag in the corner of Tessa's room.

Now, Tessa and Blake sat quietly together and listened to the Christmas music that floated in from the party taking place at a bungalow nearby. The bright Christmas lights twinkled on the tree next to them and the moment felt magical. Tessa looked up at Blake and found his eyes searching hers. She felt an uncomfortable stirring and broke eye contact as she pulled herself out of Blake's warm arms.

"What's wrong, Tessa?"

"I think we should talk about what happened while we were apart. I have to …"

Blake pulled Tessa back into his embrace before she could finish the sentence, "Shhh, there is no need to talk about anything. I have always loved you and I love you still. Let's not waste time in the past. I want to talk about the future."

Tessa looked into Blake's brown eyes, "But shouldn't we at least discuss-"

"The only 'should' that is important tonight is that we 'should' get married!" Blake slowly got down on one knee, trying not to bend the injured leg too much.

"No Blake, don't do that! Your leg…"

"Yes, I have to. I want this to be right and perfect. You deserve the absolute best." A surge of relief flooded Tessa as she realized that Blake held nothing against her. He didn't even want to talk about what had happened between her and Wayne. It was as if it had never happened.

Blake smiled a little shyly as he pulled a little black box out of his pocket, "Tessa, will you marry me?"

Tears were already pouring down Tessa's cheeks.

"Yes, I will marry you."

The ring was simple, but beautiful, and it fit her finger perfectly. Blake gently placed light kisses on Tessa's forehead, on her nose, on her salty cheeks. He whispered, "I love you Tessa, you mean everything to me. I have waited so long for this moment. It's all I've thought about…all I've wanted."

Tessa felt delirious with joy. These were the words she had longed to hear from Blake. But suddenly, just like a thief in the night, an uninvited and aggressive thought intruded into her mind. A picture of Wayne smirking as he pulled her down onto the blanket at the lake. Tessa shut her eyes tightly, trying to block out the memory. *How could I have betrayed Blake like that? If only I could go back and undo the past.* Tessa's tears of joy had now turned to tears of regret. The blanket of guilt descended onto her shoulders, smothering everything good and beautiful. "Blake, I am so sorry for doubting us, for not…"

"Tessa," Blake softly wiped the tears away with his thumb, "don't waste time on the past. Promise me that you will only think about our future. We are together, here, right now. I am discharged from the army because of my injury. We are free to get married right away. I don't want to wait anymore. Jeremiah has to go back in three days. Let's be married by then so that we never have to be apart again."

Tessa felt the sadness ebb away as she nodded her agreement. She would never think on the past again. After all, God had forgiven her, and after reading the letter of confession, Blake had also forgiven her. It was time for her to forgive herself and enjoy all the blessings that lay ahead. She looked at the ring on her finger and smiled up at Blake. "Tomorrow is Christmas, let's get married the next day?"

"Perfect. Now may I have this dance?" Blake pulled her up and took her in his strong arms. Soft music wafted in through the open window as they swayed in the glow of the enchanting Christmas lights. Tessa put her arms around Blake's neck and allowed his mouth to settle over hers. Her pulse quickened as his fingers slowly caressed her arms and then moved down her back, drawing her close to him. The kiss became more urgent and Tessa's skin felt warm where his hands lingered. Blake took a step back and Tessa looked into his dark smoldering eyes, "We should probably slow things down. I want to do this the right way."

Tessa nodded, "Me too."

"Hey, it's almost midnight; let's wake Jeremiah with our news."

Blake grabbed Tessa's hand and dragged her into the room where Jeremiah snored quietly in the corner. Blake switched on the light and threw a pillow at Jeremiah's head, "Hey, wake up. I need to ask you something?"

Jeremiah sat up on one elbow and squinted against the sharp light, "What's going on?"

"I just woke you up to ask you to be my best man at our wedding in thirty six hours from now?"

Tessa laughed, "You're counting the hours?"

Blake grinned back, "I've been counting the hours for a long time."

"Agh you lovebirds make me sick! Yes, I'll be your best man in thirty six hours but first I'm going to sleep for twenty four hours and catch up on all the hours of sleep the army stole from me." Jeremiah covered his head with the pillow and groaned, "Switch off the light on your way out."

*****

Tessa stood inside the quaint brick courthouse and looked at Blake, who stood next to her in his army uniform. Standing tall and proud, he gazed back at her and smiled reassuringly. Tessa smoothed down the new dress that she had bought an hour ago. It wasn't a wedding dress by any means, but the fine ivory-silk dress was perfect for the occasion and Tessa felt like a princess standing beside her prince. Jeremiah flanked Blake's side and looked content as the proceedings continued. Within a few minutes, it was all over and they happily descended the stone steps leading into the garden nearby. It was a beautiful summer day and Pops stood ready with his camera. He had insisted that a wedding was not a wedding without pictures. Everything had happened so quickly that Tessa was grateful that Pops had thought about this.

Pictures were taken under the giant old trees where the roots were knotted together and protruded out of the ground like huge boulders. Tessa sat on one of the tangled roots, while Blake stood behind her with his hands resting on her shoulders. Jeremiah stood in front of them pulling faces, which caused them to laugh as Pops snapped the picture. More pictures were taken on the little wooden bridge while snow white geese floated nearby. Tessa felt like she would explode with joy as she took in what was happening. She was surrounded by people she loved, and she was finally Mrs. Blake King. Pops had moved them to a new spot and now they posed, Blake and Jeremiah on each side of Tessa, under a grape vine canopy.

"Are we done yet? I'm absolutely starving," Jeremiah complained. Pops looked at Jeremiah and frowned causing the many wrinkles on his forehead to crease into deeper rivers. "My young man, this is the most important day of a bride's life. We will be done only when she is done."

Jeremiah looked at Tessa pleadingly to which she replied, "We're not done until I get one more picture with you and a picture with Pops!"

Jeremiah's exaggerated fake smile showed every tooth in his mouth. Pops put the camera down and frowned at Jeremiah again, causing Tessa to hit him in the ribs with her elbow. "Quit being a typical brother! Behave yourself and smile seriously," this caused everyone to laugh and Pops snapped the final photo of brother and sister.

Now Jeremiah reached for the camera and mumbled, "OK, smile big for the camera Pops so we can go eat!"

A half hour later they were sitting in a café across from the beach and eating chicken pies with gravy and hot chips. Tessa sipped her ice cold coke and watched the pigeon at her feet pick up bits of pie crumbs.

I am married. I am actually married. I can't believe I am married to Blake.

These were the only thoughts that swirled around in Tessa's head as she watched her brother wolf down two chicken pies and down three glasses of coke. Blake on the other hand ate more slowly, and every now and then draped his hand across Tessa's shoulder and squeezed her affectionately. When Jeremiah was finished eating he pushed back his plate and said, "Hey Pops, what do you say about some night fishing tonight? I've been wanting to fish since I got here, and I am leaving tomorrow." Pops hesitated a moment but Jeremiah winked at him and added, "It would give the love birds some time alone."

Blake laughed and Tessa blushed as Pops became quite flustered and stammered, "Yes, sure…Umm, I've also been wanting to do some night fishing."

25

Tessa woke up slowly and blinked her eyes at the harsh morning light. *It must be late already.* She rolled over onto her stomach and lay there contently as her mind travelled back to the night before. A slow smile crept over her face as she pondered how beautiful and right things had been between her and Blake. She had felt his deep devotion to her in his every touch, and it had been wonderful to fall asleep tucked safely into the crook of his arm. This was what it was meant to be like. This was the way God had designed intimacy to feel. "Hey, sleeping beauty," Blake came into the room quietly and lay down next to Tessa. He ran his hands through her hair, "Are you ready for our first day as a married couple?"

Tessa rolled onto her side and smiled, "It depends on what you had in mind, my dear husband."

Blake kissed Tessa softly on the cheek, "Well, I thought we would start with a pot of coffee and a heap of bacon and eggs. I'm famished!" Tessa nodded as her stomach growled loudly. Blake continued, "Then I think we must take Bullet for a walk on the beach. After all, I don't want him to feel neglected. You know dogs can sense if they are being replaced..." Tessa looked at him to see if he was joking but found him to be dead serious, and she couldn't have loved him more in that moment. Blake was a kind and considerate man. He was wise and giving, and her heart swelled with gratitude for having him here as her husband.

"Oh, and then Jeremiah wants to talk to us when he wakes up from his nap before he leaves tonight. And by the way, he caught some Red Roman fish last night so we will have fried fish for dinner."

Tessa leaned over and gave Blake a big hug, "That sounds like a perfect day, but only because you are in it."

"Well, get up lazy bones so that we can get our perfect day started!" Tessa got out of bed and pulled on her robe. *It already has started perfectly...*

*****

Later that afternoon Blake and Jeremiah sat at the little kitchen table drinking coffee. Champ and Bullet sat on the floor together eyeing each other. Every now and then Champ would screech and Bullet would prick his ears up, but the incessant barking had stopped... Blake gave Champ another piece of apple and offered a piece to Bullet who pushed it around the floor with his nose. Bullet eyed Champ suspiciously and only gulped the piece of apple down when Champ inched closer and closer to it. Blake laughed out loud as he enjoyed the antics of the animals. This in turn, made Tessa smile as she stood at the counter peeling potatoes for their fish fry. It was so good to see how much Blake loved Bullet and Champ and she imagined that he would be an excellent father one day. She still couldn't believe how blessed she was to have him as her husband. God had been so good to her, and Blake had been so gracious in forgiving her for her betrayal and past mistakes. He hadn't even wanted to discuss any of it...it was truly as if it didn't matter at all. Tessa's thoughts wondered back to Wayne, and she cringed at the memory of how volatile and explosive his personality was compared to Blake's. She wasn't sure how she had been so blinded, but now her heart filled with joy as she watched Bullet rest his head on Blake's knee and look adoringly into his eyes.

Jeremiah interrupted her thoughts when he walked into the kitchen and said, "Tessa, come sit with us, I want to talk to you and Blake."

"OK, what's so important my serious brother?" Tessa said as she refilled their coffee cups and joined them at the too-small table.

"I have a surprise for you. I didn't know about this until recently, but Mom had an annuity that got paid out to me. With that and the money I have saved in the military, I was able to get our house back since no one had purchased it. I want you and Blake to move back to Cape Town and move into our house."

Tessa almost choked on her mouthful of coffee. "What? You got our house back?"   Jeremiah smiled and nodded, "Yes, you can move back home."

Tessa looked at Blake, who looked as surprised as she did. She finally allowed herself to acknowledge how much she had missed her white castle on the hill. How many nights had she lain awake conjuring up memories of the foaming water and her faithful seagulls? How many days had she longed to walk along the path to her hidden cave and just hide from the world?

"Oh Jeremiah, I can't believe it," she threw her arms around his neck, "this is the best gift ever! When can we go home?"

"Well, you and Blake can go as soon as you pack up here, but I have to return to the barracks tonight," he replied.

Tessa's smile faded, "When can you come and meet us there?"

"I should be out in six months, so probably by the beginning of July, just in time for my birthday. I want you to bake me one of those four-layer chocolate and caramel cakes, and be sure to build a big fire. I remember how the Cape winds would find ways to blow through that drafty old house."

"I don't care about the Cape winds! I'm just glad I'm going back home."

For the first time Blake spoke up, "Well, this is an answer to prayer because I wasn't sure where I was going to work but now I can return to my Uncle's hardware store in Fish Hoek."

Tessa added, "And it's only two train stops to Simonstown, so you will be home in a few minutes at night. I will need to find some work, too, but I don't think I can stand going back to that stuffy salon!"

Blake laughed again and gently ran a hand down Tessa's arm, "Don't worry about that now. Let's first get settled, and then we will see what happens." He leaned over and placed his lips on hers.

"Um, I think it's time to fry that fish now. I'm getting hungry," Jeremiah chimed in.

"Some things never change; you're always interrupting us with your hunger!" Blake said as he playfully punched his new brother-in-law.

*****

Pops had offered them his old beat up Volkswagen beetle to use, and now they bounced along towards the bus station. The fish fry had been excellent, and they had all complained of being overfull. Tessa had baked an apple pie and Jeremiah was bringing an extra piece in his bag for a midnight snack on the long bus ride back to base camp. Now they sat in the old beetle and listened as the song, "Eye of the Tiger," blared out of the speakers. Jeremiah sang along and Blake played drums on the dashboard. Tessa was glad that they were all in high spirits as it would make this goodbye much easier than the last few.

As Jeremiah stood ready to board the bus, he gave Tessa a quick hug, "Don't be sad, I will be home in six months for my chocolate cake!" He then looked at Blake and said, "I can't tell you how relieved I am that you are with Tessa and will look after her."

"I will protect her with my life, my brother, with my life!" A firm handshake was exchanged and Jeremiah stepped onto the bus. Blake and Tessa watched the bus disappear around the corner before they turned back to the car.

"Let's go home, Mrs. King, and check that Bullet hasn't eaten Champ...or the other way around," Blake said as he pulled Tessa close and put his arm protectively around her shoulders.

26

Three days later at seven o' clock in the morning, Blake and Tessa drove out of Van Staden's resort and turned the car towards Cape Town. Blake had managed to buy a car and settle what they owed on the bungalow. They had packed up their few possessions and said goodbye to Pops, whom Tessa thanked profusely for being so kind to her and Bullet. "I will never forget your kindness. Please come and visit us if you ever get to Cape Town!"

Pops waved his hand in the air and shook his gray head, "I haven't left the resort for twenty years. This is where I belong. You, too, are going to where you belong; but write to me, I love getting letters." Tessa thought she saw a tear gather in the old man's eye and gave him a kiss on the cheek, "I will Pops. I promise."

Bullet lay obediently on the back seat, but Champ was determined to be in the front. He first tried to lay behind Blake's neck but soon found that uncomfortable and was now curled up on Tessa's lap. She scratched his head between his two tiny ears and heard Bullet whine from the back seat. "Oh Bullet, don't be so jealous." She turned slightly and scratched his head too.

Blake put a hand on Tessa's knee and said playfully, "What about me?"

Tessa sighed, "I have too many babies!"

"I wonder what they will do when we have a real baby one day?" Blake glanced over at Tessa who smiled shyly.

"Well, they will just have to learn that there is enough love to go around and we won't stop loving them. We will be one big happy family, and it's just what I always wanted."

Blake smiled and Tessa squeezed his hand. *I could not be happier than what I am at this moment. We are starting our life together, just as I had always hoped we would.*

The eight hour drive went by quickly as Tessa and Blake spent the time talking and enjoying the breathtaking scenery as they neared Cape Town. Table Mountain, rightly named for looking like a flat table, loomed majestically up ahead and the fragrance of the wildflowers mingled with the ocean scent. Tessa felt like heaven could surely not offer more than this. As they drove into Millers Point and up to the lofty house that stood regally at attention, Tessa was overwhelmed with joy. Blake unlocked the front door with the key that had been hidden under the pot plant nearby and pushed the door open. He grabbed Tessa by the elbow as she walked past, "Not so fast, my dear."

He swung her up into his arms and carried her across the threshold. He kissed her on the lips before setting her down in the middle of the living room floor.

Tessa turned towards the huge window and looked out over the familiar ocean below. Nothing had changed, nothing at all. The boulders still stood and resisted the waves, the seagulls squawked as if they still waited for her to bring them bread. Tessa remembered how angry she had been with God on the last day down on the beach. She now felt an overwhelming urge to put her feet on the familiar sandy shore and pray. She turned and saw Blake watching her.

"Go, I will unpack the car and show the critters around their new home."

Tessa walked down the winding stairs but instead of bouncing down two stairs at a time, she walked slowly. She wanted to savor every step and inspect the entangled foliage on the sides of the path. The air was moist and heavy. *Oh, how I have longed for this place.* She sat on a boulder in the shallow water and listened as the gentle waves lapped against the stone. There was no wind today and the water was calm. She rested her feet in the cool water, while the seagulls screeched at her from their perch nearby.

"God, I am so sorry for having left you down here all those mornings ago. I now realize that our time together is as special to you as it is to me. You long for my fellowship because you truly love me, no matter what. You are faithful, even when I am not...and you patiently wait for me. Thank you for your forgiveness and for never leaving me. I will meet you down here as often as I can and I will thank you for all you have blessed me with. I will listen too, because I now know that you also want to share your heart with me."

Tessa sat quietly on the boulder and felt more complete and peaceful than what she had in a long time. She realized that it was not enough to use God as a genie, always wanting him to produce the next thing to satisfy her. It was also not enough to pray little S.O.S. prayers when she felt pressured by life. What she desperately needed was to spend time with him, to be strengthened by his fellowship.

When Tessa got back into the house she found the bags unpacked and the tea kettle boiling. She glanced at her watch and felt a twinge of guilt. She remembered how angry her mother used to be when she dawdled down at the water and she hoped Blake would not be angry as she hurried through the empty rooms to find him.

She found him dusting cobwebs down in the main bedroom. He looked at her when she walked in, "I know how much you like spiders so I'm starting to clean up in here."

"Thank you. I'm so sorry I took so long, I lost track of time," Tessa nervously eyed her watch again," It looks like I left you to do everything. I'm sorry. Can I make you some tea?" Tessa replied.

Swatting at another sticky web Blake replied, "I never noticed. And no you can't make me tea, because I'm going to make you some tea while you relax in a nice hot bath." At first Tessa thought that Blake was being sarcastic because he was angry after all, but then she noticed his kind smile as he said, "I have to look after my new bride! Now go on and have your bath and I will bring you your tea.

Late that night Tessa lay next to Blake and watched his even breathing as he slept. It was the weirdest thing but it seemed that the more he did for her, the more attracted to him she became. While she had soaked in a bubble bath, drinking tea, he had gotten rid of all the eight-legged trespassers that had been squatting in the empty house. He had also taken Bullet and Champ for an exploration of the area.

Tessa's mind continued to pick through the memories of their first day in their new home. The house was noticeably empty and their footsteps had echoed through the hollow rooms. The windows were bare and only the old bed and worn sofa had been left in the house as furniture. Even so, Tessa had felt excited about the changes they could make to the house as time went on. Blake's easygoing spirit put Tessa at rest and she felt safe and happy here in the drafty castle. Tessa smiled at the memory that had stayed with her since she was a small child. The one where she would often look up from the beach and see the magnificent castle looming proudly out of the mountain above. The old house would always be her castle. *Well my Prince finally arrived and now we can live happily ever after in our castle.*

Tessa snuggled up against Blake and drifted off into a peaceful night's sleep.

*****

Weeks had passed since Wayne had sworn to himself that he would find and marry Tessa. But here he sat in the musty bar nursing another drink. No leads, nothing but dead ends. He had asked Aunt Rina and Charmaine everyday if they had heard word from Tessa, but the answer was always the same. Perhaps it was time to forget, time to give up the challenge. The blonde bombshell that had been eyeing him at the bar for the last half an hour finally glided over and sat down on the barstool next to him.

"Hello, handsome. Why so depressed?" She lit a long cigarette with perfectly manicured red fingernails and smiled at him. She was a beauty for sure, and Wayne toyed with the idea of responding to the obvious invitation. She swayed closer to him, "Has anyone ever told you that you have the most brilliant blue eyes in the world?"

"Yes, actually, I have been told that."

He remembered Tessa complimenting him on the unique color of his eyes, but unlike this compliment, hers had come from a clean, pure heart. He remembered how even her skin had smelled so clean, like fresh soap. Now he looked at the woman in front of him who smelled like cigarettes and cheap wine. He groaned and dropped his head into his hands. "Just go away, will you!" he spoke to the blonde without looking at her.

"Well, there's no need to be rude!" She slid off the stool and walked to the other side of the bar.

What is happening to me? I must be going crazy. Wayne couldn't tell anymore if the obsessive thoughts of Tessa were still just the thrill of the chase, or if he truly had fallen head over heels in love with her. He had never felt this vulnerable and it scared him, it scared him greatly. This in turn made him angry. One thing was sure, she held the answer to these questions and he simply had to find her. He threw down some money on the bar and walked out, leaving his full mug of beer on the counter, another thing he had never done before.

27

Tessa couldn't imagine being happier. In the two months that had passed since they had moved to Cape Town, their lives had been flawless. Blake had gotten a job at his Uncle's hardware store and had already been promoted to an assistant manager. He was on day shift now and was home by dinner time every evening.

In the mornings, Tessa kept her appointment down on the beach and enjoyed her chats with her heavenly Father, who was always there as he promised he would be. The hungry seagulls were also always there and squawked loudly as they saw Tessa descend the stairs with the bag of old bread crusts. It had taken her a while to train Bullet to leave the birds alone, but he still eyed them mischievously from time to time. Champ didn't like the beach and much preferred the safety of the fruit trees in the back yard behind the house.

In the afternoons Tessa frequented the little thrift stores in Fish Hoek and Simonstown looking for inexpensive decorations for their new home. The house now had curtains and that helped to turn the barren place into a cozy nest. By six o clock in the evening the table was set, and when Blake walked in he was greeted with cheerful smiles and a warm dinner which was followed by coffee on the balcony. This had become their favorite time of the day and they enjoyed watching the sun set over the silver ocean.

It was late now as they lay together under the floral quilt that Tessa had found on one of her shopping sprees.

"Going from being in the army to being married is one thing, but lying under this pink flower quilt is quite another," Blake feigned indignation.

"I'm wondering if you are trying to bring out my feminine side?"

Tessa giggled and laid her head on Blake's shoulder. "Not at all, I quite like your masculine side actually."

Blake slowly traced Tessa's jawbone with his thumb.

"Is that so, Mrs. King?" he replied as he ran his finger along her lips. His hoarse whisper sent shivers down Tessa's spine and then his mouth captured hers in a slow passionate kiss.

*****

Two weeks later Tessa looked around the house and smiled at how authentic her little nest looked. The colorful tapestry rugs adorned the wood floors and the old sofa had been covered with a black and white zebra print afghan. The red scatter cushions and golden candles pulled it all together. Making her own home had been a dream come true and Blake always noticed her efforts and complimented her. Everything in her life was perfect and yet Tessa felt listless and down.

"What is wrong with me?" Tessa whispered to herself. Was she simply bored because her project had come to an end? *Maybe I should go for a walk.*

It was a hot February day and she decided to leave Bullet and Champ behind. She didn't have the stamina to go chasing after them if they decided to get up to mischief today.

Tessa had thought of Nolwazi often and decided to take the path to her hut. Halfway there Tessa regretted her decision. The path had become overgrown from lack of use and the weeds and thorn bushes scraped her legs. Tessa felt stifled by the breathless heat and she thought of turning back, but it seemed closer to push through to the hut and get a drink of cold water. Her mouth felt dry and her legs burned where the tiny thorns had ripped her skin. Just when she thought she couldn't take another step she burst through into the circle of huts. Unlike the last time, Nolwazi was not outside stirring porridge, so Tessa dragged herself to the door desperately hoping she was home. Nolwazi opened the door and Tessa almost fell into the cool dark hut.

"Whatcha wrong, Chil?" Nolwazi caught Tessa as she stumbled over the dirt step. "Oh Lord help tha Chil!" Nolwazi prayed as she helped Tessa over to the little bed and then went to get her a dented tin cup filled with cool water. She helped Tessa sip the water and put a cool towel on her head.

"You sick, Chil?"

"No, no...I'm not sick. I just got hot," Tessa sat up, but still felt slightly woozy.

"Lay down, Chil!" Nolwazi scolded, and Tessa smiled slightly as she recognized that scolding voice used on her when she was a little girl who wouldn't eat her green beans.

"I missed you, Nolwazi," Tessa heard herself saying.

"Oh Chil!" Nolwazi's toothless smile widened and she patted Tessa with her fat hand.

As they sat comfortably together in the little hut, Tessa told Nolwazi that she was now married and living in the big old house.

"I coming visit you soon!" Nolwazi continued patting Tessa's hand, "And I coming help wit usana too!" Tessa knew usana meant baby in Xhosa and wondered what on earth Nolwazi was talking about now.

"What baby?" Tessa questioned.

"Usana," Nolwazi repeated again and this time she pointed at Tessa's stomach.

Tessa bolted upright causing her head to spin, "My baby?"

Nolwazi grinned, showing off her shiny gums.

"You'z eet now!" And with that, she waddled her large body to the stove and dished up a plate of maize porridge and added a spoonful of sugar to it. She sat on the bed and force fed Tessa as if she was still two years old. After setting down the empty tin dish, Nolwazi said, "See? It OK."

Tessa vaguely remembered that this was how their very last conversation had ended, with Nolwazi saying, "It OK. It OK."

And it really had turned out *OK* after all. But what would Blake say about this? They had planned on waiting a while before having a baby, but apparently their prevention plan hadn't worked very well. Yet, the thought of holding Blake's baby in her arms brought such joy to Tessa that she couldn't help smiling.

Now she lay in the cool hut and listened as Nolwazi sang an old hymn in her rich deep voice. It was a soothing sound and she drifted off to sleep in the semi dark hut. Hours later Tessa awoke with a jump and leaped off the bed. The sudden movement made her head spin, and she steadied herself before taking a step.

"Nolwazi?" she called but heard no reply. As she opened the hut door she saw that it was already dusk. Nolwazi was sitting on a mat, weaving a basket. "Nolwazi, why didn't you wake me up?"

"Is cooler now for walkin' to big house," Nolwazi replied as if the matter had been decided and settled.

Tessa had to agree that she felt better and probably would not have made the walk home in the cruel sun that had baked down earlier in the day. She hurriedly said goodbye to Nolwazi and took the path back to the house. She noticed that the thick brush had been cut back and the path was now clear. The thorns that had torn her flesh earlier were gone and she knew that Nolwazi must have spent the afternoon clearing the path which now bought her time as she quickened her step. Entering through the old rusty gate she jumped as she saw Blake out of the corner of her eye. "Oh, you gave me a fright!"

"Well I was just about to take this path and see where it leads. I've been home for hours and have been worried sick? Where have you been?"

Tessa quickly explained about Nolwazi's hut and then said, "Why did you get home so early today?"

Blake took Tessa's hand and led her back to the house, "We were all caught up and Uncle Jim let me go early. I wanted to surprise you and catch you before you started cooking. I thought we could go out to the steakhouse tonight.

Tessa's stomach churned and she felt nauseated, "Well, I'm umm...not feeling that great. Would you mind if we stayed in and ate soup instead?"

Blake put his palms out like a scale, "Steak versus soup...Soup versus steak," his imaginary scale swung from high to low.

"I'm sorry, I will get ready to go to the restaurant," Tessa said.

"No you will not! I'm just teasing you. I don't care what or where we eat as long as we are together," Blake leaned over and kissed Tessa affectionately on the forehead.

After taking a bath, Tessa heated up some soup and made them each a sandwich. They sat together at the kitchen table and ate quietly. Champ jumped around the kitchen, making it obvious that he had not been fed yet. Blake glanced at Tessa a few times and then put his soup spoon down.

"OK, what's going on? You're not yourself at all today."

Tessa didn't know how to respond. She was bursting with excitement about the baby, but she was also very nauseated. On top of that she didn't know how Blake would really feel about it. They had only been married for such a short time. Tessa had thought that they had been careful enough, but apparently not. Would Blake blame her?

"Out with it, Tess. You know there is nothing you cannot speak to me about. Remember, we are partners in everything now."

"I'm pregnant," Tessa blurted out.

"You're *what*?"

"I'm pregnant," Tessa spoke so softly it was almost a whisper.

A moment of tormenting silence followed as Tessa and Blake looked at each other. Even Champ must have sensed a shift in the room because now he sat eyeing them while twisting his tiny fingers together.

Blake stood up so suddenly that the wooden chair toppled over with a crash. He took a step forward and swooped Tessa up into his arms almost crushing her. "Really? We're going to have a baby?"

A wave of relief washed over Tessa and she laughed out loud, "Well, that's usually what happens when one is pregnant."

Blake twirled Tessa around the kitchen while making loud whooping sounds. Champ screeched and jumped across the kitchen almost colliding with Bullet who was coming to check out what all the chaos was about. Tessa was delighted at Blake's enthusiasm and wondered why she had even worried about it at all. This was who Blake was, after all. She would never compare him to Wayne again, who had called his unborn baby a 'brat'.

28

Wayne stomped into Auntie Rina's kitchen causing clods of dirt to fly off his boots and scatter across the floor. Sinethemba stood at the stove and pretended not to notice the mess he had just made on the shiny, freshly mopped floor. This was one man she wouldn't mess with. She saw that mean streak and tried to stay out of his way.

Wayne threw himself down at the long wooden table and barked, "Make me some coffee, and hurry up!" Sinethemba opened the old tin can and scooped out some coffee into the percolator that sat on top of the cast iron stove. Her hands shook ever so slightly. She didn't like it when Miss Rina and Charmaine left the farm at the same time, leaving this devil here to lord it over them. Just yesterday, he had taken his sjambok to her husband's back because he did not get the tractor started soon enough. No one knew what was eating the young man because he was worse than ever lately. Sinethemba served Wayne his coffee and fled the kitchen immediately after. She would find a way to hide from this one for the rest of the day.

Wayne slurped his coffee loudly and cursed. He hated this farm, he hated the animals, but mostly he hated himself for being stuck here. He had to get away, he needed a break. Perhaps taking a trip to the ocean would break the monotony of his life. But then again, what fun would it be going alone? He listlessly pulled over the pile of magazines and mail that lay next to him. He absentmindedly flipped through the magazine on hunting.

What can they tell me? He scoffed. *I am the best hunter around these parts. That's why no one wants to hunt with me. I'm too good.* He threw the magazine to the side which made the whole pile of paperwork fall off the table.

He cursed again. "Sinethemba! Sinethemba!" he shouted. Where did that stupid maid disappear to again? She needed to come clean up this mess before Aunt Rina got home. He bent down and scooped the papers up, dumping them unceremoniously on the table. He stood up to refill his coffee but just then his eye caught something sticking out of the pile of papers. He sat back down and pulled out a postcard and read,

Dear Auntie Rina and Charmaine,

I am sorry for leaving in such a hurry. Please forgive me. I am writing to tell you that I am moving back to the house in Miller's Point, the one down the street from the Blue Marlin restaurant you so enjoyed on your visit years ago. I have so much news and promise to write again once I am settled. But for now know that I love you and I am well!

Thank you for all you did for me...

Tessa

*****

Rocking back in his seat, Wayne couldn't believe his luck. He had found her! He smiled with pleasure. Then, just as quickly, a frown creased his brow. Aunt Rina had known about this and had not told him. Women were all the same; there was not a single one that could be trusted. But he would go and find Tessa at the house near the Blue Marlin restaurant, wherever that was, and he would bring her back here. Yes, he had made his decision and she would be his wife come hell or high water. He stuck the postcard in his pocket and walked out of the house, spraying more mud clods around as he exited the kitchen.

*****

Tessa had written a letter to Jeremiah telling him that he was going to be an uncle soon. A few days later she'd received an excited phone call from him telling her that he had the following weekend off and couldn't wait to see her and Blake. Tessa was glad that she was feeling so much better than she had been, and now energetically attacked Jeremiahs old room with a feather duster and broom. She would have to go back into town to get some bedding and perhaps a lamp and a picture for the empty walls. Tessa now understood why people said that pregnant women wanted to nest, a saying she had never understood before. She smiled as she walked past the little nursery that Blake had painted an eggshell yellow. They had already set up the little crib and changing table that they had found for sale in a secondhand shop in Fish Hoek. Tessa still needed a little quilt and a baby border for the walls, but she remembered

Blake's teasing the day before, "Tessa, we're not having the baby tomorrow. We still have lots of time to do this."

"I know," she had replied, "I just want it ready and perfect." Blake had walked over and wrapped his arms around her, "It's already perfect because you are here with me." She'd sunk into Blake strong arms and breathed in his familiar scent. Feeling safe and loved by this amazing man she had whispered into his neck, "Yes, it's already perfect!"

29

It was Tuesday morning and Jeremiah would be arriving on the weekend. Tessa pushed her cart around the grocery store, buying all the things that she knew Jeremiah enjoyed eating. She would bake a chicken pie one night and lasagna the next. Taking a cheesecake from the freezer, she laid it in the basket, then turned back and opened the freezer door again to add chocolate chip mint ice-cream to the pile of groceries, since that was Blake's favorite. The problem was that neither of these were her favorite dessert. She had been craving a rich chocolate cake, so she decided to buy flour and cocoa powder too. She would ice the cake with real caramel. Her mouth watered, and she wondered if these crazy cravings would go on very long. Yesterday she had eaten eggs for breakfast, lunch, and dinner, even though she usually didn't care for eggs at all.

Tessa hurried to the car as rain poured down, soaking her to the bone. She shivered as she drove home through the cold mist that shrouded the mountain. She pulled the car into the driveway and lugged the groceries up the steep stairs. As soon as she entered the kitchen she put the kettle on and then unpacked the groceries with blue cold fingers. A nice cup of hot tea would surely warm her bones. Tessa hurried through the house and changed into a warm pair of pajamas. It was only three o'clock in the afternoon but who would care? Blake was so laid back he didn't care about anything except that she was happy and comfortable. And these flannel pink pajamas were really comfortable and warm.

Pouring the tea, Tessa carried it to her favorite spot and sat on the ledge at the oversized glass window in the living room. She looked down at the raging ocean. Although she loved the quiet waters, her favorite days were looking out at the raging sea. The swells grew larger and larger as the rain and wind increased and crashed over the huge boulders that the seagulls usually sat on. They must have found a place to hide because there was not a seagull in sight today. Tessa remembered how she had sat on this same ledge as a little girl and had often been scared that the swells would get so big they would come up the mountain and suck her right off the ledge. She used to run through the house looking for Jeremiah who had always pacified her by saying that if a wave that big came, he would stand on the balcony and shake his fist at it, commanding it to go back down the hill where it belonged. Tessa smiled now at how she had always believed him and had returned to her ledge without any fear. Yes, Jeremiah had always been a good brother, a brother that always looked out for her. She couldn't wait to see him this weekend. She took a sip of the strong tea and leaned back against the window pane. Then the doorbell rang.

Who on earth could that be in this horrible weather? Tessa looked down at her pajamas and wondered if she had time to change but the incessant knocking sounded urgent. She hoped it wasn't bad news of some kind.

Tessa opened the door and gasped. Wayne stood leaning against the doorframe in the casual confident pose that belonged to him alone. His piercing eyes looked right through Tessa.

"So, here you are...in all your glory," he said as he looked Tessa up and down, taking in her pajamas and damp hair. Tessa was speechless and self-consciously ran her fingers along the buttons of her flannel pajama top. Her silence did nothing to deter Wayne as he continued, "I must say, you looked much better when you were with me. You shouldn't let yourself go like this."

He continued to look Tessa up and down but then waved a hand, "Never mind, I'm here now and you will be just fine when we get back home."

Tessa's mind was reeling and she spoke for the first time, "I am home."

Wayne pretended not to hear this and stepped through the door into the living room, causing Tessa to take a step backwards.

"Hope you don't mind, but it's kind of wet out there. Is the weather always so gloomy here in Cape Town?" He walked over to the window where Tessa had been sitting a moment ago and whistled, "Wow, what a view! No wonder you were miserable on the farm in Bloemfontein." He winked at Tessa and then added, "It's a good thing I was there to entertain you."

It was Tessa's turn to pretend that she didn't hear. She wasn't in the mood for these games. "What are you doing here?"

Wayne sat down on the ledge and picked up Tessa's teacup. "Do you mind?" he said as he took a swig. "That's good, but don't you have something a little stronger in this house. I think some brandy would warm me up. This sea air goes right to the bones! "

Tessa finally snapped out of her shock and replied, "No Wayne, I don't have brandy. What are you doing here?" she repeated the question again.

"Well, I'm here to see you of course." Wayne got up from the ledge and took two large strides towards Tessa, who automatically backed away. "Look, Tessa," Wayne's voice was soft and caressing now, "I'm sorry about how things ended, but I have come to realize that you mean something to me. I can't get you out of my mind. I think about you all the time. I've decided that you are the one I want. I've come to take you back. I want us to get married; we will be good for each other. I shouldn't have let you go and I'm really sorry for not telling you while you were there. And everything has worked out just fine because Sharon lost the baby." He took another step towards Tessa, "You just don't know how tormented I've been while looking for you." He reached out and cupped her chin in his hand, "You're so beautiful!"

Just then the front door opened and Blake stepped inside, wiping his wet boots on the doormat. As he looked up, he saw Tessa standing in the living room with a man he didn't know. They were both staring at him. "Oh, hello," He said, "I didn't know we had company." He shrugged off his wet coat and hung it on the coat rack.

Before Tessa could reply, Wayne took a step forward and smiled broadly, "My name is Wayne. I worked with Tessa on the farm in Bloemfontein and I am on vacation here in the beautiful Cape of Good Hope. I thought I would stop in for a visit."

Blake shook Wayne's hand, "Of course, any friend of Tessa's is welcome here. My name is Blake, I am Tessa's husband."

Wayne glanced at Tessa and she saw his jaw clench in veiled anger, "Oh, I didn't know Tessa got married." He turned to Tessa, "Tsk, tsk, tsk….and you didn't invite me to the wedding!" Wayne's voice was light and playful but Tessa recognized the murderous glint in his sharp blue eyes. "Congratulations," he leaned over and kissed Tessa on the cheek.

Blake smiled as he looked at Tessa's pink cheeks, "And what a lovely bride she is! Now, are you staying for dinner?" he asked Wayne.

"How kind, I would love to!"

Tessa groaned inwardly, "Excuse me, I need to go and get dressed."

*****

Tessa stood in the middle of her bedroom with a pair of jeans in her hands, but did not make a move to put them on. Her mind whirled in confusion as she listened to Wayne and Blake laugh together as they continued to chat like old friends. *How could that skunk show up here! And why on earth is Blake being so friendly? Has he forgotten the letter in which I told him all about what happened with Wayne? What is going on?*

Tessa picked up a brush and ran it through her knotted hair. She looked in the mirror and saw a pale face and fearful eyes looking back at her. She dreaded going back out there but finished getting dressed and stepped out of the room. On the way to the kitchen she glanced into the living room and saw the guys sitting on the sofa chatting together. It made her blood boil that Wayne was such a con man and always succeeded in winning people over. Everyone liked Wayne. Everyone, except Jeremiah. He had seen him for the snake he really was. Now Tessa found herself feeling angry with Blake. Did Blake truly not care about how Wayne had treated her before? She had told him everything, even the beating that had almost taken Bullet's life. This led to Tessa's next thought, *where is Bullet anyway*? She found him standing in the corner of the laundry room with his tail between his legs. His eyes were sad and Tessa knelt down next to him. She ran a hand over his head and hugged him. "I won't ever let him hurt you again! I promise!" She closed the laundry room door and left Bullet hiding in the dark, where she wished she could hide, too.

She heard Blake calling her from the living room and peeked her head around the corner, "Hey, could you make us some coffee please baby." She nodded as she looked over and saw Champ sitting on Wayne's lap. It infuriated Tessa because she knew this man hated animals.

She walked over and scooped Champ up, "It's time for his nap!" She felt Wayne's eyes follow her out of the room. She lay Champ down next to Bullet and closed the laundry room door again.

Taking the coffee into the living room she had a strong urge to accidently drop Wayne's coffee in his lap. He had no right to be here. She looked at Blake and said, "I'm not feeling well today, perhaps we can take a rain check with the dinner thing and do it another time?"

Blake got up and rubbed Tessa's back affectionately. He placed a kiss over the slight scar on her cheek. "Of course, baby. No problem." He turned to Wayne and said, "How about we let Tessa rest and we barbecue outside for dinner?"

Wayne glanced at Tessa and she wondered how Blake could not see the smirk there. He obviously didn't know Wayne as she did. "Sure, Blake, that sounds like fun."

"It's still raining outside, though," Tessa said pointing to the rain that splattered on the window. She desperately wanted this man gone. She wanted him gone far away!

"Don't worry Tessa, real men aren't afraid of a little rain. Leave it up to us and you go and lie down," Wayne smiled widely.

*****

Tessa lay on her bed smoldering. The only thing she could come up with was that Blake had chosen not to hold a grudge. She could only hope that Wayne would leave tonight and never come back. After all, he knew that she was married now.

Blake came into the room an hour later, "Hey, Tess, are you feeling better? We cooked some hamburgers, come and eat with us. This Wayne is quite an interesting chap. He has a lot of funny stories."

"OK, but don't encourage him to stay after dinner. I'm just not up for company today."

They sat in the dining room and Tessa forced herself to eat a piece of a burger and tried not to make eye contact with Wayne. But it seemed the more she ignored him, the more he tried to draw her into stories.

"Hey, Tessa, remember the day I taught you how to milk the cow?" Wayne put his head back and laughed as he continued, "And remember all the times I helped you feed the chickens because you always overslept."

Blake laughed and chimed in, "Yes, my bride is not an early bird, that is for sure!"

Tessa pushed her food around her plate but was unresponsive which she hoped would dampen Wayne's enthusiasm for story telling…especially stories about them.

"Hey Tess," Wayne continued, "Do you remember our day out at the pond by my house?"

Tessa choked on the sip of water she had just taken. Blake hit her on the back, "Are you OK?"

"Yes, I'm fine. So who wants coffee?"

Tessa walked into the kitchen and hung her head over the sink. She splashed cold water on her face. *What is Wayne up to?* Everything had been perfect, and now her nerves were on edge.

Tessa spoke to herself, *Pull yourself together, Tessa. By tomorrow he will be on his way home. Just get through this night.*

She put the coffee pot on and went into the laundry room to feed Bullet and Champ. After stalling as long as she could, she re-entered the dining room to find it empty. She set the coffee down and walked down the long hallway, finding Blake and Wayne standing in the nursery.

"So," Wayne spoke in a low voice, "another secret. You're having a baby?" His eyes pinned Tessa to the doorway.

"Yes," she walked over and stood next to Blake, who automatically put his arm around her, "We're having a baby."

"So when exactly are you due?" Wayne asked and Blake replied right away.

"Oh, were still in the early days. I keep telling Tessa she doesn't have to get everything ready all at once!"

Tessa turned to the door and said, "The coffee is getting cold."

30

Tessa lay awake and listened to Blake's even breathing. She tossed and turned but still no sleep came. Wayne had told Blake that he wasn't quite sure when he would end his vacation and this caused Tessa to feel unsettled. Why would he continue to hang around? She desperately needed to speak to Blake but her courage had failed her, and so she had gone to bed in silence instead.

Wednesday morning dawned with sunny skies. The rain was gone and Tessa rolled out of bed determined to make it a good day. The new day brought on a wave of relief. The fears of last night looked small in the bright daylight and Tessa was sure Wayne would be long gone by now. Besides, Jeremiah would be arriving soon. Yes, this was going to be a really good day.

After Blake left for work, Tessa vigorously attacked her to-do list. She didn't get very far when the call of the seagulls beckoned her down to the beach. She decided that the list of chores could wait. Downstairs, on the beach, she sat and prayed over her day. She fed the seagulls the left over hamburger buns from the night before and then just sat quietly, allowing the sun to sink into her skin. All was right with the world again.

"So, I figured it out! And I must say that I forgive you," Tessa jumped in fright as Wayne stepped out from behind the boulder. She shivered at the realization that he had been watching her the whole time. He still wore the same clothes from the night before, and Tessa was aware that he must have slept somewhere on the beach. He unnerved Tessa as he walked towards her, but she made a decision to stay calm and act like nothing was wrong.

"Hello, Wayne, I wasn't expecting to see you down here," Tessa said as she looked up at him now hovering over her. He did not respond but just stood there. Tessa held up a hand to shield her eyes from the sun and to get a better look at him. He looked unshaven and his eyes were red-rimmed as he watched Tessa, who broke the awkward silence by saying, "What have you forgiven me for?"

"I forgive you for getting married. You see, I figured it all out last night as I lay here between the boulders trying to sleep. I couldn't actually sleep of course, since it was cold and windy…a most uncomfortable night in fact; but it was a blessing in disguise, you see."

"No I don't see, I have no idea what you are talking about, but I must get back up to the house now; I have a lot to do today." Tessa turned to go and headed for the steps but Wayne circled her in two big strides and now stood on the first step, blocking her path.

"Don't you at least want to hear the epiphany I got while looking up at your house all night long?" Wayne asked but didn't wait for a reply. "Well, I will tell you anyway. I've forgiven you for getting married to Blake because you had no choice. You see, as I said, I figured it out. You found yourself pregnant with my child and had to marry someone quickly. So you married Blake and told him it was his child, a honeymoon baby, so to speak."

Wayne leaned on the wooden railing and crossed his long legs, he grinned and reached out to touch Tessa's shoulder, "Clever, clever girl! I always knew you were a smart one. I understand why you didn't come back to me. You thought I was marrying Sharon but as luck would have it, I can now marry you."

Wayne stood up straight and got a stern look in his eye, "The fact that you married Blake will make things a little more complicated, but he will understand when we tell him the truth."

Tessa had been shocked speechless by all the crazy things Wayne said and had at first wanted to laugh, but now as she looked into his crazed eyes a shiver of fear ran down her spine. He was absolutely dead serious. She had to reason with him; somehow she had to make him go away. Her mind raced, and she wondered if there was even a minute chance that Blake may consider this the truth? No, she had told him everything in the letter; there was nothing to hide, yet she felt an uncomfortable dread settle over her shoulders.

"Wayne, you have to listen to me. This is all a fabrication of your imagination. What happened between us was a big mistake, nothing more. I don't love you and this is not your baby. I married Blake because I love him, and this is our child. I am not going anywhere with you and I think it is best that you leave here as soon as possible." Tessa pushed past Wayne and was relieved when he kept silent and let her ascend the steps. Maybe now he would go away once and for all!

Tessa spent the rest of the day trying to work through her to-do list but her heart felt heavy and she couldn't shake the feeling that Wayne still lurked nearby. She replayed the conversation over and over again in her mind. *I should tell Blake. I know he read the letter but we should have talked about all this before now.* But no matter how Tessa tried to construct the conversation in her head, it just didn't sound like it would come out right. By the time Blake got home from work, Tessa felt exhausted from worrying all day. She set the baked fish and roasted potatoes on the table but her stomach turned at the sight of the food.   "This is delicious, Tess! You are a great chef," Blake said as he served himself a large portion of the green salad. "So, tell me all about your day," he continued. Tessa opened her mouth to say, "Well, there is something we need to talk about," but instead she heard herself saying, "Oh, nothing special...how was your day?"

Blake spoke a while about his day at work and when they had finished dinner he said, "Tessa, are you sure you are not doing too much? You look pale and tense today." He pointed at her uneaten plate of food, "And you hardly ate anything last night or tonight. You know Jeremiah won't expect you to have the house perfect for his visit." He reached over and stroked Tessa's arm.

"No, it's not that," Tessa said, feeling close to tears.

"Are you worried about the pregnancy?" Blake asked. "I know you don't have a mother or sister to talk to, but I'll try and do my best to be here for you in every way."

Blake stood up and walked over to his backpack, "Here, this might cheer you up. I bought you something today." He handed Tessa a gift bag that contained the tiniest pair of shoes she had ever seen. She also pulled out a bib that said 'I love my mommy'.

Tessa burst into tears. This husband of hers was perfect. She entered into his embrace and clung to him for a long time. She was more terrified than ever that she would lose him. "It's all going to be alright Tess," she heard Blake whisper over and over again...

The rest of the week passed by uneventfully, and not seeing Wayne again convinced Tessa that he had surely gone back home. She allowed herself to relax and on Saturday morning when Jeremiah arrived, Tessa felt overwhelmed with joy. He also came bearing gifts and now Tessa added a tiny yellow sweater and a couple of colorful baby quilts to her nursery shelves. Later in the day they had a wonderful picnic together on the beach, even the animals had been allowed to tag along.

"OK" Tessa had laughed, "but I am not going to be the one to chase them around out there." Sure enough Bullet had chased the seagulls and gotten soaking wet and covered in sand. Then Champ had gone into hiding, and it had taken them a good thirty minutes to find him. Nevertheless, the laughter and fresh air had done them all well. When they got back upstairs they enjoyed the chocolate cake that Tessa had prepared for Jeremiah. Blake also ate a big bowl of mint chocolate-chip ice-cream, and then said he had a stomach ache and went to lie down.

"Hey, Tessa, do you want to go into Fish Hoek with me? I want to buy the baby something but I want you to pick it out. How about a high-chair and a stroller?"

Tessa grinned, "Sure, it will be fun! Let's go."

31

Jeremiah and Tessa drove home in high spirits after their shopping trip in Fish Hoek. It had been a great day and they had reminisced as they walked through the familiar streets of their childhood. There had been much to laugh and talk about.

"I'm so glad you are coming home in June. You know your room will be waiting for you. The house is so big and Blake has already said that he wants you to stay with us."

"Thanks, Tess, but I think newlyweds should have their own home. Besides, I don't want a screaming baby keeping me up all night!" he laughed.

"Well, where will you stay?"

"I'll get a little studio apartment nearby, but only if I can come to dinner once a week?"

"How about twice a week?" Tessa countered.

"We'll see…" Jeremiah smiled as he parked the car in the driveway.

They headed up the stairs and Tessa noticed how even more muscular her brother had become in the last months. The military training had made him even more fit and agile, and now he carried the boxes containing the stroller and high chair as if they weighed nothing at all. He wasn't even out of breath when he reached the top step and turned around to look at Tessa who lagged behind, "Come on, old lady, you're not even carrying anything!" Then he laughed and added, "Oh yeah, I forgot, you are carrying *two* people."

They were still fooling around when they entered the front door, and Tessa's blood ran cold when she saw Wayne sitting in the living room with Blake. The room swirled a little bit as she took it all in.

Blake's face looked like stone while Wayne's held that familiar smirk. Tessa glanced at Jeremiah who looked confused and mad at the same time. The silence in the room was deafening until she heard Jeremiah speak, "What the hell is *he* doing here?"

"You know him?" Blake's voice was as stony as his features.

"Yes, I've met him," Jeremiah's voice matched Blake's.

Wayne stood up, "Well I see I have overstayed my welcome. I'll be taking my leave now." He faked a salute towards Jeremiah and then made a mockingly-low bow in front of Tessa adding "Good day, my lady." With that he swept out of the room and disappeared down the stairs.

Jeremiah dropped the parcels he was still holding and threw his hands up in the air, "What was that all about?"

Blake ignored him and looked at Tessa for a long moment. Tessa tried to read what lay behind the vacant eyes that stared at her. Jeremiah looked from one to another and then back again, "I guess I will give you guys some privacy. I'll be on the balcony putting these together," he picked up the boxes and walked out to the balcony.

Blake stayed seated but said nothing. Tessa felt like she was standing on trial and decided to sit down on the opposite couch.

"Blake, please say something," Tessa pleaded.

Blake spoke quietly, "Is it true? That's all I want to know...is it true?"

"Yes, no...I don't know! Is what true?"

"Is this *HIS* baby?"

"NO!" Tessa almost shouted out of desperation. "No, it's ours. He's lying!" Tessa repeated.

"So you weren't unfaithful to me."

Now it was Tessa's turn to sit quietly and look at Blake. She spoke in almost a whisper, "Blake, I don't understand. I told you everything in the letter. You even said the past was the past when I tried to talk to you about it in the bungalow."

Blake sounded tired, as if all the wind had been knocked out of him when he spoke, "What letter Tessa?"

Tessa stammered, "The letter that explained it all."

Blake's voice was low and his dark eyes were almost black, "I didn't get a letter, but why don't you explain it to me now."

Tessa rubbed her hands together nervously. This was not how she had wanted this conversation to be. The letter would have been much better. She only wished that she had kept a copy. She breathed a quick silent prayer, *help me Lord, and help him to understand.* "Blake, I was very lonely in Bloemfontein. I waited and waited to hear from you, but I didn't hear a single word for months."

Blake interrupted her again, "I wrote to you!"

"Yes, but I only found the letter the day I left! It had somehow fallen under the bed. When you didn't write I questioned whether there really was anything between us.

228

You had never really said it, and I started to wonder if it was all in my imagination. Then Wayne…" she stopped for a moment as she heard Blake groan and put his head in his hands.

Tessa wished she could stop speaking. She wished she could prevent the hurt she knew was coming to both of them. But it was time to get it all out, to confess everything, so she continued "…then Wayne was there and he acted like he cared. We worked together, became friends. I didn't see' til later that he was a cruel man. He beat Bullet and almost killed him." Tessa fell silent for a moment, and then she added, "I'm so sorry. I never stopped loving you."

Blake lifted his head, his eyes now penetrating, "There is only one more thing I need to know…"

Tessa dropped her eyes and looked at her hands that instinctively cupped her belly. He did not need to ask it. She knew what he wanted to know. How could this be happening now? Was there any way she could lie now and ask for forgiveness later? She looked up and uttered the one word that could change everything, "Yes."

Blake got up and walked past Tessa without a word, slamming the front door behind him as he left. A tear slid down her cheek as she listened to his angry footsteps disappear in the distance.

32

"What the hell is going on here today?" Jeremiah said as he came into the living room. "Who is slamming the doors?" he questioned and added a curse word as a punctuation.

"Jeremiah, I would prefer it if you didn't use that language around here. You're going to have a niece or nephew that is going to repeat everything you say someday."

"Sorry, Tess, just a bad habit I picked up in the army." He sat down next to Tessa as he noticed her tear-streaked cheeks. "What is going on? Where is Blake and why was that snake, Wayne, here today again?"

Tessa felt her throat burn with unshed tears, and she leaned her head on Jeremiah's shoulder and cried.

"Jeremiah, I am ashamed to tell you, but Wayne and I..." Tessa covered her face with her hands and sobbed, "We..."

"I know Tessa; you don't have to say anything. I read all about that in the letter."

Tessa lifted her head, "In what letter, Jeremiah?"

Tessa knew Jeremiah well enough to recognize the guilty look that crossed his handsome face. He cleared his throat and said, "Well, Blake was in the hospital and I recognized your handwriting and read the letter, in case it was something important. I didn't think he needed to read it because that was in the past, and I knew he had already bought you the ring."

Jeremiah looked at Tessa's accusing eyes and ended feebly, "I burnt the letter. I didn't think it would matter."

"Well, apparently it did matter and now he's gone! I married him, thinking he knew. You had no right to do that Jeremiah!"

"I know, Tess, I was only trying to protect you."

"You can't keep trying to protect me from everything; this has just made everything worse. What if Blake leaves me now? I couldn't stand that." A fresh flow of agonizing tears cascaded down Tessa's cheeks.

"Tess, Blake loves you, just give him some time. I'll go out and look for him and explain about the letter."

*****

An hour later Tessa was still pacing the living room floor. Her eyes were swollen from crying and she continued praying for God to soften Blake's heart. The phone rang and Tessa lurched for it, hoping that it was Blake.

"Hello, beautiful," she recognized Wayne's voice.

"Wayne, can't you understand? I want nothing to do with you. Leave me alone!"

"Well, the way I see it…that boyfriend of yours won't want anything to do with you now that he knows the truth. I saw it in his eyes….I bet he is already on his way out of your life. So I will give you a day to pack, and then I will come and pick you up. Its best you just come home with me. I'll see you soon."

"He is not my boyfriend, he is my husband! Stop tormenting me! There was nothing between us but a mistake."

Click

Hello? Hello?" Tessa slammed the phone down. *The nerve of that man to put the phone down before she could finish telling him off.*

"That was him, wasn't it?" Tessa almost jumped out of her skin as she heard Blake's voice from behind her.

"Yes, he just won't leave me alone."

"I understand now Tessa. I just had a long talk with Jeremiah and I almost punched him in the face when he told me he burnt that letter!" He reached out and took Tessa by the hand. "But he also told me that he had asked around about Wayne in Bloemfontein, and he is well known for his abuse towards women and animals. He is also known for his seducing ways." Tessa dropped her head, but Blake put his finger under her chin and lifted it up, forcing her eyes to meet his, "But none of that matters. While I was out walking on the beach the Lord reminded me that not one of us is without sin, and yet he forgives us and throws our sins into the sea of forgetfulness. I should not have gone off to the army without declaring my love for you more clearly. I choose to forgive you and to throw this all into the sea of forgetfulness. I love you and I love our baby."

Tessa clung to Blake, "I'm so sorry. I love you."

Blake put a finger on Tessa's lips, "Let's forget about all this now," he bent down and kissed her. Tessa pulled Blake closer and fiercely responded to his kiss. The kiss deepened and then they heard Jeremiah's voice coming from the front door, "What the hell…" but then he caught himself, "I mean, what the heck is going on here today? Fighting and kissing! I just can't keep up! I think we should all go to our rooms and call it a day. See you guys in the morning." He walked past them faking a big yawn and closed his bedroom door.

Blake rolled his eyes, "I guess we've been ordered to go to bed, Mrs. King." Tessa giggled, "I think that's a good idea, Mr. King," she said as she led him to their bedroom and shut the door.

*****

Tessa woke up to the smell of bacon and eggs frying and she heard her stomach grumbling. Had she really slept the whole evening and night away without stirring? She got out of bed and stretched. She couldn't remember when last she had felt so refreshed and light. She knew now that, although the situation with Wayne had been bad, God had allowed it to work out for the best because a weight had fallen from her shoulders. She had a quick shower, threw on a dress, and smiled as she brushed her long hair, remembering how Blake had run his hands through it the night before. She felt closer to him now than she ever had before. It was truly an amazing feeling. Yes, everything had worked out for the very best.

Stepping into the kitchen she was met by quite a sight. A huge heap of toast stood like a pyramid in the center of the kitchen table. It was surrounded by platters of bacon, eggs, fried onions and tomatoes. The coffee pot was filled to the very brim and Jeremiah was tossing some pancakes in the air from an iron skillet. Blake was kneeling on the floor giving Bullet and Champ their morning treats. He laughed as he tried to trick them by giving Bullet a piece of apple, and Champ a piece of bacon.

"Look here, Tess, they are so clever! They throw it down and switch!" Tessa could just imagine how great Blake was going to be with his children.

"Umm, I see that. Very clever! Are we making food for an army?"

"Nah," Jeremiah said, "We're just starving since someone didn't give us any dinner last night, but we won't say who!"

Tessa playfully boxed Jeremiah on the arm, "Hurry up with those pancakes, I'm starving too!"

Blake got up from the floor and wrapped his arms around Tessa. "Yes, and I want you to rest and eat today. You have to look after yourself." He kissed her on the forehead.

"Ugh, enough already. This is just too much PDA for me!" Jeremiah said as he slid another pancake off the griddle.

"What's PDA?" Tessa asked as she bit into a piece of bacon?

"Public Display of Affection. We heard enough about that in the army. Problem is, I haven't had anyone to have any PDA with!" Jeremiah turned around and swung a dish cloth at Blake who was pulling faces, "Quit it! It wasn't too long ago that I had to listen to your lovesick whining. All I heard was, 'I wish Tessa would write. I wonder what Tessa is doing. Tessa…Tessa…Tessa.' "

Tessa smiled at Blake, "Really?"

"Oh, he's exaggerating… but just a little."

Tessa sat down on Blake's lap and put her arms around his neck. "I'm so glad we never have to be apart again!"

Jeremiah set the pan down too loudly on the stove and said, "I'm so glad I am leaving tomorrow night so I don't have to watch all this kissing, especially before breakfast."

"We'll talk again when you..," Blake pointed his fork at Jeremiah for emphasis, "...find the girl of your dreams. Then we will see who waits till after breakfast for a kiss."

Tessa laughed as the boys teased each other, and she made sure she tucked every single thing about this morning deep into her memory. She never wanted to forget anything about this perfect day. Champ must have sensed her reflective mood because he jumped up and curled himself into her lap. She looked over at Bullet to make sure that he didn't feel left out, but he was contentedly fast asleep on the kitchen floor, his stomach full of the bacon Blake had fed him.

33

Tessa listened carefully to the preacher as he spoke. His message ironically was on forgiveness. He opened his Bible and quoted from Psalms 103.

"He has not dealt with us after our sins nor rewarded us according to our iniquities...As far as the east is from the west, so far has he removed our transgressions from us."

He expounded on the passage and then made a powerful statement, "God cannot love you any more than he does right now. God doesn't just choose to love, He IS love!"

How wonderful that God always finds a way to remind me of his love, no-matter what. Tessa felt Blake squeeze her hand, and she knew that he was listening carefully too. She looked over at Jeremiah who sat on the other side of her; his attention was not on the preacher or his message, but rather on the girl who sat quietly on the piano stool in the corner. After church Jeremiah asked Tessa and Blake to hang around a little while, and it didn't take much time for them to figure out why. As soon as the girl stepped out from behind the piano, Jeremiah bolted over to see her. In fact, he almost gave her a fright with his enthusiastic approach, and she took a quick step backwards.

"Can I help you?" She managed to stutter, as she held the music book to her chest like a shield.

Jeremiah obviously sensed that the whole meeting had gone wrong and he mumbled, "Yes…I mean no, I don't need anything."

Tessa groaned at the impossibly awkward exchange and heard the girl say, "Excuse me then," before stepping around Jeremiah to head for the back door.

Tessa felt she owed her brother this much and stepped in front of the girl with her hand extended, "Hello, I am Tessa. What is your name?"

The girl looked suspicious but replied, "Mindy."

"Well Mindy, excuse my brother but he has been away with the army for too long. He has forgotten how to talk…you know, living with all those boys." This brought a slight smile to Mindy's serious face, and she glanced up at Jeremiah for just a split second before looking back at Tessa.

"Anyway," Tessa continued, "his name is Jeremiah and he just wanted to tell you how much he enjoyed listening to you play the piano."

Mindy smiled shyly at Jeremiah who had thankfully found his tongue and said, "Yes, I wanted to tell you how much I enjoyed listening to you play the piano." He repeated Tessa word for word. Rolling her eyes at him, she made signs to show him to keep talking. "Thank you," Mindy replied and then stood there for a minute in the uncomfortable silence that followed. She turned to walk away again and Jeremiah saw Tessa mouthing him something he couldn't decipher.

"Ummm...Mindy?" He spoke in a louder voice than he had intended, causing a few of the old ladies standing nearby to look up at him.

"Do you give piano lessons at all? I've always wanted to play piano you see." Tessa dropped her head into her hands in dismay. She had never ever seen her confident brother so awkward before.

Mindy looked at Jeremiah for a second as she appeared to weigh the question. She caught Jeremiah by surprise when she said, "When do you want to start?"

"Well, there is no time like the present. So how about today? Now?"

Jeremiah's confidence seemed to have returned and Tessa smiled at him. He looked so dashing as he stood looking hopeful before Mindy who questioned, "You mean right now?"

"What he means is, would you like to come to our house for lunch and then give him a piano lesson afterwards?" Tessa interrupted.

"Oh no, I couldn't impose," Mindy shook her head, blonde curls bouncing on her shoulders.

"No imposition at all, we have more than enough, and I personally would love some girl company!" Tessa smiled.

"OK I will follow you to your house then," she nodded at Jeremiah who grinned back.

In the car, on the way home, Tessa turned to Jeremiah, who was sitting in the back seat,

"You know you have a small problem right?"

"What's that?"

"Well, we don't have a piano!"

Blake looked at Jeremiah's expression in the review mirror and burst out laughing at the top of his lungs as he saw the realization hit Jeremiah.

Tessa laughed, too, as she saw Jeremiah's shocked expression.

"What is wrong with me? I never even thought about that! What am I going to do? She is going to think that I'm an idiot."

"Maybe we can say we've been robbed while we were at church, and the only thing they took was the piano?" Blake keeled over the steering wheel as he howled with laughter.

"It's not funny, Blake! What am I going to do?"

Tessa turned around and patted Jeremiah on the knee. "Don't sweat it. Just tell her that you thought you had to do some theory first before sitting at an actual piano."

"Good idea, Sis. Thanks!" Jeremiah sat back now and rested his hands on his knees, which bounced up and down in a jittery motion. Tessa faced forward and had to smile as she realized how much he really liked this girl.

*****

Tessa lay in bed and looked at the clock. It was ten o' clock, and she felt grateful for the sweet day they had all shared together. Breakfast had been fun with the boys cooking up a storm, church had been good, and their afternoon had been pleasant. There was nothing to complain about, yet a thought kept niggling at Tessa. She thought about the many times she had tried to engage Mindy in conversation throughout the afternoon. As soon as she asked any questions about Mindy's family or childhood, she sensed an iron door being shut between them and Mindy quickly changed the subject. She had also noticed that Mindy was not willing to maintain eye contact. Tessa had wondered if Mindy did not like her, but she noticed it when Jeremiah spoke to the girl as well. Tessa had tried to bring up the subject after Mindy had left this evening, but Jeremiah was on cloud nine and would not talk about anything serious. "She's probably just shy," was his only comment.

Jeremiah and Mindy had sat at the table together and gone over some piano theory. Jeremiah had feigned deep interest, but Tessa had watched him taking in every aspect of Mindy's profile as she bent over the paper, drawing new notes with her sharp pencil. Whenever she looked up and saw him watching her, Jeremiah would drop his gaze to the lined paper and say, "I understand."

They had all enjoyed a walk on the beach and a simple sandwich for dinner before Mindy had left, but not before Jeremiah had asked her to come back the next day, which happened to be a public holiday.

"You're teaching me how to read music, and now I want to return the favor and teach you how to snorkel and read the ocean," Jeremiah had said with a proud grin. They all agreed that the next day would be a lovely day for a picnic on the beach and playing in the blue surf. It was finally warm enough to go for a swim and Tessa looked forward to the next day. She sighed as she looked back at the clock, the red numbers *10.35* now glared back at her in the dark room. She curled up next to Blake who was sleeping peacefully, and within a few minutes drifted off to sleep herself.

34

Tessa stood at the front door in her white beach dress and blue flip flops.

"Come on Bullet," Tessa called again. She knew that Bullet would never miss a moment on the beach and he was usually the first one out the door, but today he didn't come as she called. Putting down the basket she held in her hand, she went to look for him. She switched on the light in the laundry room and found him lying in his bed.

"There you are, lazy bones! We're going down to the beach, are you coming?" He lay his head back down as if to say, "No thanks, I'm taking a nap." Tessa heard Blake calling from the front door and knew they were waiting for her.

"OK then, I'll see you later," she turned off the light but didn't close the door, thinking Bullet would bounce up and follow her out.

"Come on, slow poke, let's go!" Jeremiah waited anxiously in the living room. He had been up early and Tessa smiled at his impatience as he paced the floor in his swimsuit and tank top. His muscles were bulging as he quickly scooped up the four chairs and umbrella.

"Can I help you with those chairs?" Blake asked.

"No, I've got it, they're light" Jeremiah replied and hurried down the stairs. "Mindy should be here any minute, and I want us to be set up on the beach by the time she gets here." Tessa and Blake exchanged a knowing look as they headed down the stairs and onto the beach. Jeremiah was undeniably smitten!

Tessa unpacked the picnic basket onto the red and white checkered tablecloth and watched the others splash around in the water. It must still have been quite cool by the sounds the guys were making as they dove under the blue waves. Popping a grape into her mouth, Tessa laid out the sardine sandwiches and chips. She set out some apples, grapes, and oranges before unwrapping the four slices of dark chocolate cake she had brought down for dessert. Today she would not have to guard the food as carefully because Bullet was not on the beach. *I wonder why he didn't want to come down to the beach today.* Tessa worried that Bullet may not be feeling well. Quite frankly, since the beating Wayne had given him, he never quite trusted strangers and perhaps he didn't care for Mindy.

Tessa glanced over to where Mindy had been floating in the blue swells but noticed that she was now making her way back up to where Tessa sat. Her lips were almost blue from the cold and she hugged her towel around her shoulders. "Now I know why you didn't go in! Jeremiah convinced me it would be nice once I was in…"

Tessa smiled and looked at Jeremiah diving in and out of the waves. "He believes it gets better once you are in but I think it only gets better for *him,* because he doesn't stop moving for a second."

Mindy looked at Jeremiah who waved at her and she waved back. He didn't see the big wave sneak up behind him and it broke over his head, throwing him under the white churning water. Mindy laughed unguardedly and Tessa found her laughter to be melodious.

"Did you have a piano when you were growing up?" Tessa heard herself asking as she peeled an orange.

"No," came Mindy's one word answer.

"Oh, then how did you learn to play?"

Mindy stood up and said, "I'm going onto the sand to look for shells while we wait for lunch." She didn't wait for a reply from Tessa but hurried down the steps onto the sand. Tessa again found herself wondering what she had said to run Mindy off. It had just been a simple question! However, she soon forgot about it because Blake came running up the stairs and put a crab right in the middle of the tablecloth. The big orange crab snapped his blue claws together angrily and swerved from side to side, trying to make an escape around the oranges and apples that blocked his way.

"Blake, no!" Tessa slapped him playfully, "Take it back down to the water!"

"Well, I'm starving and want to make sure we have enough to eat up here. Those apples and oranges aren't going to do it for me! I need some protein, some meat! Maybe some crab?"

The crab had inched its way around the fruit and now scooted closer to Tessa who jumped up shouting, "Take it away!"

"OK, OK but you better feed me some meat when I get back, woman!" Blake scooped the crab up and brought it close to Tessa's cheek, making a pecking sound with his lips.

"That's enough you weirdo!" Tessa giggled and pushed Blake's arm away.

By the late afternoon they had eaten every morsel of food Tessa had brought down for the picnic, and she heard the boys complaining.

"There wasn't any protein on those tiny sardine sandwiches. We're hungry. We're growing boys, we need some meat! This woman is starving us to death."

Tessa was lying on a towel and soaking up the last of the sun's rays. "What? All you guys think about is eating. I'm also hungry again, but I have an excuse, I'm eating for two."

"Well, there you are! We will definitely have to go up and grill some steaks because we are all hungry!" "Yes, let's have a barbecue on the Barbie then? What do you say Sheila?" Jeremiah's Australian accent was perfect.

He waited for Mindy to respond and laughed when she asked, "Who is Sheila?"

"All women are Sheila's in Australia!"

"I don't understand, how can they all have the same name?"

"You mean you've never heard the term, 'Sheila'?" Jeremiah asked as Mindy shook her head. "It's their slang word for all women. What about their other sayings like, 'No worries' or 'What's up Mate'?"

Mindy looked uncomfortable and quietly said, "No, I haven't heard any of those sayings."

"How is that possible, Mate? Did you grow up in a dungeon or something?" Jeremiah asked incredulously.

Mindy got up and folded her towel, "I have to go now. I forgot I have something to do tonight."

Tessa sat up and said, "Please stay."

Mindy stuffed her towel into her beach bag, "No, sorry, I have to go."

"Well, let me walk up with you. The boys can stay and pack up the chairs and stuff."

Mindy gave a quick wave to Blake and Jeremiah and turned quickly towards the steps.

Jeremiah called out, "Don't go. I'm sorry; I won't ask you any more questions about Australia..."

But Mindy was already climbing the stairs and didn't turn around. Tessa decided not to broach the subject and pretended that nothing had happened down on the beach. Mindy stayed silent as they climbed the stairs together. When they reached the top and Tessa saw Mindy walking towards her car, she said, "I really could use some help making the salads. The boys are determined to braai outside tonight. Would you stay?"

Mindy put her key into the car and unlocked the door. She looked at Tessa and then hesitated, "I guess I could stay and help you."

"Thank you," Tessa hooked her arm through Mindy's, and playfully dragged her up the stairs into the house.

*****

Even though it had been cool on the beach, they had all gotten some sun. Tessa now stood in the kitchen and broke off a piece of the Aloe Vera plant that sat in the windowsill. She rubbed it on her pink shoulders before sprinkling salt into the potatoes. Mindy stirred the curried rice salad and poured a few more raisins into it. Her white tank top showed off the sunburn she had gotten and her back was as red as her burnt nose. Blake had teased them earlier as his olive skin had not burnt at all. Now he came in and stood behind Tessa. He took the aloe plant and gently rubbed it on her back. Jeremiah bounced into the kitchen from outside and brought with him the wonderful smoky aroma of steak sizzling on the fire. He grabbed the aloe plant out of Jeremiahs hand and walked up to Mindy.

"May I, M'lady?" he soothingly rubbed some aloe on Mindy's shoulders and she smiled shyly.

"That actually feels really good. It's been stinging."

Blake winked at Tessa who smiled and turned back to the counter. She handed Blake a bowl of food for Bullet and some chopped fruit for Champ. "Won't you feed the four legged ones for me tonight?"

"Sure, but then I better get back to the meat since someone has left his post!" He looked at Jeremiah who pretended that he had not heard and continued to rub the aloe down Mindy's arms. Tessa watched Jeremiah and was glad that he had found someone he liked so much. She liked Mindy too, but she just hoped that Mindy would not end up breaking his heart. A wave of sadness passed over Tessa at the thought that Jeremiah would be leaving soon, to go back to the base. She reminded herself that he would be home in a few months and that it would pass by quickly as she got ready for the baby.

Jeremiah turned around and caught Tessa looking at him, "Hey, Sis," He leaned over and dabbed the gooey aloe on her nose, "You need some, too?"

Tessa swatted a dish towel at him with one hand as she wiped her nose with the other. "I'm just going to miss you when you leave."

Mindy whipped her head around, "Leave?"

With that one-word question, Tessa instinctively knew that although Mindy was trying to stay blasé, she too felt something for Jeremiah.

"Yes, I'm leaving at the end of the week, but I will be home by June," Jeremiah said as he turned toward the back door.

"I better get down there and save the meat or we will be eating potatoes and rice for dinner. He flung the back door open, letting in not only a cloud of smoke, but also the blaring music that floated up from the back yard. He danced his way out the backdoor to the sound of *the beach boys* singing, "I wish they all could be California girls."

Tessa and Mindy looked at each other and burst out laughing. It was a moment that bonded them together and Mindy allowed herself to drop her defenses for the first time that day, "Well, I guess that leaves us out right?"

Tessa laughed again, "I guess it does."

*****

The steak and salads had been delicious and the four of them lingered over dessert. After a while Jeremiah stretched and got out of his chair. He walked over to the window and looked out. Turning he said to Mindy, "It's a full moon. Come and see how it falls across the ocean like a beam of light." Mindy got up and stood next to Jeremiah.

"It's so beautiful!"

"Let's go for a walk by the water, it's even better down on the beach."

"Now?" Mindy questioned hesitantly. Then she smiled slightly, "OK, let me get my sweater. It's always cool at the water."

As she walked into the living room to get her sweater, Blake pointed a finger at Jeremiah and in a mocking fatherly tone he said, "Now see here young man, what exactly are your intentions with that young lady?"

"Well, sir, my intentions are completely honorable. But I do intend to give her a first kiss that will make her weak at the knees." Tessa threw her head back and laughed at Jeremiah as Mindy walked back into the kitchen.

"What's so funny in here?"

"Oh nothing, Blake was just trying to tell a cheesy joke and Tessa felt obligated to laugh...Old married couple, you know?" Jeremiah said as he led Mindy to the door. They walked out of the house and down to the beach. "It's true, the moon on the water is even more beautiful down here," Mindy commented.

Back upstairs, Blake leaned over and gave Tessa a slow kiss. "Well, my dear, even though we are an old married couple by their standards, I would like to take you for a walk, too."

"No, let's give them some privacy."

"Of course. But my walk is a short one, and we are going in a different direction." He pulled Tessa up and led her through the living room to the bedroom. The moon streamed in through the window and fell across the blue and white quilt on their bed. Blake shut the door and kissed Tessa passionately. When she could get a breath she said, "I dare say, Mr. King, I believe I am the one left weak at the knees tonight."

"Just as I planned," Blake whispered and swung Tessa into his arms as he carried her over to the moon bathed bed.

35

Although it was not Monday morning, Tessa felt like it could definitely have been a blue Monday. Everything that could have gone wrong, had! First, she had gone to let Bullet out and found that he had not touched a single bite of his dinner from the night before. He also had had diarrhea all over the laundry room floor, and somehow Champ had stepped in it. Now Champ was sitting down and looking at Tessa with accusing eyes, while pulling his foot up to his nose from time to time.

Bullet had obviously not been well the day before and that is why he had not wanted to go down to the beach. Tessa felt guilty for not having checked on him last night. She had just assumed that he had eaten what Blake had given him.

Tessa called the vet and set up an appointment for later in the morning. Her stomach heaved as she tried to clean up the mess and she found herself hugging the toilet bowl. Now she was starving and put on a pot of mielie meal. She and Blake had fallen asleep early last night and had not come back to the kitchen to clean up the dishes from dinner. Tessa loathed facing a dirty kitchen in the morning and tried to scrape the hardened potato salad off the plate. Nolwazi was meant to have come up to the house this morning, but she had sent a little boy with no front teeth to tell Tessa that she was sick and would not make it. Now Tessa turned around and stood in another pile of poop that Bullet had just left in the kitchen. Her stomach lurched again, and she prayed that she wouldn't get sick again. Champ kept jumping up and down screeching kek-kek-kek at the top of his lungs. Tessa scolded him, "Quiet Champ, stop making such a racket!" This just made him screech louder and caused Bullet to slink away with his tail between his legs.

She desperately wished that someone were here to help her, but Blake was at work and Jeremiah had taken a train into Cape Town to finalize some paperwork. A company was looking to hire him when he completed his service in a few months. The telephone rang at that very moment and Tessa hobbled on her heel to the phone. She heard Blake's voice, "Hey Baby, I have a minute and just wanted to check on you."

Tessa quickly told Blake the details of the morning, ending with, "I'm really worried about Bullet, he doesn't look good."

She looked over at Bullet who lay against the wall in the kitchen, not moving and looking pale, even for a dog.

"He won't eat or drink anything," she continued.

"I'm sure he will be fine, Tess. I have a customer waiting so I have to go now, but call me when you get back from the vet. I love you."

"I love you, too."

Tessa put down the phone and heard her stomach rumbling. She turned toward the porridge on the stove, "Oh no!" Yanking the lid off the mielie meal, she smelled the burnt porridge.

"Oh no!" she said again. What more could possibly go wrong in one morning? Tessa wiped away the tear that slid down her cheek. "Stop being silly," she spoke to herself, "crying won't help anything!"

But the tears continued to fall, and Tessa saw Bullet pick his head up and look at her. Even feeling sick, he wanted to comfort her as he always did. Tessa sat down on the floor next to Bullet and laid his head on her lap. She stroked his head and spoke to him through her tears, "Good boy, Bullet. You are such a faithful friend. You have to get better you hear? I love you so much." And there, with the stench of burnt porridge, dirty dishes, unwashed laundry, and a sick dog, Tessa sat quietly and gently stroked Bullet's head.

A few minutes later the doorbell rang. Tessa groaned, "Seriously? Who can this be?" She tiptoed to the door, and relief washed over her when she found Mindy standing on the step.

"Jeremiah is not home this morning," Tessa greeted her with a hug.

"I'm not here for Jeremiah. I'm here for you. I ran into the hardware store this morning for some light bulbs and Blake told me about Bullet. I came by to see if you needed some help; and no offense, but by the smell of it, you do!" Mindy waved a hand in front of her nose.

Tessa was too relieved to be prideful and smiled, "Yes, I desperately need your help. Just wait 'til you see the kitchen. It looks like a bomb has hit it. I am so overwhelmed, I don't know where to start and I don't have any energy anyway...and I'm worried sick about Bullet."

Fresh tears escaped as Tessa acknowledged out loud her fear for Bullet.

"Well, firstly we need to take care of you. Let's put on some fresh porridge, and let me see about Bullet. You know I worked at a vet clinic for a few years."

Tessa had a newfound respect for Mindy as she watched her take charge of the situation. She flung open the windows in the kitchen and living room causing a fresh breeze to blow through the house. Then she put on a pot of porridge and quickly soaked the dishes in some hot soapy water. Within minutes the washing machine was swirling and the floor had been cleaned and mopped. Now Mindy knelt next to Bullet who allowed her to examine him. Tessa noticed Mindy's gentle touch and tranquil voice. The thought occurred to her that Mindy would be a good wife to Jeremiah, and she knew that Mindy would be a good friend to her as well. She still wondered however, why Mindy sometimes seemed so skittish, like she was ready to bolt out the door for no reason at all.

Tessa sat down with her bowl of creamy porridge and stirred some golden syrup into it. She called Champ over, whose feet were now washed and cleaned, thanks to Mindy. His tiny fingers held tightly to the piece of apple she handed him, and she wished that Bullet could be enjoying his breakfast like he usually did. Tessa felt much better as she spooned the smooth cereal into her mouth. She was so grateful for Mindy's help. After the laundry was put out to dry and the dishes were washed and packed away, Tessa and Mindy quickly worked on putting a pot roast in the oven for dinner.

"This way," Mindy said, "it can cook slowly all day and dinner will be ready when Jeremiah and Blake get home." Tessa nodded in agreement as she sprinkled garlic and rosemary on the meat. She chopped carrots, potatoes and onions and put them decoratively around the meat in the pot.

"You will stay for dinner, won't you?" Tessa asked.

"I don't think so," Mindy replied without any explanation. Tessa slid the roast into the oven, "Well you simply have to, you don't have a choice! No one is allowed to help me cook and then not eat the food. I have to make sure you didn't poison it after all."

Tessa started laughing but noticed that Mindy said nothing as she bent down and looked at bullet. "What's wrong, Mindy?"

"Now that you mentioned poison…" Mindy said as her eyes travelled towards Bullet.

Tessa looked at Bullet and her blood ran cold. She hadn't even considered that. "Bullet…poisoned? How?" Tessa's questions poured out of her, but Mindy had no answers and just shrugged her shoulders.

"Earlier I thought it was just an upset stomach, but now I'm thinking I might be wrong. I didn't want to upset you, but I don't think we should wait for the vet's appointment. We should probably get over there now."

36

Tessa had a hard time getting Bullet down the stairs. Dizzy and disorientated, he stumbled down the steps and for the first time, she allowed herself to think about the fact that Bullet may not make it.

"Come on boy, you survived once before, you can do it again. Don't you dare give up!" Tessa spoke to Bullet all the way to the vet while Mindy drove.

Two hours later Tessa paced the reception area of the vet clinic. She felt aggravated. What was taking so long? Mindy sat quietly and watched Tessa pace.

"Why don't you sit down a while and rest?"

"I can't. I need to know that he is going to be alright."

"Well here, sit down in my place and I will pace instead; that way you know one of us is pacing and worrying."

Tessa stopped pacing and looked at Mindy as if she had had an epiphany. "You're right. I haven't actually prayed for Bullet. Instead I've been pacing and worrying! And that's not how I'm supposed to be handling this crisis."

Mindy just nodded wisely but didn't say anything else.

"Please excuse me for a few minutes, I need some time alone." Tessa walked out onto the grass behind the clinic and found a quiet bench. She sat down and bowed her head for the first time. She prayed for Bullet to be healed and to survive. She prayed for peace to come to her own heart and confessed her fear and worry. She finished praying by declaring her trust in God and confidence that he was concerned about everything that touched her life, including the wellbeing of her four legged friend.

Just then the door swung open and Mindy called her inside. The vet confirmed that Bullet had indeed been poisoned, but they had been able to treat him successfully.

"I'm sending him home with these meds," the vet said. "He needs a dose twice a day, and I'm sure he will recover completely."

Tessa was delighted and didn't forget to thank God for answering her prayer. Back at home she made Bullet a bed in her room. Now he lay down with his head on Mindy's lap, while Tessa went to make them a cup of tea. She sighed as she poured the boiling water over the tea leaves. Although the morning had started off horribly, everything had turned out all right after all. Tessa smelled the pot roast simmering in the oven, and the delicious aroma, mixed with the freshly-mopped floors and the fragrance of clean clothes flapping on the line nearby, caused Tessa to smile. All would be well.

Walking into the bedroom Tessa almost dropped the tray of tea and chocolate cookies. She steadied her arms just in time and slowly put the tray down on the nightstand.

"What are you doing here?" She said to Wayne who sat casually on the bed. Now he leaned back and propped up his head with the pillow. "Come now, Tess. That is not a very nice welcome. I came to visit and found the front door open, so I came to look for you and instead found this delightful creature."

He winked towards Mindy who pretended not to hear or see him. She continued to look down at Bullet and rub his head. Tessa may have believed that she was not affected by Wayne's comment, but her bright pink cheeks spoke otherwise.

Tessa looked back at Wayne and an awkward silence followed as Wayne stared back into Tessa's eyes. Needing to break the unveiled intimate stare, she turned her gaze away and asked Mindy how Bullet was doing. "He's drugged and sleepy, but peaceful."

Wayne sat up and took the teacup nearest to him, lifting his little finger into the air he said, "Cheers!" This was followed by a big swallow of tea. He reached for a cookie and stuffed it into his mouth. Talking around the cookie in his mouth, he asked, "What's wrong with the mutt anyway?" Another big gulp of tea followed.

Tessa felt disgusted as she observed Wayne's behavior. How could she ever have been attracted to this man? "He is sick, and I think you should leave now so I can see about him."

"Actually that dinner you have in the oven smells delicious. I'm starving."

When Tessa didn't reply, Wayne took another cookie and stuffed it into his mouth as he looked over at Mindy.

"You know Tess...I've come a long way to see you, and I don't know anyone else here. But since you have been so unwelcoming, perhaps you could introduce me to your pretty friend here and I can have dinner with her tonight."

"Wayne, I'm sorry, but this really isn't appropriate. I am married now and it's best for you to leave and go back home."

Tessa glanced over at Mindy, who gave her head an almost unnoticeable shake, but it was enough for Tessa to add, "And my friend here is dating my brother so she will not be available for dinner either."

Wayne stood up and stretched, he looked at Mindy and Bullet, "That's OK, I don't want to date a mute who can't speak for herself, and definitely not one who's another dog lover."

He strode to the door and turned around to blow Tessa an exaggerated kiss, "Don't miss me too much; I'll be seeing you soon."

With that, he slammed the door shut and was gone.

Tessa held her hand to her beating heart and leaned against the door that still seemed to quiver in the hinges. She looked at Mindy who seemed shaken too and said, "I'm sorry. Just ignore him."

"Who is he?"

"It's a long story, but not one worth telling." Tessa rubbed her stiff neck. She walked over and sat down on the floor next to Mindy and Bullet. He slept quietly now.

"Tessa," Mindy spoke quietly, "Be careful."

Tessa questioned Mindy with her eyes and Mindy added, "He is dangerous."

"Why would you say such a thing?" Tessa queried.

Mindy took the question as a reproof and immediately pulled away and said, "I'm sorry. It's none of my business, I shouldn't have said anything."

She started to get up but Tessa stilled her with a hand on her arm. "Please...I need to know what you are thinking."

Mindy sat down and nervously rubbed Bullet's soft ears. When Tessa had almost given up hope that Mindy would speak at all she heard the first stilted words. Mindy told her story haltingly at first, weighing every word carefully.

"I am an orphan. My real father died when I was three years old and I barely remember him, except that he had very kind eyes."

She fell silent again and Tessa tried to stop herself from saying, "And?"

After a few more minutes Mindy continued, "My mother remarried two years after my father died, and I remember everything about my step father. At first he seemed kind but then little things started happening, you know?" She turned and looked Tessa in the eye. Tessa wasn't sure what to say so she just nodded and said, "Go on."

The words came faster now, as if they had been bottled up for years and years. "He turned out to be a drunk. The more he drank, the more unpredictable he became."

Bullet opened his eyes and whined, distracting them for a moment, but then he lay his head down again.

"Whenever he drank, I took to hiding. One dark night I hid in the closet under the stairs. I didn't think he would look for me in there because he was a very large man, and the closet was narrow. It was pitch dark that night when I shrank back into the corner and my back hit into a doorknob. I turned the doorknob and it opened, but I couldn't see anything. I sat down and scooted forward an inch at a time until I found a staircase. I held onto the rickety banister and pulled myself down."

Tessa held her breath as she relived this story with Mindy who seemed to be reliving it herself.

"By then, my eyes had grown accustomed to the darkness and I found myself standing in a room. I ran my hands along the old wooden shelves and miraculously stumbled upon a candle and some matches." Mindy smiled for the first time as she continued, "That night I found my salvation."

She stopped talking as if the conversation was over, but Tessa prompted, "What do you mean?"

"The piano. I found an old German upright piano down there. My stepfather never allowed any music in the house, calling it unnecessary noise. But down in the fortress, I could make music. Of course, I didn't really know how to play anything, but I spent so much time down there that I taught myself a lot of things. My music teacher at school noticed my passion and offered to help me during my breaks. I begged her never to mention it to my parents, and somehow she understood that the music itself was my hiding place."

"Didn't your parents wonder where you were all the time?"

"My mother was sad a lot and didn't seem to notice my absence. *He* didn't seem to notice either, and he simply didn't care. The less he saw of me the better, it seemed. So I raised myself in the basement which no one knew was there. I made a little house for myself down there and only came up for meals and a bath. I sometimes saw my stepfather glaring at me, and his stare would make me shiver. He was a bad man. I couldn't wait to get down to my fortress. My music was my constant companion. But that is over now. I finally escaped." Mindy sighed and closed her eyes.

37

"How did you end up here?" Tessa asked Mindy as they sat together on the floor watching Bullet sleep.

"My mother died when I was sixteen. The doctors called it something else, but I think it was from a broken heart. I didn't go back home that night. After the funeral I walked until the night grew dark. I walked aimlessly the next day and the day after that. But it had gotten so cold, so very cold. I couldn't feel my feet as I stumbled along, and that is when I saw it. I crawled through the wires at the back of a vet clinic to lie in the dog crate I saw back there." Mindy snickered, "I remember hoping there wasn't a bull terrier waiting for me in that dog box. But I was cold and tired, and then I almost wished there was a big mean dog in there that would finally end my useless life." Although Tessa had seen some bad days too, she tried not to look shocked at this candid confession.

Mindy smiled again, and Tessa saw how truly beautiful she was in these unguarded moments. "Instead the vet himself found me curled up in the dog box at six o'clock in the morning and took pity on me. He was an old man with a long snow-white beard. For a minute I thought I had actually died and was meeting God himself. Then the smell of the kennel hit me, and I knew heaven surely couldn't smell that bad," Mindy laughed before she continued. "Doc gave me breakfast and then offered me a job. I love animals, so I was very pleased to accept the job of cleaning the kennels and feeding the dogs. I ended up renting a room behind the clinic and I got paid extra to do the night shift...You know, checking on dogs that were sick. I eventually got promoted to the head vet technician. Soon I could afford to go to some night classes at the local college. I followed my dream and studied music. After I finished school, I got my own apartment and started teaching piano lessons."

"How did you get into church?" Tessa asked.

"My mother had taken me to church when I was a little girl, but that stopped around the time I turned seven. My stepfather said religion was a waste of time and that I should spend my time learning how to serve a man instead. On Sunday mornings, he would make me polish his shoes and wash his car. I hated Sunday mornings from then on and learned to clean quickly so that I could disappear again."

"I noticed what would have taken me hours this morning, you did in half an hour," Tessa said.

"But you know," Mindy continued with her story, "the things I learned in church as a little girl never left me, and I found myself searching for God. The vet and his wife invited me to church and after a dozen invites, I finally went with them. I gave my life to the Lord and accepted Jesus as my Savior. But I must admit that it took a long time before I was ready to forgive my parents. I know it sounds crazy, but I had to forgive my mother, too,   for deserting me when I needed her most."

Tessa put her hand in Mindy's hand, "I'm glad we found each other. We both don't have a mother and perhaps you would let me help you sometimes, as you helped me today."Mindy's eyes lit up as she said, "It would be such a gift just to know that I have a true friend." Mindy squeezed Tessa's hand. "I haven't told anyone else my story. It feels really good to have shared it with you. I just hope you don't see me any differently."

Tessa saw the vulnerability in Mindy's eyes. "Are you kidding? No, I only have more respect for you than ever!" She leaned over and the girls gave each other a heartfelt hug.

Mindy stretched and wiggled her numb legs, "Gosh, what got us started on this conversation?"

"*Wayne* got us started on this conversation."

"Yes…Wayne," Mindy replied. Her expression had changed to concern again as she added, "He reminds me so much of my stepfather. I don't trust him, Tessa. He literally gave me the chills."

Mindy was looking at Bullet as she spoke but then suddenly lifted an eyebrow at Tessa.

"What is it?" Tessa asked.

"Well, I've just been wondering how Bullet got poisoned," Mindy responded.

Tessa gasped, "I just assumed he got into something. Do you think *someone* poisoned him?"

"I don't know, but it is a possibility," Mindy said as she saw Tessa's shocked face.

"No, it can't be. I think he just ate something poisonous," Tessa said.

Mindy decided not to say anything more about it, "Let's go and check on dinner. I'm starving since *you-know- who* drank my tea and ate all the cookies!" She pulled a face that made Tessa laugh out loud.

38

It was silent around the dining room table as they all ate their food hungrily. Jeremiah had not had any lunch and came home famished. Blake had been kept out on a job all afternoon and was dizzy from hunger when he came in the door. Tessa caught Mindy's eye and they smiled at each other, knowing what the other was thinking. *It's a good thing we put this pot roast in the oven.* The boys wolfed their food down as if they were in a competition.

"Well Mindy, I guess the old saying is true! The way to a man's heart is through his stomach," Tessa smiled.

"Yes, it seems like it," Mindy replied as she watched Jeremiah scoff his food down.

He looked up for a second and spoke with a full mouth, "What? I'm still a growing boy!"

"No Jeremiah, you are six foot four inches tall and have bulging muscles. I don't think you are growing anymore," Tessa said.

Jeremiah ignored this comment by asking, "Are there any more potatoes in that pot?"

Blake pushed back his empty plate and rubbed his stomach. "Well, that was about the best meal I've ever eaten. Thanks to all the cooks involved!"

He leaned over and gave Tessa a kiss on the cheek. "Who wants some coffee?" Three hands went up and soon after Blake brought in the coffee and cookies. They decided to recline in the living room and while they sipped their coffee Blake said, "I'm relieved that the vet said Bullet would be fine, but I can't help wondering what poisoned him."

"I know," Tessa said and looked at Mindy. "We were just talking about that a while ago." Mindy stayed silent and Tessa added, "I think he ate something poisonous. You know how inquisitive he is sometimes."

Jeremiah took Mindy's hand and kissed it, causing her cheeks to redden as she saw Tessa and Blake watching them. "Thank you for staying today and helping my sister. And I have a great idea. Why don't you stay over in the guest room and help me make pancakes in the morning?"

Mindy laughed, "You know perfectly well how to make pancakes!"

Jeremiah looked at Tessa, "Tess, ask her to stay. You may need help with Bullet in the night."

Tessa stifled a big yawn, "I am actually exhausted. I wouldn't mind a good night's sleep."

"OK I will stay and keep Bullet in my room tonight," Mindy pointed a finger at Jeremiah and added, "but only because Tessa needs my help."

Jeremiah faked a serious expression when he replied, "I would never assume that you would stay for me. I know you are a very independent woman." As Mindy took another sip of coffee, Jeremiah winked at Blake and Tessa and showed them thumbs up. Tessa smiled at her brother who could be such a jokester at times. He would be good for Mindy, and she would be good for him.

The next morning Tessa walked into a very different kitchen from the day before. Instead of chaos, the coffee pot was happily percolating, pancakes sizzled in the pan, and Bullet stood eating over a small plate of food. Champ sat on Jeremiah's shoulder as he flipped another perfect pancake, and Mindy was setting the table.

Jeremiah kissed Tessa on the cheek, "Good morning, sleeping beauty. Blake left for work already and said he wanted you to rest, so he didn't wake you."

"Actually I feel wonderful today. I think I'm going to go down to the beach for a few minutes. I will be back before breakfast is done."

"Don't take too long. The coffee and pancakes won't be good cold, and then you will say that I am a bad cook," Jeremiah said as he flipped another pancake.

"To tell you the truth, I'm more worried about your helper there," Tessa said pointing to Champ, "Are you sure he washed his hands this morning?"

"Hey, he is the cleanest monkey around. Don't worry about his little fingers."

As if on cue, Champ started parting Jeremiah's hair as if looking for fleas.

"Umm, I see what he is doing with those little fingers. Just make sure he doesn't touch my pancakes," Tessa said.

Mindy shook her head and laughed, "Don't worry, Tessa, I'm watching those two."

*****

Blake heard his name being called over the intercom at work. It was only nine o' clock in the morning and he wondered who was calling him.

"Hello?"

"Blake, its Jeremiah. I think something has happened to Tessa."

Blake doubled over and he found it hard to breathe. "What do you mean? What's happened? This better not be a joke Jeremiah or so help me…"

Jeremiah's voice was serious and he sounded worried, "I wouldn't joke about something like this. Tessa went down to the beach early this morning, like usual. She said she would be back upstairs to have breakfast with me and Mindy, but she didn't come back. I've searched all the spots on the beach that I can think of, but she is nowhere to be found. Something is wrong, I can feel it."

"I'm on my way," Blake put the phone down before he even heard Jeremiah saying goodbye.

39

As Tessa had stepped out onto the road from the winding pathway, she felt hands grab her from behind and push her towards a rusty green truck. She tried to scream but a firm hand came up around her mouth, silencing her. She was shoved into the passenger side of the car, and then she saw her abductor.

"Wayne, what on earth are you doing?"

He didn't answer but locked her door and jumped into the driver's side.

Tessa repeated her frantic question, "Wayne, what are you doing?"

He leaned over her, his face so close to hers that she felt his unshaven cheek brush against her own. He reached up and pulled her seat belt down, clicking it firmly into place. Tessa smelled the whiff of alcohol on his breath and looked at the time on the dashboard:

8:34 a.m. - and he was already drinking. Wayne battled to get the old truck into gear and the gears grated loudly. She could only hope that the noise would draw Jeremiah's attention. The truck finally lurched forward, leaving behind a plume of black smoke.

"Wayne, where are you taking me?" Tessa heard the fear in her own voice. It was his silence that unsettled Tessa more than anything else. She had no way of knowing what he was thinking if she didn't get him to speak. He lifted a bottle wrapped in a brown bag to his lips and took a long swig. He didn't look at Tessa but held the brown bag out to her. She didn't take it and he gave a harsh laugh then, "Oh, I forgot, you're pregnant and you shouldn't be drinking."

Then he added in a British accent, "You're right old chap!" Wayne hit the dashboard with his hand and laughed hysterically. Tessa realized now that he was already drunk. In this state he was even more unpredictable than usual, but she had to try and reason with him. "Wayne, let's stop for some coffee. We can sit and talk awhile....about us and the future." She hoped that she could derail this runaway train by acting as if she actually wanted to leave with him.

At least this got him talking and he replied, "No stopping. We have many hours to travel, and there is nothing to talk about. I'm taking you home with me like I promised you I would. I'm taking you back to where you belong." Wayne looked at Tessa and she saw pure hatred in his eyes as he added, "I waited for you all day yesterday but your body guards were hanging around all day! You can be lucky that boyfriend of yours left early this morning. I was going to have to put his lights out for good if he kept hanging around."

They were now on the narrow road that led over the mountain pass and Tessa looked down the steep side at the rocky coastline below and breathed a prayer, "Help us, Lord. Keep us safe."

Wayne looked at Tessa with piercing eyes, "I was angry that you didn't come and meet me yesterday like we had planned. Your boyfriend must have kept you busy."

Tessa decided it would not be a good idea to correct him and remind him once more that Blake was her husband. Instead she replied sweetly, "No, we had a guest for lunch and I just couldn't get away. I'm sorry."

Wayne's eyes softened, "It's alright, baby, I forgive you." He laid his hand on Tessa's leg and she tried not to cringe. He put the bottle to his lips again but found it to be empty. Cursing violently he threw the empty bottle out of the window, the glass shattering into a thousand pieces on the road behind them.

"You know I've decided I won't live without you. And I've told you before that when I want something…Well, I simply must have it!"

He leered at Tessa with his red-rimmed eyes. His hand moved up her thigh. Tessa willed herself to stay calm. It wouldn't do any good if she tried to fight him. She spoke calmly and quietly, "You look tired. Did you not sleep well last night?"

His British accent returned out of nowhere, "Who can sleep well on the blasted beach?" He winked at Tessa, and she glimpsed the Wayne she had met on the farm, the terribly handsome one. He had been a bad boy and unpredictable from the start, and that had made him all the more attractive to her when she had met him. Now his appearance and touch repulsed her as she saw what misery it had caused her. Wayne continued in character with his flawless British accent, "Cor Blimey Mate, it was blasted chilly on the beach. That is why I had to go into town and get a nip of something to warm my icy bones." This seemed to remind him of something, and he dug down next to his seat and pulled out another bottle of whiskey.

"This here does the trick. Cheers, Mate!"

The truck veered over the double lines and Wayne jerked at the steering wheel as he swallowed another gulp of the whiskey. His overcorrection drove them onto the gravel next to the road and Tessa squeezed her eyes shut in terror, "Wayne, I'm begging you, please slow down!"

She should have known better than to say anything, because Wayne put his foot on the gas and the truck peeled around the corner. "Why? Do you think I don't know how to drive? You're always criticizing me."

Tessa tried to speak calmly, "No, Wayne, you drive better than anyone I know. I just don't feel well today."

Tessa felt the truck slow down and she took a shallow, ragged breath. They had finally reached the highest point on the mountainside and now they started descending. *Maybe everything will be alright after all*, Tessa thought. But no sooner had the thought crossed her mind when they rounded a sharp bend and found a troop of monkeys crossing the road. Wayne slammed on brakes but the truck continued to skid forward. Tessa screamed as they hit a monkey who flew up in the air and landed behind the truck. Wayne tried to gain control of the truck and pulled the steering wheel hard to the left. The truck flipped over twice and landed right side up with the front wheels dangling off the cliff in front of them. There was nothing below but rocks and ocean.

40

Tessa opened her eyes and looked over at Wayne. He groaned and put a hand up to his head, the blood trickled through his fingers and onto his white shirt. "You need to put pressure on that," Tessa reached for a shirt that now lay on the floor at her feet. As she unbuckled and leaned down, the truck creaked and tilted forward like a seesaw. Tessa screamed as she pictured the truck tipping over the steep mountain edge and crashing on the rocks below. Wayne groaned again and leaned his head back, the blood from the cut on his forehead streamed down his cheek. Tessa was shaking now, and praying, "Oh God, oh God, please help us." Was this the end of her life? Would she not get to see Blake hold his baby in his arms, or get to say goodbye to Jeremiah?

She continued to mumble, "Oh God, have mercy on us." The wind had picked up slightly and the truck creaked as if it was old and tired and wouldn't mind saying goodbye to the world. Wayne looked at Tessa out of one open eye, the other covered in blood.

"Stop praying, Tessa. God doesn't hear us. We're all bad." Tessa looked back at Wayne and noticed how still everything was around them. The sky was bright blue. There were birds chirping in the trees nearby, and yet their lives hung in the balance. Then she heard the still small voice. *Be still, and know that I am God.*

A peace came upon Tessa then and she stopped shaking so violently. She thought about death and knew that at least she would be in heaven. But what about Wayne? Would he enter the gates of hell today? She had to make sure that would not happen.

"Wayne, God hears me because I am his child. And yes, we are all bad at times and we mess up and sin, but he promises to forgive us and make us as white as snow. His mercy is new every single day."

Wayne's eyes were closed now, and she reached out slowly and touched his arm. "You have to make right with him. He loves you. Accept Jesus as your Savior today. Let him come into your heart and make you new. We can live with him forever, here on this earth and then...in the afterlife."

At first Tessa thought that perhaps it was already too late. Wayne was so pale and still, she couldn't even tell if he was breathing. Then he whispered, "I want that Tessa. I want to be washed clean. I feel so filthy, and I am so ashamed of how I have lived my life." A single tear slipped down his waxen cheek. "I have hurt so many people and lived so selfishly. Do you think it is too late for me?"

Tessa felt the famous Cape gusts pick up and the wind blew through the broken windows of the truck. Her hair twirled around her, but she was too scared to move in the slightest, in case it would topple the truck forward.

"It's never too late, Wayne. The Bible says that they who call on the name of the Lord shall be saved. Do you want to pray with me?"

Wayne nodded ever so slightly and whispered the prayer that Tessa led, "Jesus, please forgive me for all my sins. Wash me in your precious blood. I accept you today as my Lord and Savior. I am now your child. Amen."

Even in the terrible situation they were in, Tessa felt the quiet peace that surrounded them. Then, the quietness was disturbed by car doors slamming, and she heard Blake's frantic voice calling "Tessa! Tessa!"

Blake and Jeremiah ran up and stood at the side of the truck.

"I'm OK, but Wayne is hurt," she called out since they couldn't see her. The front end of the truck still slightly teetered up and down over the edge.

"Hold on Tessa, were going to pull the truck back," she heard Jeremiah shout.

"Hurry, please hurry!" Tessa shouted as her hope for survival was renewed at hearing Blake's voice. Tessa heard a car start behind them and then felt a tugging. At first it seemed as if the old rusted truck was stubbornly going to refuse to be rescued, and then it suddenly gave in and they were lurched backwards. Tessa felt herself being dragged out of the car and Blake held her firmly in his arms. He kissed her, and her tears mingled with his own. Jeremiah knelt down next to them and asked, "Are you all right?"

"I'm fine, Jeremiah," Tessa hugged her brother. "Just a little shaken and bruised." Tessa looked down at the little cuts that ran up and down her arm from the splintered window. Blake pointed at her leg where the large swelling on her bone was already turning purple. "We need to have you checked out," he said and Tessa could tell that he was worried.

Now that the initial shock was wearing off, her mind turned to the baby and she was sure that it was adding to Blake's concern. They heard Wayne moan and Jeremiah stepped in that direction. Tessa said, "I don't think Wayne should be moved."

Jeremiah's eyes became fierce, "Well, I think he should be moved. Right down that mountain side to the rocks below! He almost killed you, Tessa."

"Jeremiah," Blake interrupted, "Tessa is alive. We have to help him."

They opened the truck door and saw that Wayne was now lying down on the seat. He managed to slightly open his eyes and look at the three of them standing there.

"I'm really sorry," he whispered and coughed. Blood leaked from his mouth as he uttered his final words, "Please forgive me."

He slowly closed his eyes and his bloody hand fell away from his head. His face relaxed as he left the earth behind and stepped into eternity.

Tessa crumbled to the ground, sobbing. She was overtaken with sadness that Wayne's life had ended with this tragedy, but she was also relieved as she pictured him entering onto the streets of gold, in heaven. She was so grateful that she had been given the opportunity to lead him to Christ, and her tears of sorrow mingled with tears of joy. Wayne could finally be at peace. The boys stood back and looked at each other, not sure what to say or do. Blake put his arms around Tessa and picked her up. She lay her head on his shoulder as he walked away from the truck. She felt his warm breath on her neck as he whispered, "It's over now, let's go home."

41

Eight months had passed since *that* day. It was early in the morning and Tessa sat at the kitchen table, watching the steam swirl out of the teapot's spout. Autumn lingered in the air and she rubbed her chilly arms. Walking over to the bassinet that stood under the sunny window, she tucked the pink blanket tighter around the little bundle that slept there. Bending down she placed a soft kiss on her daughter's cheek. Leigh was six weeks old and every day she brought them so much joy. Blake hurried through the house when he arrived home from work at night and scooped her into his arms. Tessa never got tired of the scene as she watched him hold his daughter. He whispered the same thing every night, "Daddy loves you so much."

She would surely be spoiled by the end of it because if Blake wasn't holding her, then Jeremiah, Mindy, or Nolwazi had her in their arms. Even Bullet was very protective over her and lay close to the bassinet. Only Champ feigned disinterest and ignored the baby completely. Blake said that he was probably jealous because he was used to being the baby and that they should be sure to give him his usual attention.

Tessa now looked at the clock and chided herself for daydreaming. Today was going to be a very busy day. It was Jeremiah's wedding day and there was much to be done before the guests arrived. The chairs had to be set out on the beach and the tables would be laden with food. Tessa had tried to talk Jeremiah out of planning a wedding on the beach in autumn, since no one knew what the weather would do from day to day. His response had been, "Have a little faith, sister. It will be a beautiful day!"

So here they were, and indeed it was going to be a beautiful day. There was no wind, and everything was still and peaceful.

Nolwazi pushed open the back door and clapped her hands in excitement. She loved to cook and now pulled out the trays of chickens that she had been marinating since yesterday. Soon they would be baking in the oven. There would be heaps of peeled potatoes on the table and different desserts lined the length of the kitchen counters. Tessa hugged Nolwazi's soft body, "I don't know what I would've done without you. Thank you so much for helping me like this Nolwazi."

Nolwazi's fat face broke into a grin, "I'z happy, I'z happy!"

"Me too, me too," Tessa repeated herself as Nolwazi always did, and Nolwazi grinned back at her. Tessa's mind went to all the dear faces she would see today. She was overwhelmed with gratitude for all her blessings and felt tears of joy well up in her eyes.

*****

The violinist in the purple dress played a tune that caused the atmosphere to feel enchanted. Tessa watched her for a few minutes, and then her eyes drifted to the ocean where the waters splashed lightly over the boulders. The candles flickered along the pathway and the late afternoon sun splattered the sky in orange, yellow, and red paint. Even the seagulls stood to attention along the sand as if they, too, were part of the wedding party.

Tessa drank in the beautiful scenery and couldn't imagine a more perfect setting.

Jeremiah stood tall and handsome in a black tuxedo and waited for his bride. He had finally completed his time in the army and was more than ready to be married. In his absence, Mindy had been a regular visitor and she and Tessa had become great friends. She was always willing to help babysit Leigh, Bullet, and Champ, and this had given Tessa and Blake quite a few nights free to go out together. Mostly they just packed a picnic basket and spent it in a quiet cove down at the water. Neither Tessa nor Blake liked crowds, so this suited them both well.

Tessa's thoughts returned to the present as everyone stood and the violinist started playing the wedding march. Mindy walked slowly down the sandy isle and Tessa noticed her choking back tears. She knew that Mindy so desperately needed a family and she had confessed to Tessa that this was a dream come true. Not only was she marrying someone like Jeremiah, but she was gaining a whole family. To not be alone anymore, was more than she could have hoped for.

Jeremiah lifted Mindy's veil and gently wiped away her tears. "You're so beautiful," he whispered loud enough that everyone heard, which was followed by a few giggles. Tessa had always told him that he had never learned the art of whispering quietly. Once Mindy's hand was hooked into Jeremiah's arm, her tears stopped and a beautiful smile radiated from her.

The ceremony was beautiful and now Tessa looked over the crowd as they mingled together near the food tables. Ginger stood with a glass of champagne in her hand and nodded her head as Pops explained something to her. Tessa was so pleased that Ginger had sent her a post card a few months ago with her return address on it. By the looks of things, Pops was thoroughly enjoying Ginger's company. He had come in from Van Staden's and had brought his dog, who was overjoyed to see his old friend Bullet and now chased him up and down on the beach nearby. Ginger's hat, with the fruit on it, had been replaced by one that held an enormous grey feather. Every time she moved the grey feather would sway from side to side, making her look like a strutting peacock. Apparently Pops didn't mind as he smiled shyly at her. Tessa smiled too as she wondered if there would be another wedding shortly.

Auntie Rina sat eating a piece of pie and was asking Nolwazi about the recipe. Charmaine was scouting out the party for any available young man to dance with. She looked beautiful as usual. Her long blonde hair glimmered in the sunlight, and her tight fitting red dress showed off her perfect figure. She wore cowboy boots with the dress…*Well, only Charmaine can pull that one off,* Tessa thought.

Leigh was fast asleep in Tessa's arms when Blake walked up. He looked so handsome in his black suit and starched white shirt. He took the baby out of her arms and brought her to Nolwazi, letting her hold Leigh. Striding back over to Tessa, he held out his hand. "May I have this dance?"

Tessa rested her head on Blake's shoulder and enjoyed breathing in his familiar scent as they swayed to the slow love song. Everything in the world was right tonight and Tessa looked up into Blake's eyes. "Thank you for... everything."

Blake frowned at her, "I need to thank *you* for everything. I can't imagine my life without everything you have brought into it."

Tessa grinned and said, "Like what exactly?"

Blake stopped dancing and started counting things off on his fingers. "I have a crazy dog, a sulking monkey, and a beautiful baby who keeps me up all night." Blake laughed but continued to count, "I also have a gorgeous wife who loves me, and my best friend has become my brother. Plus," he finished off by adding, "I get to live in a white castle with you!"

Tessa felt playful and replied, "Yes, sir, it does seem like you have to thank me for all that chaos." They both laughed and looked at Bullet who was now digging a hole to China, it seemed.

"Well, I was thinking..." Tessa said.

"Uh oh," Blake sighed loudly, "this sounds like trouble."

Tessa playfully slapped Blake's arm, "Stop, this is serious."

"OK, let me hear it."

"I was actually thinking that Bullet needs a friend. Look how he has been playing with Pops dog. Champ teases him a lot, but he needs another dog to play with."

Blake laughed, "I see where this is going! Once we get another dog, you are going to say that Champ is lonely and needs another monkey...and then Leigh will be lonely and will need a brother or sister."

"Well, you just said you were thankful for living in the white castle. Why not fill the old place with as many critters as there is space for?"

They looked up from the beach and their eyes settled on their big white house that stood like a magnificent castle against the darkening skies. Blake smiled as he thought about how good it was going to be to fill up the rooms of that old house with the pattering of paws and little feet. He pulled Tessa closer and whispered, "Yes, I'm glad we have the space for extra critters. Let's do our best to fill up the castle."

ALSO BY JENNY HEWETT SMITH

COMING SOON: *LESSONS MY DOGS TAUGHT ME ABOUT GOD.*

ABOUT THE AUTHOR

Jenny Hewett Smith was born the second of four children to Loretta and Theodor Jerry Hewett in Cape Town, South Africa. There she grew up during the years of violence in turbulent South Africa, where the many divisions in the country created a fear based society.

Jenny's parents moved to New Orleans in America in 1992 and Jenny and her husband followed soon after. While raising two young daughters, she felt the need to write her story so that her children would not take for granted the many freedoms they had in America. The true story took on a life of its own, and her first book 'A Land Far Away' was born.

 Jenny and her family now live in Daphne, Alabama, with their two crazy dogs, Mitzi and Sweet Pea. She works part time at a Health Food Store and writes whenever she can carve out a quiet hour or two. Besides reading, she loves long walks and picking up shells on the beach.

I'd like to hear from you. Visit me at www.jennyhewettsmith.com or connect with me on my Facebook page.